(continued on next page)

Also by Joanna Trollope

THE CHOIR

A VILLAGE AFFAIR

A PASSIONATE MAN

THE MEN AND THE GIRLS

THE RECTOR'S WIFE

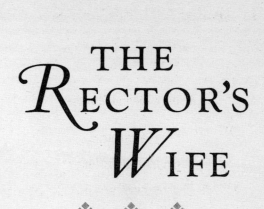

Joanna Trollope

BERKLEY BOOKS, NEW YORK

THE RECTOR'S WIFE

A Berkley Book / published by arrangement with
Random House, Inc.

PRINTING HISTORY
Originally published in Great Britain by Bloomsbury Publishing Ltd.,
London, in 1991
Random House edition / October 1994
Berkley edition / October 1996

The Putnam Berkley World Wide Web site address is
http://www.berkley.com/berkley

ISBN: 0-425-15529-3

BERKLEY®
Berkley Books are published by The Berkley Publishing Group,
200 Madison Avenue, New York, New York 10016.
BERKLEY and the "B" design
are trademarks belonging to Berkley Publishing Corporation.

PRINTED IN THE UNITED STATES OF AMERICA

10 9 8 7 6 5 4

For Antonia

THE
RECTOR'S
WIFE

Joanna Trollope

1

❖ ❖ ❖

AS USUAL, THERE were five of them on the village green, waiting for the school bus. Also as usual, they began to talk differently as Mrs. Bouverie approached, louder, more self-consciously, and the younger two, in their all-weather uniform of jeans, and bare feet thrust into stiletto-heeled shoes, put their cigarettes behind their backs. It was, Mrs. Bouverie thought, as if she were a headmistress. But she was worse than a headmistress; she was the Rector's wife.

Every weekday afternoon in termtime, the school bus from Woodborough stopped at Loxford village green and decanted nine children. The reception committee of mothers was always waiting, partly out of maternal duty, but mostly because those ten minutes on the village green filled the same gossiping function as ten minutes at the village pump had for earlier generations. When the children clattered, yelling, down the bus steps, their mothers regarded them with a mixture of disgust and pride, as if amazed anew each afternoon that they had managed to produce children of such spectacular offensiveness.

The last child—and the oldest—was always Flora Bouverie, who came trailing down the bus steps burdened with splitting carrier bags and fragile, half-made artefacts, peering about her blindly for her mother. She took her glasses off, every journey, because, if she did not, they were taken off for her and thrown out of the bus window into a hedge. Mrs. Bouverie knew this, and she also knew that the Loxford mothers despised her for meeting a child of ten. If she had said, But I meet her as miserable compensation for enduring Woodborough Junior, which is quite the wrong school for her, they would have despised her even more.

"Intolerable," Flora said, dropping her bags on her mother's feet.

She scrabbled about in her duffel-coat pockets until she found her glasses. "I hate this coat. I look like a train spotter."

Anna Bouverie thought with revulsion of the bags of jumble lurking in the Rectory garage. "I know. But the alternatives are even worse."

Flora put on her glasses. She looked up at her mother with eyes enlarged and blurred by the lenses.

"What does cretinous mean?"

"Literally, mentally defective."

Flora looked round at the village children swirling, screaming, across the green, like gulls round the ships of their mothers. "Exactly!" Flora shouted after them.

One mother turned back. She worked most nights in the pub, and was the self-appointed keeper-up of the village spirits, relentless in her jollity.

"See you tomorrow, Mrs. B! Don't be late!"

They all cackled with guilty laughter.

"What does she mean?" Flora said, staring after her.

"I'm usually late for the bus. I have to run. They watch me running. That's all."

"Frankly," Flora said, stooping for her burdens, "I think it's intolerable."

"You're full of huge new words—"

"English," Flora said briefly. "We had to find six words out of a newspaper. We always do everything out of a newspaper for English." She paused. "I found flatulence. It means burping—and the other one."

"Farting," Anna said. Woodborough Junior's familiarity with rich obscenities had overlaid Flora's natural vocabulary with an anxious and reacting gentility.

"Yes," Flora said, looking away.

Anna bent to disentangle a bag or two from Flora's fingers.

"Come on. Tea. It's starting to rain."

Ominous little gusts of wind were digging playfully in the nearby litter bin and scattering crisp packets about. They blew damp draughts against Anna's and Flora's faces and veiled Flora's spectacles with infant specks of rain. The mothers and children were out of sight now, reduced to no more than faint yelps from among the council houses built on rising ground above the green, and there was no-one else about, and would not be, until the men began to come home at dusk.

"Why," said Flora, in the dead and hopeless tone of one who has uttered a particular, heartfelt question over and over, to no avail, "why does school have to be so horrible?"

Loxford church was medieval, with a square tower and a Norman tympanum over the south door of the Harrowing of Hell. Loxford Old Rectory was Georgian, built of

3

the same blond stone as the church, and it sat behind grand double gates whose posts were boastfully crowned with new stone eagles. Loxford New Rectory was red-brick and had been built in the early sixties. It had, Anna Bouverie's mother said, all the quiet charm of a bus shelter.

Its redeeming feature was its setting. It had been built on a piece of glebe land behind the church, with a narrow drive running up beside the churchyard wall, separating it from the lane, isolating it from other houses. Its front windows looked towards the church, and its back ones over farmland to a series of gentle green hills, the furthest one crowned with a low, dark copse, like a pool of spilled ink. When Peter and Anna had come for interview, Anna had looked at the hills with hunger, and not at the cramped kitchen or the meanly proportioned sitting-room, and had urged Peter to accept. "Oh, we must," she had pleaded. "You must. Please."

He had been doubtful. He was doubtful about being sole incumbent in five parishes—he had visualized a team ministry—and even more doubtful about the rural ministry in itself. Did he . . . Was he . . .

"While you are waiting for God to write it down for you in capital letters," Anna had shouted finally, exasperated out of all diplomacy, "I shall decide for you both. We are going to Loxford."

To Loxford. Loxford with Quindale, Church End, New End and Snead. After six years in a Birmingham slum parish, Anna thought, you became desperate not to have a front doorstep strewn with down-and-outs and to have a back garden littered with worms, not discarded syringes and used condoms. Six years! Six years of bringing up Charlotte and Luke with chicken wire tacked across inside their bedroom window, and a security sys-

tem worthy of Alcatraz so that the parishioners who
needed to get to you never could. Flora had been conceived the minute they reached Loxford, out of sheer
relief. Anna supposed that she should then have had another baby, to keep Flora company, but had found that
she felt as unlike having another baby as she had once
felt like it.

Walking up the drive beside the churchyard wall,
Anna said, "What happened to Marie? I thought she was
your friend."

"She went to Germany," Flora said, stopping to peer
at the wall, where moss was beginning to swell into new
plump spring cushions. "With her father. He's a cor-
poral."

Half Flora's school were Army children. They lived
briefly in the great camps round and about, and then
vanished. Flora envied them because all the things she
craved in life they could buy cheaply in the NAAFI.
They seemed to take money for granted. Flora, accustomed to a life of bare sufficiency, knew differently.

She put down a bag and dislodged a green dome of
moss.

"Look—"

Flora had always dawdled. Toddler walks with her
had been a superhuman test of patience as she squatted
by every puddle, slowly stirring the water with sticks,
and picked up myriads of stones, tenderly brushing them
free of earth and inserting them with infinite laborious-
ness into pockets already grinding with pebbles. She
roared with fury if helped or hurried.

"It really is raining now," Anna said.

Flora must be fed, the sitting-room fire lit, the dining-
room tidied for tonight's Parochial Church Council
meeting, supper organized. And then, there was her

translation. Paid by the page, Anna translated German and French technical books into English. It was dreary work, but it was private. Peter had discovered that his five villages would not like him to have a working wife.

"You will find," Colonel Richardson of Quindale House had said, not unsympathetically, "that it would cause a lot of resentment. A lot. Particularly among those who don't go to church"—he eyed Peter—"but might?"

Peter did not repeat this to Anna. There would have been no point; she would simply have laughed. Her natural vivacity, her particular charm, had led her too often into thinking that people would be drawn into seeing things her way, with disastrous results. At least, Peter had found them disastrous, and he would find them so again if Anna chose to try and charm Colonel Richardson out of his opinion of working clergy wives. So, to avoid this, Peter merely said that for the moment, he'd appreciate it a lot if she'd keep working a bit quiet. She had taught in a language school in Birmingham three mornings a week, a language school with a creche, run by an enlightened Belgian woman, where Charlotte and Luke had gone until they were old enough for school. She said to Peter, "Teaching is very quiet. Isn't it?"

"No," he said. "Not invisible enough."

They had been in Loxford six months then. She was happily pregnant and still sustained by the hills. She saw the advertisement for a technical translator in the newspaper. It was easy to learn the vocabulary, as easy as it was dull. So strange, she sometimes thought, to have all this engineering knowledge in three languages and still be so unable to apply a single word of it that she could scarcely change a plug without helpful diagrams. In order to make a weekly sum of money even dimly visible to the naked eye, she had to translate fifty pages a week, a drudgery she tried to regard as ineluctable as brushing her teeth or washing the kitchen floor. A decade of it now, ten years at two and a half thousand pages a year. Best not to think of it, in case her temper slipped out of gear and, as once she had done, she threw a bowl of apples at Peter. She had missed; the bowl had broken. It was a blue-and-white pottery bowl Peter's mother, Kitty, had brought back from a timeshare holiday with a friend in southern Spain. The apples had rolled everywhere, gathering bruises and fluff. She had found one months later under the vegetable rack, shrunk to the size of a nut, dark wizened brown, and smelling of cider.

"Where's Daddy?" Flora said, setting her moss down carefully on the kitchen table.

"Gone to see the Bishop."

"Wowee," said Flora. She pressed the moss and watched a trickle of earthy water ooze out of it. "Why?"

Slicing bread, Anna said untruthfully, "I honestly don't know."

The Bishop had been to Woodborough Junior once, to take prayers. Flora, unwisely, told her class he would wear a purple robe and a great cross round his neck and a huge ring like a winegum. He arrived in a dark suit and a black shirt buttoned down over his dog collar and kept his hands folded so that nobody could see if he had on a ring at all, let alone one like a winegum. It had been a humiliating day for Flora and she bore the Bishop a grudge in consequence.

"Would you like cheese in your sandwich?"

"What I would really like," said Flora, knowing there wasn't any, "is chocolate hazelnut spread."

Recognizing the game, Anna waited.

"Or black cherry jam. Swiss jam."

Silence.

"Or smoked salmon," Flora said inventively, never having had any.

"Or cheese."

"OK," Flora said, "cheese."

"Cheese, please. I can't think why I'm making this sandwich for you. Why aren't you making it yourself?"

Flora stuck out her hands and her lower lip.

"Search me."

"Flora," Anna said, "have you got prep?"

Flora put her hands over her ears and began to jump about all over the kitchen.

"Shut up, shut up, shut up, shut up—"

Again, Anna waited. She watched Flora with exasperation and pity. Charlotte and Luke had managed school perfectly well, had made friends, had slipped effortlessly in and out of all the required fads and fashions. Charlotte had gone on to university; Luke was now at sixth-form college. Flora was different. She was cleverer than either of them, more elusive, more fragile. She said sometimes, of school, "But I can't make the right conversation," and it was true. Something uncompromising in Flora prevented her from understanding where she went wrong. Her frustrated jumping, which sent her thick, straight, dark hair—Anna's hair—flying up and down like dog's ears, was no more than a maddened expression of how she felt when reminded of school, of a world where she was doomed to remain odd.

Anna put the sandwich on a plate, and then put the plate on the table, beside the moss.

Flora stopped abruptly, and said, "I forgot my flute."

"Does it matter?"

"Yes!" Flora said on a rising note. "It's my lesson tomorrow, I must practise—"

8

The telephone rang.

"I'm so sorry," Anna said into the receiver, "Mr. Bouverie is out just now. He should be back by six; could you—oh. Oh, I see. Are you sure he said he would call? All right, I'll tell him. Mrs. Simms, 7 New End. Goodbye."

She put the receiver down.

"Daddy apparently forgot to go and see Mr. Simms in Woodborough General."

The telephone rang again.

"No," Anna said, "Mr. Bouverie isn't back yet."

Flora came up close and mouthed, "My flu-u-u-te. My flu-u-u-te."

"A wedding in May. I'm afraid he has his diary with him. Could you call back? Before seven-thirty, he has a meeting. No," Anna said, "no. He won't mind that you aren't churchgoers."

"He will, actually," she said when she had put the receiver back. "He will, but he can't."

"My flute—"

"Flora," Anna said, pushing her fringe off her forehead, "I can do nothing about your flute. Daddy has the car. And now I have to do an hour's work."

Flora turned away and cast herself, face down, across the table, narrowly missing the sandwich.

"It's the end of the world," she said. "It's intolerable."

She kicked one of her bags. Very slowly, its side seam split open and a flute rolled quietly out on to the floor.

Anna worked at a little table in their bedroom. It was an Oriental table, donated by her mother, who was an actress of the old school and given to lavishness of gesture. The table was made of bamboo, lacquered scarlet,

9

and the top was painted with gilded peonies. It bore its load of textbooks incongruously, and a typewriter that a parishioner had given Anna, a weekender who worked on a London newspaper, and who had sworn, positively, that she had outgrown the thing, didn't need it. "Chuck it in a jumble sale," she had said to Anna, trying to make it easier to accept.

"I've got pride," Anna had replied, taking it, "but no false pride. Thank you very much indeed."

It was electric. It produced smooth, bland sheets of text that Anna's publishers greatly preferred to the characterful efforts of her previous old portable. She sat down in front of it and looked at the half-page she had typed that morning. She thought of Peter. He would by now have left the Bishop, would be crossing the Close to find his car, would know what lay ahead for them both. She looked out of the window and saw the brown strip of plough, and then the line of willows marking the river, and then the green slopes rising, dotted now with the first sheep of the year. In a month, she thought, in just a month, I might be looking at quite a different view. And what is more, I might never ever have to look at German again except on a menu in a restaurant on the Rhine, where we might go, like other people do, for a real holiday instead of borrowing mildewed cottages and cardboard holiday-houses from people to whom we then have to be disproportionately grateful. She looked up at the bedroom ceiling, where a pale stain recalled a burst pipe nearly fifteen months ago. Through that ceiling, and through the roof above it, lived God, omniscient, omnipresent God. "You try living your adult life on nine thousand a year," she said to Him, and bent, with a sigh, to her typewriter. The telephone rang.

• • •

Luke Bouverie missed the last bus out of Woodborough to Loxford, so he thumbed a lift. This happened most nights and he had grown to think that it was an easier and more interesting way of travelling, particularly as his looks and his load of schoolbooks and his thinness caused people to stop. They were mostly local people, often men from the villages who worked in Woodborough. Only once, last autumn, had there been an unnerving lift, a well-dressed man in a Mercedes, who had wanted Luke to drive on towards Devon with him, had offered him dinner and a night at a hotel, had put his hand high up on Luke's thigh, and been altogether menacing. Luke, who had a reputation for staying cool, had panicked. He had heard himself squeak in a long-outgrown pre-pubertal voice, ''You be careful, my dad's a vicar!'' and the car had stopped and the man had sworn at him viciously, using some phrases Luke later regretted not remembering, and Luke found himself shaking on the dark verge a mile out of Snead. He had had to walk home, three and a half miles, but luckily his parents were out, at some deanery get-together, and Trish Pardoe, who helped in the shop, was babysitting Flora. Trish never asked questions; she was only interested in telling you things. That night, she'd said, ''If you'd come out the Quindale way you'd never've got through; it's flooded right across the road from Briar Farm to the old water tower, three feet deep, burst water main,'' and Luke had said, ''Yeah,'' and gone out to the kitchen to raid the fridge.

This evening, his lift was Mike Vinson, who worked as an electrician for a firm in Woodborough and ran the Loxford cricket team. He and his wife had so done over a cottage on the green that its original simplicity had been quite obliterated in an orgy of DIY neo-Georgian.

Mike Vinson had a respect for the church. He never darkened its doors, but he thought it was the proper place for weddings and christenings and funerals, and he was always prepared to rig up lights for the annual parish nativity play, with a dimming spotlight to beam sentimentally on the Virgin Mary. He would say, casually, to his wife later that night that he had given young Luke Bouverie a lift home. "Nice lad," he would say. "Nice manners." He would go to bed with a small satisfaction at having given a lift to the Rector's son.

Luke said, "I'm hopeless. I always miss the bus."

"You'll be driving soon," Mike said. "Own car, and all. Change your life."

"Yes," Luke said, suddenly miserable. He had practised in the car, but there was no money for lessons and as for a car of his own! Even the family car had come from some Church-loan scheme. The application form for a driving test had lain, unfilled in, in the muddle on his bedroom table since his seventeenth birthday. Anna had promised him lessons—when they knew. Knew what? "Just wait," she said, smiling. "Not long now."

"And what'll you do with your life?" Mike said. "Vicar like your dad?"

Loyalty just prevented Luke from saying, "No fear!" He said, "I want to do art."

Mike tried to imagine it, and failed.

"Stage sets," Luke said, to help him. "Theatre design."

Mike nodded. He had no vocabulary to ask what he felt were appropriate questions. "Nice boy," he planned to say to Sheila later, "artistic, too. Interested in drama." Sheila liked drama. When he had found her, on holiday in Bournemouth, she had been very keen on amateur theatricals. She'd stopped for him, though. He

didn't like the thought of her kissing other men, even in
Show Boat.

"Father approve?"

"I think so," Luke said.

"And your mum?"

Mike's voice was elaborate with nonchalance. In his
view—a strictly private view aired neither to Sheila nor
to the lounge bar of The Coach and Horses in Quindale—Anna Bouverie was, well, something; not just a
looker, but something more, something—

"She's all for it."

Mike took a grip on himself. "Been here a long
time—"

"Yes, since I was seven."

"What happens," said Mike, abruptly interested,
"what happens to vicars? I mean, do you get to climb
the ladder?"

"What?"

"Chances of promotion. That's what I mean. Where
does your dad go from here?"

Luke thought.

"Well, he's rural dean, so I suppose the next thing is
archdeacon."

Mike slapped the wheel.

"He'll be a bishop one day! What d'you reckon?"

"I don't know," Luke said. His whole soul had been
so given over to dreams of leaving Loxford recently that
he was startled to think his father might share them.
"He's happy here," Luke said stoutly. He did not want
his parents to leave Loxford; just him to leave. He
wanted them to be where he could visualize them.

The Loxford sign gleamed briefly from the black
hedgerows.

"Lovely village," Mike Vinson said, "smashing. I

grew up in Harlesden. You don't know you're born, growing up here.''

Courteously, he drove to the far end of the green and let Luke out by the church.

"Really kind of you," Luke said, getting out. "Thank you."

He turned up the drive. The Rectory's windows glowed behind drawn curtains. His father couldn't be home yet because he would have turned half the lights off again. Some evenings, his parents almost seemed to circle round after one another, his mother turning lights on, his father switching them off. "It's the tiniest luxury," his mother would say and his father would reply, without looking at her, "No, it isn't. It's provocation." Luke thought that as his father plainly was not home yet, he would use his absence to do a little preliminary softening up of his mother, about plans for the summer.

She was in the kitchen. She was wearing the huge red skirt she had made out of some curtains someone had sent to the jumble, and a black polo-necked jersey, and she had tied her hair up with the Indian scarf Luke had given her for Christmas. She was slicing onions. Beside her, with a music book propped against a milk bottle, Flora was playing slow, unlovely exercises on her flute.

Anna stopped slicing and offered Luke a cheek wet with onion tears.

"You missed the bus."

"But not Mike Vinson."

Luke gave Flora a mild cuff. She squealed.

"Where's Dad?"

"Not back yet," Anna said.

Luke put his books on the table, where they toppled sideways against the milk bottle, which tipped over and spilled milk across Flora's music book. Anna took no notice. She picked the onions up between cupped hands and dropped them into the frying pan on the cooker. Luke began to mop clumsily at the pool of milk with a teacloth. Flora stood frozen, torn between wishing to scream and giggle. Her dilemma was solved by the telephone ringing.

"Do get it," Anna said, "I'm oniony. Say Daddy isn't back yet. Say don't ring till nine, after the meeting."

"Say don't ring ever again," Luke suggested.

"Hello, Ga," Flora said with pleasure into the receiver. "No, I've had an intolerable day. No, I'm not! I'm not! OK. I'll get her." She held the receiver away from her with distaste. "Ga says I'm a little tragedy queen."

"It's not put on, you know," Anna said to her mother, retrieving the telephone. "She isn't making it up."

"Is he back?" Laura Marchant hissed. "Is Peter back?"

"No."

"Hades. I left ringing till now because I was sure that he would be. Do you think his being so long is a good sign?"

"I simply don't know."

"Oh, such wild celebrations there'll be! You can remove poor Flora from that sink of a school and send her to some nice nuns."

"Tonight's celebration," Anna said, "is the Loxford PCC meeting in the dining-room. The secretary, who also organizes the church flower rota, has just resigned in a huff, because she says the Sunday school has taken over some shelves in the vestry flower-vase cupboard without asking, so I have to take the minutes.''

"My poor darling. Shall I come down and bring a breath of life and urban decay?''

Anna shifted so that her shoulder was comfortably propped against the wall.

"I wish you would.''

"Next weekend—''

Luke dropped the sodden cloth back on to Flora's music book.

"Here's Dad. I heard the car—''

"Peter's back,'' Anna said. "I must go. I'll ring you.''

"Yes,'' Laura said, "yes. He must have it, he must. Or it's to hell in a handcart.''

Anna put down the telephone and waited. Luke and Flora waited too, by the table. They heard Peter slam the car door, then pull down the groaning metal garage door, then approach the house along the path of concrete slabs, which were lethally glazed all year round with slippery green. He opened the kitchen door and came in and shut it before he turned to face them. He looked wholly unhappy.

"It seems—'' he said, and then he stopped. "It seems I am not to be Archdeacon of Woodborough. The next Archdeacon of Woodborough is to be someone from the north, someone called Daniel Byrne.''

2

❖ ❖ ❖

KNEELING IN THE Rectory pew of Loxford church, Anna watched Peter preparing deftly for communion. He looked tired, in the bruised way that people who are physically slight do look tired, but not so much so that any of the congregation would notice. Anna was inclined to think that most of them would only notice if he looked disgustingly well, when they could say suspiciously to one another, The Rector looks all right, doesn't he, wonder what he's been up to? The rest of the time, they were not disposed to look at Peter as a human being, but only as a rector, a creature of whom standards of motive and conduct were expected that they did not expect of themselves. Anna's one great clerical friend, a woman deacon in Woodborough, said that it was being a village congregation. "Towns are much more forgiving. Villages are crippled by people who can't bear to have the veil torn from their fantasy of idyllic retirement."

Poor Peter. If anyone was crippled just now, it was Peter, by disappointment. In the three days since his in-

terview with the Bishop he had scarcely been able to
speak for the bitterness of his blighted hopes. He had
lain wakeful beside Anna in the bed that had not been
quite wide enough for twenty years and felt himself to
be all at once boiling with misery and quite immobilized
by it. A change of parish, the Bishop had suggested, a
spell of team ministry, perhaps. He had not said,
Frankly, Peter, you are not up to being Archdeacon, he
had instead emphasized the need for someone from outside the diocese, for someone with ecumenical experience in urban work, for someone accustomed to
ministerial care. Burble, burble. Peter lay in the dark and
hated the Bishop. It was the only small luxury he could
discover. He had telephoned the present Archdeacon of
Woodborough, a valued friend, the friend who had indeed suggested and supported his application, and he
had said that he simply did not know why Peter had
been turned down, he had no idea. He was so sorry, he
said, so very sorry. But then, he was going on to be a
suffragan bishop in East Anglia and his sorrow and his
support would go with him.

"I'm not moving," Peter said to the Bishop. "I'm
not leaving Loxford."

The Bishop waited.

"I am Rural Dean, after all," Peter said, with a small
defiance.

"Indeed you are."

Peter looked round the Bishop's study, which was entirely lined with books. An academic, Peter thought with
angry scorn. An academic! He's never even had a parish.

The Bishop, reading Peter's thoughts, would have
liked to have put his arms around him, would have liked
to have said, I cannot make you Archdeacon because
you have insufficient judgement and experience, but you

are a good priest, a conscientious priest, and I am wretched to disappoint you. Instead, he said gently, "When you have thought it over, you must come straight to me if you would like a change."

"I won't change," Peter said.

The Bishop's wife had shown him out tenderly, as if he were ill. He imagined them putting the kettle on afterwards, making tea, saying, Oh dear, what an unfortunate business, so glad it's over. They did indeed put the kettle on, but then the Bishop took it off again and said he needed a drink more, oh, that poor fellow; and his wife said, "And his poor wife."

"It would have doubled his stipend," the Bishop said, looking sadly at the remaining inch in the gin bottle.

"Don't," said his wife. "How old is he?"

"Forty-five."

"And will he never go further?"

"I don't think so."

"I'd share your gin," the Bishop's wife said, "except that it would make me further inclined to cry."

Anna had not cried. It had all gone too deep for crying. She rather thought Luke had cried and Charlotte certainly did, on the telephone from Edinburgh. Peter did not think Anna should have told the children anything about it, but she was not, as she frequently said to him, that kind of mother. She hoped she had given Peter the chance to cry, if he had wanted to, but he had not taken it. Flora roared, without knowing why, just knowing something was violently the matter. Anna said to God, while she dug her prolific vegetable patch, "I think You are a toad." Now, kneeling on one of the Jubilee Year hassocks organized by the county Women's Institute, she was not inclined to think differently. She looked at Peter's back—she had not, she observed, done a perfect job this week on ironing his surplice and old Miss Dunstable, who was Mistress of the Robes at the Cathedral, but lived in Loxford, would both notice this, and point it out—and wondered what would become of him. Not in a career sense, because the leaden weight that lay on her heart told her that his career was now Loxford with Quindale, Church End, New End and Snead until relieved by the trumpets of Doomsday, but as a person. He would be changed by this; he couldn't avoid that. Even the gradual assimilation of his disappointment would leave scars and blights, like a landscape after fire. What a thing to do, Anna accused God, what a thing to do to someone who serves You. God said nothing. He held Himself aloof. Anna looked at Peter again and said to herself in a guilty whisper, ''Will he become even more difficult?''

She wondered if a stranger could tell that he was difficult, just by looking at him. Would such a person, watching Peter now, reading the prayers of Rite B in his level, pleasant voice, notice that resentment lay, like his blood, just under his skin, because the life he had chosen had not turned out as he had expected it to? Anxiously, Anna had sometimes wondered if Peter had lost his faith. As for herself, she was uncertain she had ever had any, and yet, for all that, she sometimes joyfully felt that she knew what it was about. She had tried to explain this fleeting instinctive comprehension to Peter, but he had said, ''I think you are confusing faith with emotion,'' so she had not tried again. Peter had grown afraid of emotion; he considered it messy stuff that could lead one into a fatal labyrinth of self-forgetfulness. He had once said to Anna, in a touching burst of confidence, ''You know what's the matter with me? I'm just clever enough, and no more.''

Those limitations had been a great attraction to Anna, when they first met. The only child of parents whose steady outrageousness was charming only to outsiders— oh, the luck, Anna used to think as a child, oh, the sublime luck of being an outsider!—Anna, at university, sought out friends who seemed to be defiantly normal. Even the dullness of her room in a hall of residence possessed, for her first year at least, a kind of charm. Reality, in the form of banality, seemed very precious to Anna, a token of having stepped out of a nightmare into the sanity of the waking world. This overreaction was not to last, but while it was still strong upon Anna, while she briefly favoured neat cardigans and regular library hours and institutional meals, she chanced upon Peter Bouverie.

She liked his name. She liked his quiet manner, his bookish looks, his thin hands emerging from the voluminous sleeves of jerseys knitted for him by his mother, who plainly, in her mind's eye, saw him as a strapping youth of six foot two. He was reading theology, a subject which seemed to Anna both mysterious and sophisticated. He too was an only child, the son of a widow: his father had died of cancer when he was seven. Mr. Bouverie was a solicitor, Peter said, but he had wanted to be a priest, had intended to try for ordination if cancer had not prevented it. His mother was called Kitty. He showed Anna photographs. Kitty Bouverie looked like an eager little lap dog, bright eyes hopeful under a curly fringe. "My father adored her," Peter said.

He made it plain, quite quickly, that he was poised to adore Anna. She rather liked it, not least because it was wonderful to have someone of her own, someone she could talk to. One of Peter's best qualities was his ability to listen. Anna told him about her childhood, about the house in West Kensington that resembled a gigantic, filthy theatrical props cupboard, smelling of face powder and cats and old ashtrays, where a five-foot plaster saint, dumped on the drawing-room sofa three years before, as a joke, by one of her mother's lovers, had subsequently never been moved. The same lover had made palm trees out of Edwardian ostrich feathers and tied them to all the newel posts of the four-storey staircase. They were thick with dust, Anna said, but they too would never be removed. Peter said, "My mother has never had a lover. I don't think she is interested in men now. I think there was only ever my father, for her."

"But your father wasn't queer," Anna said.

Peter, who was drinking coffee, stopped drinking. "Is yours?"

"Yes," Anna said loudly, full of pride and shame.

Peter looked at her speculatively.

"Then how—"

"Oh, he can do it with women," Anna said. "He'd just rather do it with men. So the house is always full of men. Men for my father and men for my mother." She was suddenly overcome by the drama of her situation. "Don't sit there like a stuffed owl!" she shouted at Peter. "Say something! Do something!"

He put his arms round her. Then he kissed her. After a while he took off her cardigan and his jersey and then the rest of their clothes, and made love to her on the folk-weave bedspread of her university bed. Anna did not say that she was not a virgin, that she had been to bed with two of the men in West Kensington and had been, at seventeen, much inclined to suppose herself in love with one of them. She liked Peter's smooth, clean skin, and his childhood-smelling hair, and the way he gazed at her with huge eyes without his glasses.

22

"I'll look after you," Peter Bouverie had said to Anna then. "We'll do things together."

He had wrapped her in a blanket off her bed and made her more coffee. "Which saint is it," he had said, "the one on the drawing-room sofa?" And his question, making Anna laugh, drawing off the poison, sealed the success of his courtship of her.

Anna's mother loved him. She treated him as a malnourished curiosity, swooping down on him with tender cluckings, and seductive titbits—a crab claw, a lychee, a chocolate truffle—asking him to describe God, or Heaven, or sin, treating him as a confessional, trying to dress him up as a cardinal, showing him off to her friends. To Anna's amazement, Peter did not mind. He did not seem to like it very much either, but he was perfectly good-natured and only jibbed at the dressing up. He even showed a quiet courage.

"Say it," Laura Marchant demanded of him. "Go on, little padre, say it. Say this is the most toweringly revolting house in all Christendom. Don't just sit there and ooze the thought at me. Say it!"

"It's so disgusting," Peter said calmly, "that I'd rather not have meals here, and sometimes I have to put my shirt on my pillow."

Laura adored that. She embraced him in a clash of bracelets and beads. He then, with equal calm, cleaned part of the kitchen. "For Anna and me to use," he said. Anna's father, an actor of no great distinction, said to Peter, "Marry me. Marry me at once. You are wasted not being a wife."

Peter made Anna, for the first time in her life, fond of home. Lifelong bogeys became jokes; the long tunnel of what had always seemed to her exaggerated behaviour and elaborate unorthodoxy had a light at the end of it, the light of a life with Peter. She was certain his faith would be infectious; that, like maternal love being born fiercely with the baby, her belief would spring to life with marriage. Her future mother-in-law, peering worriedly at her, said, "You're sure you can cope with God? I mean, He's very full-time."

"Oh yes," Anna said, not understanding.

"You know best," Kitty Bouverie said, fidgeting the flowers she was arranging. "You know your own mind, a clever girl like you. But between you and me, I'm not sure I could have managed. With God, I mean. Perhaps it's a blessing—" She broke off. "There now. All that messing about and I've broken a lily."

Little Kittykins, Laura called her. Anna's father called her Madame Bovary. She perched in the drawing-room beside the recumbent saint. "Completely flat-chested, you see," Anna's father said, indicating the saint, and offering a jaggedly opened tin of caviar and a kitchen spoon. "So she must be St. Agatha. Breasts sliced off—" he held out a glistening spoonful; Kitty bienched—"for refusing to submit to the lustful wishes of one Quintian. Eat up, Madame Bovary, eat up." He licked his lips.

Kitty said, in her little voice, "I'm afraid I can't bear caviar."

Joyfully, the Marchants elected Kitty to the same category of quaint but endearing knick-knack which they had devised for her son. Like Peter, Kitty did not seem to mind. "Your mother," she said to Anna, "thinks you are so clever to have found us."

Anna said hastily, "She doesn't mean to be patronizing."

"Of course not!" said Kitty in surprise. "She is so kind."

24

Anna stared.

"And brave," said Kitty, taking out her needlepoint.

"Brave?"

Kitty unwound skeins of pink and beige wool.

"Brave. I'm not brave, so I always spot it in others."

A fortnight before Anna and Peter were married, Anna's father was knocked down in the Fulham Road at two in the morning by a van driving without headlights. His companion managed to drag him into St. Stephen's Hospital, where he died within the hour. Anna, neither knowing what she felt, nor what she would like to feel, went to her mother expecting to find Laura in a similar confusion of relief and distress, and treating her loss as occasion for a fine theatrical flourish.

But Laura was sad; deeply, quietly sad. She sat in the dishevelled shabby glamour of her bedroom and stared out of the window for hours at a time. Gently, Anna tried to suggest that a life free of an ageing queen had a great deal to recommend it. Laura said simply, in reply, "But I loved him."

Anna said, "How—" and stopped.

"If I had not loved him, I should have left him," Laura said. "But I did love him. And he loved me. He loved me more than anyone."

In consequence of his death the wedding was very quiet. "Barely audible, Kittykins," Laura confided, putting on a brave show of a scarlet hat and a velvet coat stamped with heraldic signs in gold. Kitty wore powder-blue. Anna wore a short cream dress, from which her long legs emerged, seemingly, for ever.

After the service, Peter said, "I wish we hadn't slept together. I wish tonight was the first night."

"Are you being romantic or religious?" Anna asked, wanting to know.

He looked at her. "You should know me better than to have to ask that."

They had a peculiar little wedding breakfast in West Kensington. St. Agatha was lifted from the sofa and stationed at the window in a bridal veil, to the electrification of passers-by. They sat, with some of the lovers, and with Peter's startled Uncle Roland, at an improvised round table draped in shawls, and ate seafood and drank Guinness and champagne. Anna felt, with a sudden pain, huge affection for her mother, for the house of her childhood, at last for her dead father. She looked at Peter, gravely answering the teasing of one of the lovers, and wondered if what she felt for him was the same quality of feeling that her parents had known and relied upon. Then Kitty kissed her, and gave her a pearl brooch, shaped like a lily of the valley, which had been her mother's and they climbed into Peter's Morris Minor and drove away to Wales, for a honeymoon. They stayed in a pub, near Penmaen Pool, and walked for miles and miles each day. They only had a week. On the last day, Peter bought Anna a Welsh wool shawl she had craved, striped like the summer sea, and, when they packed to go home, she deliberately left all her cardigans behind, in the rickety chest of drawers of the pub bedroom.

At theological college, near Oxford, the docility of most of the wives of other students irritated Anna. She said to Peter, "I won't be, in inverted commas, a 'clergy wife.' " She said sometimes to the other students' wives, "I married the man, not the job." Only the older ones, the ones whose husbands had been engineers and farmers and management consultants first, agreed with her. They often looked very strained to Anna, as if they were holding on to their loyalty for dear life. Loyalty was not yet a problem for Anna. She worked in a language school in Oxford, and returned home at night with coffee and flowers from the covered market, and a fine little air of independence. Peter admired her for it; he liked the way she stood out from the other wives. She made a friend at the language school, a fellow teacher called Eleanor Ramsay, who was married to a young don and wished to be a writer. In turn, Eleanor introduced her to someone else, a young woman named Mary Hammond-Heath, who had been at Oxford with Eleanor, and who was not much interested in being married. She had read law as an undergraduate and was now reading for the Bar. She came home to Oxford at weekends, and she and Eleanor and Anna spent Saturdays together, and often the husbands joined them for supper. Peter called Mary and Eleanor The Friends. They were Anna's first women friends of significance.

When Peter was made curate in a northern suburb of Bristol, Anna celebrated the event by becoming pregnant. Eleanor Ramsay did not become pregnant until three years later. Anna and Peter had a small, yellow terraced house with a garden, and Anna worked part-time as a clerk in the almoner's office of a nearby hospital; the Ramsays had only a flat, off Norham Gardens in Oxford, and even less money than the Bouveries because they were supporting Eleanor's widowed mother-in-law, who had senile dementia. Mary Hammond-Heath, still not a qualified barrister, lived in a room in a house in Clapham, and came to see the Bouveries on the long-distance bus, because it was cheaper. They none of them had much money, but the Bouveries had a house, for which they did not have to pay rent. It was also a pleasant parish, and the vicar's wife was very kind to Anna and shielded her from exploitation.

"She is so young," she said to her husband. "And she's such an appealing girl. I don't quite know what it is, but it's more than looks. It's a kind of sparkle, and it would be such a shame to extinguish it with duty. She hasn't had time to have any freedom yet."

That brief curacy was to be the best of her freedom. When Charlotte was born, Anna stopped working. The parish was very interested in Charlotte, and supportive, but Anna could no longer be independent. Her baby and the parish, like water flooding slowly across low-lying land, began to claim her, as did a new and unwelcome preoccupation with money. Without her earnings, and with the addition of Charlotte, money seemed to have dwindled to nothing. Anna was twenty-three.

It was the first occasion in her life that she had had to take stock of it. She had no idea whether she was early or late in doing so, and was inclined to chastise herself for self-indulgence. She wrote a long and intimate letter to Eleanor describing her state of mind and her new and disturbing sense of isolation, but Eleanor was working on the first draft of her first novel, and replied at length but not to the point. The lives of her characters were more preoccupying to her than Anna's life. Anna read the letter with incomprehension, then put Charlotte into her secondhand pram—donated by the Young Wives' Group—and went out for a long and significant walk.

It was significant because during the course of it two things became very plain to Anna. The first was that, although several people recognized her and stopped her and peered into the pram saying "Ah," to none of them could she have begun to say what was on her mind. In none of them, even in the young woman who was almost her age and who had a baby Peter had just christened, could she confide. They were friendly and nice, but she was the curate's wife and somehow, therefore, in a separate category of human being. If she had entrusted one of them with her secret thoughts, made one of them into a particular friend, it would have created immediate parochial difficulties, rifts and divisions and jealousies. There was, Anna saw with clarity, no possibility of intimate friendship within the parish, and never would be. Later, much later, when she had occasion to meet a policeman's wife, a woman who had been beaten up by her husband for taking a lover on the nights he was on duty, the wife said to her, "Well, you ought to understand. You should know how lonely it is for us."

The second thing that struck her was on a different plane, but was another restriction. She was suddenly hungry, being young and having pushed Charlotte for several miles on a cold October afternoon, and longed for a bar of chocolate. She had braked the pram outside a newsagent and was just stooping to pick up Charlotte and take her inside for the chocolate, when she thought: I mustn't. She had enough money with her and the chocolate wasn't going to be expensive, but chocolate was not what her money—Peter's money, their money—was for. She took her hands away from Charlotte and thought of the half-loaf at home. She must go back and eat that. She must get into the habit of using what she had, loaves instead of chocolate, herself instead of other people.

She was not, at twenty-three, in the least cast down by either of these realizations. Pushing Charlotte home in the dusk, she felt rather exhilarated, as if she had made a discovery. It did not cross her mind—and would not, for several years—that Peter could not supply a complete companionship and that she would intermittently always yearn for metaphorical chocolate. When she got home, she answered an advertisement in the parish magazine for a baby minder (how simple; why had she not thought of it before—she was at home minding Charlotte anyway, so why not several more?) and offered herself to the Vicar's wife for parish duties. The Vicar's wife gave her the magazine to edit and type up.

The moment she had settled to this, Peter was given his first parish, a little parish in a country town to the south of Bristol. The vicarage was half a huge Victorian house—once it had been the whole—and the parish was elderly and sedate. Within weeks, it became perfectly plain that the parish was in the inflexible grip of a powerful and intractable laity, who would not let go. Peter, unable to bear such a pedestrian first appointment (he saw himself in those days as a fervent worker priest), chafed almost from their arrival. He badgered his local rural dean, wrote letters to the nearest archdeacon and then to the Bishop, complaining of his frustration and begging he might be relieved of it.

Infected by his impatience, Anna grew restless too. There were no small industries around the town, so few working mothers, so no call for the baby minding she had grown accustomed to. There seemed to be nobody to teach, and the quiet, firm lay organizers of the parish were not about to allow a girl of twenty-four to interfere with the way things were done. They disliked having so young a couple in the vicarage and they made that plain. When Laura came to stay, and swept into church in an Easter bonnet of her own devising which quivered with artificial lilac, and laughed out loud at a tiny joke in

Peter's sermon, to encourage him, one of the church-wardens wrote to the Bishop.

Bored and thwarted, Peter and Anna turned to one another. The result was Luke, born two weeks after Anna's twenty-fifth birthday, and almost called Benedict, whose Rule Peter was then enthusiastically studying. They argued contentedly about which saint emerged as the more attractive personality: St. Benedict won on grounds of religious influence, St. Luke on those of influence over secular life, because of his gospel. In the end, Anna won. Benedict Bouverie, she said, was affected in any case, because it alliterated. The day she brought Luke home from hospital Peter was offered a slum parish in another diocese, in Birmingham; sole charge, a mighty challenge. They celebrated in the cavernous vicarage kitchen with a shop pork pie and a bottle of local cider, both of which later gave five-day-old Luke colic.

To The Friends, Anna's life in a slum had radical chic. Eleanor's husband had secured his first lectureship, and her first novel had been acclaimed in literary circles. They had bought their first house and were expecting their first baby. They drove to Birmingham occasionally and were deeply, seriously interested in the problems of such a parish as St. Andrew's. Mary Hammond-Heath had distinguished herself as junior to a QC in a fraud case that had made national headlines, and was inclined to regard the Bouveries' life as an excellent test case for some of her theories. She had also become agnostic, and could see no sense in expecting a God to take the slightest interest in St. Andrew's. But she quoted the Bouveries in London, as the Ramsays quoted them in

Oxford. Anna, knowing nothing of this, and battling to come to terms with the violence of her surroundings, while The Friends seemed to expand and achieve by the month, succumbed every so often to the demon envy.

It was also evident that St. Andrew's was almost too much for Peter, even from the beginning. He took everything too seriously, and was apt to shoulder all burdens, all responsibilities, to initiate too many schemes for battered women, delinquent children, alcoholics, drug abusers, prostitutes, the old and the destitute. Anna, determined not to be able to reproach herself for not trying, took on the women and children. There was no peace. The kitchen and the one spare bedroom were constantly, noisily occupied, the doorbell rang at all hours, and once, when she answered it, a man she had never seen struck her on the side of the head with an empty bottle and told her to leave his wife alone.

They put a chain on the front door and bolts on the ground-floor windows. Anna only went to her meetings if she was accompanied, and never after dark because she trusted no-one else to guard the children. One Guy Fawkes' night, she found the children's bedroom window shattered and a half-brick on the floor, so Peter tacked chicken wire across the frame inside. Anna was so frightened she grew furiously angry with Peter and screamed at him and accused him of putting God before herself and the children. He said, "I am doing what I have to do." Incoherent with rage and terror, she threw a dictionary at him and caught his temple. He bled copiously and went about the parish for a week adorned with a large piece of sticking plaster, like a clown. But he emptied the house of its demanding lodgers, some of whom subsequently abused him, when they saw him in the street. In the eyes of the more docile he read their unsurprised acceptance of the fact that even God would not help them. He wondered sadly aloud to Anna whether experience could finally make one more robust. Anna, worn through to her nerve ends, said she thought one would probably drop dead before one ever knew. "I'm sorry," he said. Anna put her hands over her face. "Please don't be. I haven't the strength left to comfort you."

One day, taking the children into central Birmingham, Anna saw from the bus window the name of the language school she had taught at, in Oxford, on a board outside a small office block. She got off the bus at the next stop, and went back to the building, pushing the children in a collapsible pushchair, which had a propensity to collapse only when occupied. Yes, it was the same school, just another branch. Yes, there was a vacancy for part-time work. Yes, Anna might apply for interview. Anna went home via St. Andrew's Church, where she apologized to God and then thanked Him. She then went home—there was a man asleep on the doorstep whom she took care not to waken—and apologized to Peter. He said, "It's hard, isn't it? I never knew it would be so hard." They held each other soberly, and Anna noticed he was as thin as a ruler, all bone.

He's too thin now, Anna thought, kneeling in Loxford. St. Andrew's nearly killed both of us, in various ways, but Peter couldn't say so. He had asked to be tested. Now, in a way, he has asked to be rewarded. He failed the test and the reward has gone to someone else and it is not, Anna said fiercely to herself, pressing her palms to her closed eyes, it is not fair that he should never know what he cannot do, that he should always set himself targets he can't achieve, that he should never be allowed to progress.

Around her the congregation rustled to its feet, indicating that she should go up to the communion rail first, as was fitting, as was customary. Peter did not look at her as she walked towards him up the chancel: he stood waiting, holding the paten, the first moonlike communion wafer ready between finger and thumb. She knelt in front of him and raised her crossed hands. There is no gaiety in Peter, she thought, bending her face to the wafer, no real pleasure in living, just an anxious shrinking from everything except duty; obligation has become his Rule, he clings to it, it stops him drowning. The communion wafer glued itself to the roof of her mouth. She pressed it with her tongue, as she had pressed hundreds, thousands now, over twenty years' worth of these papery discs stamped with crosses, made by nuns. I take communion too often, Anna thought, I take it to show the flag, Peter's flag, and I never think what I am doing.

"The Blood of Christ," Peter said softly, stooping to her with the chalice. She took it in both hands. She loved the chalice, made in 1652, used in Loxford church for over three hundred years. She took a sip of wine, sweet and strong. Peter, with a square of folded white linen, laundered by Anna among all the Rectory sheets and pillowcases, wiped the place on the chalice that her lips had touched, and moved on.

3

❖ ❖ ❖

MISS DUNSTABLE DECIDED to say nothing about the Rector's imperfectly ironed surplice. She decided this on Monday afternoon, having seen Anna digging manfully in the vegetable garden she had made behind the Rectory. The apple trees beside it, to Miss Dunstable's eye, also looked properly pruned. Miss Dunstable surveyed this evidence of—to her mind—most proper domestic industry, from a hundred yards away, on the footpath to her favourite walk, and made up her mind on the side of tolerance. So firmly did she make it up that she even waved her stout walking stick in the air, and hallooed at Anna.

Anna straightened up, looked round, and hallooed faintly back. Triumphant and satisfied, Miss Dunstable marched away. Anna returned to the task of removing the last fibrous old leeks of winter, which would make, oh groan, yet more soup. She was proud of her ability to make things grow, a new skill, developed at Loxford, but a garden was a tyrant as well as a satisfaction, and this garden was regarded by her family as very much

35

her business. Luke would mow, or sweep leaves, very occasionally, but with the air of one earning himself exemption from such tasks for months to come. Flora was only a nuisance, stopping after seconds of weeding to write her name in pebbles on the lawn (all ready for the tender teeth of the mower blades) or float daisy heads in a puddle, and Peter was never so galvanized by holy necessity calling from the far side of the parish as when the garden was mentioned. Anna thought he did not much notice the country, earth, growing things; but then he had not observed city things much, either.

"What are you thinking about?" Isobel Thompson said.

She had rung the doorbell, but as no-one had come she had walked round the house to the garden. She wore a fawn mackintosh and a scarf patterned with neat flowers. Straightening up for a second time, Anna thought Isobel looked more like a librarian than a deacon. Was one of the problems with the public perception of women deacons the fact that they did, often, look so like librarians?

"Peter," Anna said.

Isobel stepped on to the earth, and kissed her. "That's why I've come."

"It's really nice of you, but if you say one word about the Will of God, I shall hit you with my fork."

Isobel said, "Would you like me to dig too, or will you stop and make me a cup of coffee?"

"You can't dig," Anna said. "Not with your little white deacon's hands. And you've got trim little parish shoes on."

Isobel Thompson took off her scarf and ruffled her grey curls. "Goodness me. You are cross."

"I'm angry. And miserable. Peter deserves better."

"Shall I go away?"

"Please don't."

Isobel said, "I don't expect Peter minds as much as you do."

"Why? Because of his vocation?"

"Exactly."

Anna stuck her fork in the earth and scraped mud off her boots against it. "I think you overestimate vocation."

"How is Flora?"

"Much the same."

"And Luke?"

"He wants to travel, this summer. Some friends have clubbed together to buy an old van and they think they are going to drive to India. I don't blame him, but we can't help him. I wouldn't mind driving to India."

They began to walk back towards the house. Isobel put her hand on Anna's arm.

"I'm sorrier than I can say. Truly I am. But might it not draw you and Peter together?"

"Not so far."

"Anna," Isobel said pleadingly, "Anna, don't so set your face against things—"

Anna whirled round.

"My face! My face is set against nothing! It's the damned Church, Isobel, that's what it is! Slammed doors, refusals, hierarchy, muddle, divisions, loneliness. I'm sick of it. And I'm sick of seeing what it's doing to Peter—" She stopped and took a breath. "It's a prison, you see," she said in a calmer voice. "It may not be spiritually so, if you are lucky, but socially it is a prison. I can't be myself. I can't be an individual, only someone relative to Peter, to the parish, to the Church. I'm forty-two and I don't expect I ever will be myself now. The parish has become the other woman in my life—our lives—I don't blame Peter for that, he has to believe in its importance in order not to feel he has wasted everything. I expect that for other clergy wives whose husbands are less disappointed than Peter, God is the other woman. Do you understand me? Are you listening?''

''Oh yes,'' Isobel said sadly.

They had reached the back door and the muddle of trugs and boot scrapers and milk-bottle crates that lay outside it.

''Of course I'm not tidy,'' Anna said, following Isobel's gaze, ''of course I can't be. I'd go mad if I had to be tidy as well as everything else. Come in and I'll make you coffee.'' She paused and opened the door. ''Actually, I think I shall go mad. It seems to me the only thing to do.''

When Isobel had gone—dear, patient, wise Isobel whom she loved and to whom she was often so unreasonable—Anna ran water into the empty coffee mugs and stood them in the sink. It was two o'clock. There was time to start on the parish magazines before the school bus came, a job which had reverted to Peter because he was not good at asking people to do things he did not like doing himself. So Anna did it, on foot, delivering the magazines to the twenty-seven households in Loxford who took it, chiefly, Anna suspected, for the useful directory on the back page of plumbers and decorators and taxi services. They also liked it—as did the other villages—for the spiteful inter-village competitiveness that lay under the seemingly innocent accounts of the Snead Women's Institute going on an Easter outing to Weston-super-Mare, while the Quindale branch could only muster a local dried-flower expert whose crisp and solid arrangements, adorned with bows of florist's ribbon, they could all have recognized in their sleep. There was also the monthly parish draw—top prize, £5—a "Children's Corner" (rabbits and a cross to colour in this month) and Peter's "Letter from the Rector," which Anna had given up reading because she could not recognize the man in the message. "Is it a myth that the Church is just for Sundays?" he had written. Exchanging her shoes once more for Wellington boots, Anna wondered if he found such phrases in a "How to . . ." book.

She carried the magazines in a plastic bag from Pricewell's, the supermarket in Woodborough. It was the combination of the carrier bag and the boots and the voluminous purple cloak that had been a present from Laura that attracted the attention of the man at the first-floor windows of Loxford Old Rectory, the man who had decided to buy it.

Patrick O'Sullivan, whose Daimler stood at the elegant, twin-leaved front door below, turned to the present owner of the house and said, "Who is that?"

Susie Smallwood peered out under the festoon blind. As was usual with Susie, she was being uprooted by her restless husband the moment the last blind was in place, this time to Oxfordshire. She didn't particularly mind leaving Loxford. At least the new house was close to the M40 and thus to London. She said, "Oh, that's the Rector's wife."

"Are you sure?"

Susie turned away from the window. "She always dresses like that. Causes a lot of talk. Her mother's an actress."

Patrick O'Sullivan went on watching as Anna walked along the lane.

"What is the Rector like?"

Susie had never been to church.

"He seems all right. Bit dreary." She sighed. "Do you want to see the main bedroom again?"

Anna walked on, swinging her bag. It was a dead time of day in Loxford, with only a handful of people out in their gardens—she would have to have the usual shouted conversation with Mr. Biddle among his brassica stumps, and a whispered one with Mrs. Eddoes, who treated life as a giant conspiracy—and nobody in the shop or on the green. She always began her delivery among the less picturesque groups of cottages on the south side of the green. These cottage front doors were never used—some even had rows of flowerpots across the sill as a deterrent—and Anna had to go round to the back to find a resting place for the magazine. There was no sentimentality about these cottages. Their back doors were protected by makeshift porches of ribbed plastic, and the gardens grew as many derelict motor bikes as they did dahlias and cabbages. Only the windows had been modernized, with the old, many-paned windows replaced with blank sheets of glass through which Anna could see the inhabitants, burrowed deep in the comfortable fusty layers of their living-rooms, mindlessly absorbed in the relentless quacking of the television set. These were the people, Anna thought affectionately, who knew the rules of village living, as of old. She wedged their magazines between old paint tins and imperfectly washed milk bottles and towers of flowerpots, and crept away.

The north side of the green was another matter. The prettier cottages here faced south, and were divided from the green by a stream, which necessitated a little stone bridge to every garden gate. Here the Vinsons lived, and the Partingtons, and the Dodswells, all newcomers to country life who had decided ideas, gleaned chiefly from magazines, as to how to live it. Their cottages had scarcely survived their attentions. It gave Anna real pain to post magazines through one new front door hinged and studded so as to resemble part of the set for a pantomime of *Robin Hood,* and then another, moulded and classically pedimented, between half-pilasters made of fibreglass. The third had a goblin lantern, and stone frogs cemented (for fear of theft) to the little bridge and a nameplate which read "The Nook." Yet Elaine Dodswell, who inhabited The Nook, produced the annual Sunday-school Christmas Play, and organized the parish hospital-run for those visits to out-patients' departments at Woodborough so cherished by three-quarters of the population. "You," said Anna to herself, squeezing a magazine into The Nook's small and fancy wrought-iron mouth, "are a snob. God is not a snob. God values Elaine Dodswell because she does what she does with a good grace. Which is more, my girl, than can be said for some."

The Nook's door opened.

"I'm so glad to catch you," Elaine Dodswell said. She wore a tracksuit and an expression of deep sympathy. "I heard. I just heard. I'm ever so sorry for you both but of course I'm ever so relieved. We don't want to lose you."

Anna stared.

"Colin heard in Woodborough. In the pub, he said. The Coach and Horses."

Anna leaned weakly against the varnished door jamb.

"Nothing's private, is it? You can't breathe in a village—"

41

"Come in," Elaine said. "Come in and have a coffee."

"I can't. I've got eighteen more houses before the school bus. But thank you."

"Is Peter ever so upset?" Elaine asked cosily.

"Oh no," Anna said, "I think he's relieved. He was advised, you know, but he loves it here." She stood upright again. "It would have been an awful wrench."

Elaine nodded.

"Yes. Yes, I'm sure it would. I'll tell Colin, then." She began to push the door to. "He'll be ever so glad. We were so worried, that Peter'd mind."

The door closed and then Elaine pulled the magazine in, from inside, causing the letter box to snap shut smartly. Anna made a face at it before she turned away. Damn, damn, damn. No face to save, no place to hide. She crossed the bridge between the frogs and set off for the far end of the green, where the lane led up into the council estate. As she turned uphill, a dark-red Daimler slid by, and blew its horn at her. She stood and stared after it.

"It's the new chap!" Mr. Biddle bellowed from his potato bed across the green. "It's the chap that's bought the Old Rectory."

Anna waved in acknowledgement. Poor Susie Smallwood, she had always said to herself, poor Susie, with her discontented little face and her sports car and her Rolex watch; but now enviable Susie who could, and would, albeit with a show of petulance, leave Loxford and begin again.

" 'E give four 'undred thousand!" Mr. Biddle shouted. "Bloody crackpot!"

Anna turned away from the green and climbed the hill towards the council houses, in whose gardens interminable lines of washing were guarded by yellow-eyed German shepherd dogs. She could not help reflecting, as she pushed a magazine into the first letter box, that a world in which Daimler drivers could pay four hundred thousand pounds for a country house while she could not even muster a couple of hundred for Luke's modest share of an old transit van had a certain imbalance to it.

The school bus was late, so Anna was on time. Someone said to her, "Made it all right today, then, Mrs. B?" and she said, "I know. It's a bit of an achievement, isn't it?" and bravely smiled. They had watched her, in the council estate, they knew what she had been doing. They were not unkind people, not mean-minded, but it would never have occurred to them to offer to help. The parish magazines were Church business: Anna was the Rector's wife.

When the school bus pulled up, there was the usual avalanche of nine children, and then a pause. It was quite a long pause. Anna moved towards the bus steps and saw the driver looking behind him down the length of the bus, waiting. After several seconds, Flora came, as slow as a snail, bumping her bags down the steps, head bent.

"Flora," Anna said. "Darling—"

Flora raised her head a little. Her face was blotched and swollen with crying.

"Oh Flora," Anna said, holding out her arms.

Flora stopped in front of her, and leaned tiredly against her, still holding her bags. The village mothers and children watched in uneasy silence. Flora said something. Anna could not hear it. "What?" she said, stooping.

Flora whispered, "I can't bear it any more."

Holding her, Anna looked up at the others. They began to shift and move away. One of them, taking the lead, said loudly, "It's a shame. Poor kid. You want to tell the headmaster, Mrs. B. That's what you want to do."

"I've got a deanery meeting," Peter said.

He stood in the kitchen, half into his depressing mackintosh.

"Will you be late?"

"Nine-ish—"

"On the way to your meeting," Anna said, piling supper plates, "would you think about Flora?"

Peter shrugged on his second sleeve and began to button himself up, collar neat, belt buckled.

"Please—" Anna said in exasperation. "Please."

"What?"

"Must you do yourself up so—so *trimly*? Must you look so utterly suburban?"

"I am suburban."

"Flora," Anna said. "Just think about Flora."

"I was. It was you—"

"I know. I know, I'm sorry. I'm on edge because of Flora."

Peter finished buttoning and buckling.

"What do you suggest we do?"

"Take her away from Woodborough Junior and send her to St. Saviour's."

"But that's Catholic!"

"Same God."

"No," Peter said.

"So bullying is better?"

"Why St. Saviour's?"

"Because it's the cheapest private alternative in Woodborough."

"How cheap?" Peter said.

"Six hundred pounds a term."

He let out a yelp. "Six hundred!"

"Yes," Anna said. "Kind nuns. Small classes."

Peter seized the black document-wallet he always took to meetings. "You must be mad. Where can we find six hundred pounds three times a year?"

"Borrow it," Anna said, beside herself, not caring if the remark were a red rag to a bull.

Peter gasped. He glared at her, wrestling with himself, then he went out to the garage, banging the kitchen door behind him.

The telephone rang at once.

"Anna?"

"Yes—"

"Anna, it's Celia Hooper here. Just rang to remind Peter—"

"He's gone. Just left."

"Oh good. Splendid. Just rang to make sure. You know."

Celia Hooper, secretary to the Deanery Synod, one of what Anna thought of as Peter's groupies.

"Thank you, Celia."

"Not at all. Must fly. Bye!"

If we haven't got the money, Anna thought, putting the telephone down, and we can't borrow it, we must make it. She visualized more hours at her red lacquer table. Well, if needs must, they must. She considered telephoning Laura, and Kitty, both of whom were long on sympathy and short on cash—so strange that Peter's orthodox solicitor father should have left his widow quite as poorly provided for as Anna's unconventional one had left Laura—and decided that it would be unfair. What could they do, except be made miserable by impotence?

She went upstairs. Flora was lying on her bedroom floor doing her homework. Through the wall came the thump of rock music, which was Luke's required accompaniment to doing his.

"Flora," Anna said.

Flora rolled over and peered up at her mother. She looked terribly tired. Anna sat on the edge of Flora's bed. "Look," she said, "I think you've had enough."

Flora waited.

"I don't quite know how we'll manage it," Anna said, "but we will, somehow. You won't have to stay at Woodborough Junior much longer. I promise."

"St. Saviour's?" Flora said. She had seen the nuns in Woodborough. They had appeared to her like grey gulls, mysterious and soothing.

"Is that where you would like to go?"

Flora considered. Girls at St. Saviour's wore dark-green skirts and jerseys, not their own clothes.

"Could we afford the uniform?"

"I should think so. Secondhand, of course, but we're used to that."

Flora, suddenly flooded with relief, said stoutly, "But we always have new toothbrushes." She got up from the floor and sat on Anna's knee. "Soon?"

"I have to do a bit of planning. And talk to Sister Ignatia. You'll just have to bear it for a little while longer."

Flora leaned back and Anna put her arms around her.

"Did you pray?"

"No," Anna said.

"I did. I expect Daddy did. If you had, I might have gone to St. Saviour's last term."

"It isn't as simple as that."

Flora wasn't listening. She began to play with the string of amber glass beads round Anna's neck (Oxfam Shop, Woodborough).

"Perhaps I'll have a best friend," Flora said.

Laura came down from London on the long-distance bus. She had never learned to drive and disliked the train because, she said, you were too low in a train to see properly. A coach was just right; like being on a very tall horse, or even an elephant. And nowadays coaches had lavatories and armchairs and dear little hostesses whom Laura liked to induce to tell her their life stories.

"Do you know, Anna, my darling, that the poor child longed, only longed, to be a concert pianist but was literally forced by her ogrish father to nurse him while he died of drink and now her spirit is quite broken and all she can bring herself to do is dispense plastic cups of repellent coffee to OAPs going to Ferndown to see their married daughters?"

Laura travelled in style. She had a leather suitcase which bore the remains of labels from pre-war Oriental hotels, a hatbox and an immense carpet bag which sighed out little puffs of dust every time it was set on the ground. She also had a tattered travelling rug— "Purest cashmere, darling, just feel, adorable little goat's tums"—and a string bag full of books and apples. As the bus came to a halt in Woodborough bus station, Laura slid open the window and lowered her string bag down to her son-in-law.

"Darling. Too thrilling. Take this, do. Reminds me of Port Said, and you're a little bumboy in a boat."

The travelling rug followed the string bag, and then the driver came round the bus to release Laura's other luggage from the boot. She swept down the steps and embraced Peter warmly.

"Oh my darling, I've wept for you. I can't bear it."

Leaning against her with an almost childish relief, Peter said, "I'm not at all sure I can."

"And Anna?"

"What do you think?" Peter said. "What else can she feel but utterly let down?"

"Not by you."

"Oh," said Peter crossly, freeing himself and seizing Laura's luggage. "Who else could it be but me?"

Laura opened her mouth to say, The Church, of course, and shut it again. Tact, as she often proudly said, was as alien to her as hygiene—"The sign of a bourgeois mind"—but this was an occasion for affection above even a fine disregard for tact. If Peter were encouraged to despise and disbelieve the very authority he had given his life to, where would that leave him, but spinning in an abyss? So instead, Laura said, "She's just desperate with disappointment for you."

Peter, half hearing, said, "Oh, I'm desperate all right," and gave a little barking laugh, and set off across the bus station to the car park, grasping Laura's luggage.

Dear heaven, Laura thought, trotting after him with her string bag and her blanket. Dear merciful heaven, is this what happens to a thwarted man of God? She cast her eyes skywards, muttering soft curses. A man, passing her, took one startled look and reflected anew what a very unwise policy was the current one of closing nineteenth-century asylums and turning the inmates loose into an alarmed and inadequate society.

• • •

By bedtime, Laura was exhausted. She lay in Charlotte's bed and looked up at the ceiling that Charlotte had festooned with shawls and old curtains and Indian bedspreads (there was a definite small weight in one of those hammocks: what lay there? The body of a—mouse?) and considered the household now shut away around her in the spring darkness. They had all come to her, one by one, during the evening, an evening harried with telephone calls—"I don't think," Anna had said at one point, "that we have eaten an uninterrupted meal in twenty-one years"—and they had all explained to her how awful they felt, and how guilty they felt about feeling awful, because it wasn't anybody's fault, and that made it worse, having nobody to blame.

"I know Mum and Dad can't help with the van," Luke said. "And I'd like to make the money myself, I mean, I could, easily, at the Quindale garage, but I haven't time because of A levels and the others are all going at the beginning of July."

Laura, thinking privately that she would telephone Kitty and propose £100 each (St. Agatha must be worth something, silly to hang on to her for sentiment, even though she had now become something of a friend, someone waiting when Laura came home to what was, to be honest, a deeply, darkly dire apology for a decent flat), patted Luke and said, "Mmm."

Luke said, "I don't suppose you think it matters."

She turned huge eyes on him. "But I do! I'm plotting."

"The thing is," Luke said, encouraged, "I don't want to give Mum a lot of grief about it, but you do get hacked off with being patient, a bit."

"Wait!" Laura held up a forefinger burdened with an enormous cameo ring. "Just wait! And trust!"

49

"Sounds like a bloody dog," Luke said, grinning.

If Luke needed £200, Flora needed a uniform. It had not crossed Flora's mind that St. Saviour's might need payment for teaching her, only that her place there depended upon her ability to have the right uniform, all the uniform, down to the last sock, garter, and science overall.

"They must be green," Flora said to her grandmother, "with my name here"—she patted the left side of her nightie-clad chest—"in chain stitch. Mummy can't do chain stitch."

"Immaterial," Laura said, gesturing. "Chain stitch, satin stitch, feather stitch, stump work, back stitch, smocking, tacking—"

"Chain stitch," Flora said loudly. She had been in the habit of anxiety and tension for so long that she could not stop now, merely because the menace was being taken away. "Chain stitch, chain stitch," Flora cried, bursting into tears. "It has to be, I've seen one—"

Chain stitch, Laura thought, eyeing the weight in the ceiling cloth (had it moved?), chain stitch and £600 a term. She could only sell St. Agatha once, and there was precious little left besides to sell.

"I don't mind more work," Anna said, "but I have to confess that my heart does rather quail and fail at the thought of three times as much French jacquard-weaving machinery specifications to translate as I have already."

"Defy the village," Laura said. "Take pupils! Teach French!"

Anna, sitting on the side of Laura's bed wrapped in a bath towel, looked miserable.

"If it was just defying the village I wouldn't think twice. But if I defy the village—the parish—I automatically defy Peter. And truly I can't do that to him now, on top of everything.''

"I'll think," Laura said, shutting her eyes. "I'll cudgel my brains. Cudgel, cudgel.''

"Don't get me wrong," Anna said, standing up, "I'm not giving up. I'm just stuck. I can't think what to do next, except the same things. The same old rather fruitless things.''

Me too, Laura thought. Whither now, at sixty-five, with an agent who sends me postcards from abroad as conscience sops, but never telephones because what work is there for such a one as I (or is it me)? And is it better to be poor Kittykins, in that dull ground-floor flat in the wrong part of Windsor, for whom life's highlights have dwindled to pension day and nature programmes on the telly box? Gnash teeth, thought Laura, roll eyes, tear hair. She turned on her side so that, if the mouse on the ceiling began a stealthy movement, she would not see it. And then, as was her wont, she began to declaim ''The Lady of Shalott'' to herself, to chant herself to sleep. "God in his mercy, lend her grace," she muttered, thinking of Anna, her Anna, who had grown from being such a dull child into a truly engaging woman, a woman so richly deserving of being lent a little of God's grace. And why, why in hell's name, didn't He?

On Saturday morning, Peter went off to do his rounds of parish patients at Woodborough Hospital. Luke went with him, to see schoolfriends and to get out of Loxford. Flora sat in the kitchen, laboriously practising chain stitch on a rag torn from an old shirt of Peter's, and Anna, who was in charge of the cleaning-rota, went off to the church to see if it actually had been cleaned. Being medieval, she thought it was unsuitable for the church to be visibly glittering, but, if the pews and the brass weren't polished, it quickly looked sad and Anna did not like it to look sad. She had an affection for the building, as if it were a sturdy and uncomplaining beast that had stood and endured human volatility and neglect since 1320. It demanded very little and gave a good deal in return. When she was alone in it, she would, in affection and gratitude, pat the squat stone pillars that held up the nave roof. Laundering its altar linen and hoovering its aisle carpet often seemed like the instinctive care she gave to anything dependent of which she was fond. Today, only the altar candlesticks had been forgotten (it was Elaine Dodswell and Trish Pardoe's week and they could at least be relied upon) so Anna gathered them up and took them home to polish. On the way back, she met Miss Dunstable with an armful of pussy willow intended for the church porch.

"Action, action!" cried Miss Dunstable, indicating the candlesticks. "Good for you! Only way!"

"Only way to what?"

"Get anything done!"

"I think," Anna said a minute later, setting down her brass burden on the kitchen table, "I think I have had a little revelation."

"An angel!" Laura said.

"A tweed one," Anna said, thinking of Miss Dunstable. "A tweed one in a mackintosh hat. Action, she said, action. I've got to act—"

Flora, whose notions of acting were confined to the village nativity play, tugged in puzzlement at her sweaty chain stitch.

"As long as I do something *outside* the parish," Anna said, "does it matter what I do?"

"Teach again—"

"I can't. My qualifications aren't enough for state teaching, only for private language schools."

Laura flung out her arms.

"Does it matter? Petrol pumps, shop assistant, filing clerk, who cares?"

Anna looked at her.

"I don't," she said. "Not anymore."

4

❖   ❖   ❖

THE *ADMINISTRATION MANAGER* at Pricewell's
seemed to Anna very young. He was slim and dark and
he told her his name was Steve. (His office door—an
office the size of a cupboard—had "Mr. S. Mulgrove"
on it.) He said consolingly to Anna, "The lack of experience isn't a problem. Most of our school-leavers
don't have any experience."

It had been an impulse, appealing to Mr. S. Mulgrove.
Anna had been suddenly struck, as she pushed open
Pricewell's double glass doors, by the "Vacancy" notice pasted to the inside of it. "General staff wanted,"
it said, "Full- and Part-time, Stock and checkout assis-
tants. Apply the Administration Manager."

"May I take your name and address?" Mr. Mulgrove
said. Anna gave it. He did not flinch when she said "the
Rectory." Perhaps he didn't even realize what the im-
plication of living in a rectory was.

"I don't mind what I do," Anna said.

He said delicately, "Stock involves quite a lot of ladder work, in the warehouse . . ." as if Anna might not be up to such physical strenuousness.

"I think I'd rather climb ladders than sit at a check-out."

Mr. Mulgrove rather wanted to say that her voice and appearance would be an asset on the checkout, good for Pricewell's public image (a cause dear to his heart), but he was uncertain how to put this.

"I wouldn't like you to be in the wrong situation . . ."

Anna, emboldened by the energy of taking action, said, "Would I be paid more for one than the other?"

He shook his head.

"What would I be paid?"

As Anna was the sort of person Mr. Mulgrove associated with being a customer rather than a member of staff, he was suddenly embarrassed. He flicked, with much throat-clearing, through a plastic-sheeted folder.

"Three twenty-one an hour."

"Three pounds and twenty-one pence—"

"Yes."

"Heavens," Anna said. "You see, I need to make at least fifty pounds a week for thirty-six weeks a year."

He could not look at her: he was overcome by her directness. He said, "That would mean twenty hours a week as a part-time assistant. Four hours a day for five days."

There was a little pause.

"You're on," Anna said. She held her hand out to him. He took it doubtingly.

"You're sure?"

"Yes." She smiled at him. "Yes. It also means no Church and no village for twenty hours a week."

He did not understand. He wondered if he were making a mistake. He said, "Of course, there has to be a three-month trial—"

"Oh, of course."

"And you will have to work under supervision for the length of that period—"

"Why do you think I might be difficult?"

Mr. Mulgrove went scarlet. Give him a school-leaver any day, or a nice, motherly woman going back to work once her children were grown-up, or an obliging pensioner, prepared to collect trolleys from the car parks . . .

"I won't be difficult," Anna said gently, to comfort him. "I need a job and I'd be really grateful if you would let me have one."

He looked at her, for the first time. Why on earth did she need a job? What was she doing? Bravely he said, "You're not having me on?"

"No," Anna said, "no. My youngest child is being bullied at school and I want to send her to St. Saviour's. That's all."

Mr. Mulgrove relaxed. His sister had been to St. Saviour's. He stood up.

"If you'd like to come this way, Mrs. Bouverie, I'll show you the warehouse and the rest room." He held the door for her to squeeze past. "There's a bonus scheme, of course," he said, "for good work. Some people get awarded it before the trial period is up. It would mean an extra ten pence an hour."

"I can go in on the morning bus with Flora," Anna said, "and home on the early-afternoon one to Quindale. It's perfectly simple. And they were so nice. They said I could work just in termtime as long as I give them notice of the definite weeks a month in advance." She looked at Luke. They were sitting either side of the kitchen table, in the debris of supper. Peter had gone to the New End PCC meeting. "I will wear a navy-blue overall with a checked collar and cuffs, and a little badge saying, 'I'm Anna. Can I help you?' " She waited for Luke to laugh.

Luke did not laugh. People who are drowning in mortification do not find it easy to laugh. Luke would have said that politically he stood way to the left of his mother and way, way to the left of his father, but somehow he could not reconcile himself to the thought of his mother stocking shelves in Pricewell's. With a badge on. He had a lump in his throat and he felt his skin prickling with shame at the thought of his friends and his friends' mums going in to Pricewell's and seeing Anna unloading ketchup bottles with "Can I help you?" pinned on her overall.

"Oh Luke," Anna said. She used the tone of voice she had used when he was little and she caught him doing something he had been expressly forbidden to do. "Won't your principles stand being acted upon?"

"Shut up!" Luke shouted. He glared at her. She'd promised him money for the van, which she would make wearing that bloody badge. He didn't want money made that way; he didn't want the humiliation.

"I'm sorry," Anna said, "I didn't mean to tease. But really you must try to be a little consistent. And practical." She stopped. She had been about to say, You're just like Daddy, but that, though true, would not have been fair, or kind. So she said, "What's so different about my working in Pricewell's from your working at the garage?"

Luke squirmed. He could not say that the garage was macho and Pricewell's was naff, because she would

58

tease him again. He was unable to imagine what she was
after, why she had chosen this way out, why she seemed
so bloody cheerful.

"I'm not qualified to do much else," Anna said, in
the gentle voice she had used to Peter. ("It's deliberate,
isn't it?" Peter had said. "Just rubbing my nose in it.")
"It won't be for ever."

"Why can't you do something where people can't
see?"

"Ah," Anna said, "I see. You do think like Daddy,
don't you?"

"What's Dad think?"

"That I'm doing it to show off. That it's Ga coming
out in me, a kind of exhibitionism. Why can't I go and
be a clerk in the Council offices where no-one can see,
is that it? Well, I'd rather work in a shop, among people."

"But—"

"Luke," said Anna, leaning forward, looking intently
at him, "Luke, I want to be *normal.*"

He held her gaze for a couple of seconds, then
dropped his own.

"Yeah."

"This doesn't have to be a big deal. This has to be a
practical way to rescue Flora and get you to India or
wherever. You and Daddy seem to expect a freedom for
yourselves you have no intention of awarding me."

Jesus, Luke thought, I'm going to cry.

"If your friends' mothers despise me for working in
a supermarket, then they are to be pitied. But they won't.
They'll understand. Women do," Anna said with vehemence.

Luke rubbed his hand across his eyes and nose.

"You ought to know," Anna said more gently, "you

59

ought to know by now that things you want don't just fall off trees. There's Charlotte on the most basic grant, you dressed entirely from the Pakistani stalls in Woodborough market, Daddy miserable because he can't just magic up school fees for Flora. It's a struggle, isn't it? You know that."

Luke nodded. He understood all right, but he had a dim feeling that dignity was all the same compromised by what Anna proposed to do. He thought he would not begin on all that, so he got up from the kitchen table.

"Well, Flora seems pretty happy—"

Anna smiled. "Now she has cracked chain stitch, she's fine."

"I liked Woodborough Junior."

"You're a very different kettle of fish from Flora." She paused, and then she said, "And from me."

Luke turned in the kitchen doorway and said suddenly, "Mum, you OK?"

Anna nodded. Luke looked relieved. "I'll go up then," he said, and went.

On Anna's first morning at Pricewell's, she caught the early bus with Luke and Flora. Flora clung to her, like a limpet. As the bus swung slowly round Loxford green, Anna saw that two immense removal vans were parked in the drive of Loxford Old Rectory. The Smallwoods were off to Oxfordshire. Anna made a mental note to go in that evening and wish them well: Peter would like it; poor Peter, who had broken down in bed the night before, and wept that he had failed her, failed her as well as—but he couldn't actually articulate that.

"It's not your fault," she had said, hardly knowing what she meant.

"It is, it is. I've failed everything I've attempted."

"I don't think so," Anna said. "I think the goalposts have been moved. Godly goalposts."

It was two in the morning. She had been downstairs to make tea.

"Are you lonely?" she said to Peter, handing him a mug.

He seemed reluctant to answer, doubtful. He said at last, "I've got you," in a slightly hearty voice. She waited for him to ask her if she was lonely, but he didn't, merely drank his tea obediently, like a child with hot milk.

"Do you want," Anna said, embarking impulsively on the thinnest ice, "do you want to reconsider everything? I mean *everything*? Our lives, where we live, even—even what you do?"

He stared at her.

"Heavens, no."

"Sure?" she said, persisting. "I wouldn't be afraid, you know."

"No," he said loudly. He set the mug on the tray. "I can't just throw it in because I haven't succeeded yet. The test is part of it all."

"Part?"

"Part of holiness," Peter said rapidly. "To be tested is to suffer. Suffering is part of spiritual progress. You know that, that's child's stuff."

"So is listening."

"Listening?"

"To me," Anna said. She jerked a glance upwards. "To Him."

Peter made an impatient noise.

"So you think I don't pray?"

Inside herself, Anna shrank away. They had had this kind of conversation before and it always ended with her frustrated and him defiant.

"No," Anna said tiredly, "I don't think that. I was only trying to help spring you from a trap if you felt you were in one."

"I'm not in a trap," he said, "I'm just in a dark bit of the wood."

"Sure?" she said for a second time.

"Oh, quite."

He'd slept then. In the morning he looked hollow-eyed, but he'd gone off, with dogged cheerfulness, to take prayers at Snead Hall, a sad, second-rate little girls' public school, where he was Chaplain, and the rest of them had caught the bus. He had not, Anna tried to remember, wished her luck.

Flora had to be detached from Anna physically as the bus approached her school. Luke had to pull off her hands, one by one, and half carry her along the bus and down the steps. When he got her on to the pavement, she sagged against the school wall and would not move. Luke shouted up to Anna that he would take Flora in, and then walk on to the sixth-form college. "You're a hero," she mouthed back. She felt sick, and tearful at Luke's goodness. He waved and grinned at her and jerked a thumb upwards. The bus pulled away from her children and headed for the market-place.

"Anna," said Mr. Mulgrove with an effort (he would so much have preferred to call her Mrs. Bouverie), "this is your supervisor."

"Hi," said the supervisor. He looked about sixteen. He had red hair and a bad complexion and huge ears. But he was smiling broadly. "I'm Tim."

"I'm Anna," Anna said, anxious to do what was expected of her.

"We're on grocery," Tim said, "we're doing bottled sauces and mustards this morning." He waved a batch of papers at her. "Stock reports," he said enticingly.

Rustling in her stiff new overall—Mr. Mulgrove's administrative eye had rested in disappointment on the extra foot of Anna's grey corduroy skirt that hung below it—Anna followed Tim out of the warehouse and down a grim cold staircase on to the shop floor. It was like coming on stage in a theatre, out of the dark wings into warmth and light. Tim loped off down an alleyway lined with pet food, and halted before a tier of shelves of bottles, brown and red bottles, ochre and copper and olive-green.

"Got to do your facings," Tim said.

Anna nodded.

"Know about facings?"

Anna thought about the needlework classes of her schooldays, in which she had been such a conspicuous non-success. Facings had been something of a nightmare then, a closed book of mysterious rites that led, finally, her teacher assured her, to the temple of tailoring.

"No," Anna said with complete honesty to Tim, her supervisor, who was certainly young enough to be Tim, her son, "I know absolutely nothing about facings."

Tim looked delighted. He turned behind him to a metal trolley where neat regiments of jars and bottles waited breathlessly under sealing plastic. Tim considered them, glanced back at his shelves, noticed a gap and pounced upon a rectangular block of tikka masala sauce.

"Now," he said. His ears glowed with satisfaction. "Check your stock sheet. Column one: numbers of items in case." He held out the block; this was a game for

Anna to play with him. She counted obediently.

"Twelve."

"No need to look. Stock sheet tells you that. Second column: shelf allocation?"

Anna peered.

"Two?"

"Right. Twelve jars to go two abreast. And the front two," Tim said with emphasis, "must touch the shelf rim exactly—that's called presenting—and," he paused, "they must all face the front. That's called facing up. Now you put them on the shelves, and I'll check you."

It was not, Anna reflected, unlike doing the church flowers, except that Tim was being so much nicer to her than Miss Dunstable or Freda Partington ever were. He stood three feet behind her with his adolescent arms folded inside his blue overall sleeves and said, "That's right. You're getting there. Cheers," at intervals.

When Anna stepped back, she said, "I think I'll go straight home and face and present the larder."

Tim did not understand. He said, wagging a forefinger, "No coffee break till ten-thirty-five!"

At ten-thirty-five, a stout woman in a blue overall with plain, pale-blue collar and cuffs to denote her seniority came up with a clipboard and said, "Tim and Anna. Ten minutes coffee."

Anna said, "I'll just finish the teriyaki sauces." They had a pretty label with almond blossom and a blue cone of oriental mountain printed on them. Tim and the stout woman looked astonished.

"It's coffee break," Tim said reprovingly.

He led Anna back up the gaunt staircase to the dining-room Mr. Mulgrove had shown her when she came for interview. "Two-course lunch with fruit juice, ninety-five pence," Mr. Mulgrove had said, and then, indicating a brightly coloured graph on a notice board, "Our wast-age display. We try and beat it every week." He had looked very grave at the thought of all those rotting star fruit, those superannuated pies and fizzing yoghurts.

"Smoke?" Tim said.

Anna shook her head. She was surprisingly pleased to sit down.

"Getting engaged, Easter," Tim said, lighting up and drawing deeply.

"Are you? How are you going to ask her? Have you planned it?"

"I didn't ask," Tim said. "Her mum said why didn' we get engaged Easter so we said yeah." He pulled a photograph out of his shirt pocket inside the overall, and held it out to Anna. "She works at Crompton's, on the industrial estate. Wages clerk."

Anna looked at a plump little person with a deter-mined mouth. She wore jeans and a black leather jacket.

"Will you be married in church?"

"She wants it."

"Don't you?"

"Bit old-fashioned, i'n'it?" Tim said.

"You could excuse God for thinking He was perhaps beyond fashion—"

"Come again?"

"Sorry," Anna said, "thinking aloud."

Tim looked at the clock.

"Time's up."

Later, silently passing each other little stone jars of French mustard, Tim said, "I never heard anyone say God 'cept for swearing. Seems a bit rude to say it oth-erwise."

"God and death," Anna said, marshalling jars, "two of the rudest words in the world."

This was going too far. Tim said loudly, to quell her, "We run six'n a half thousand lines in Pricewell's. Six'n a half thousand."

He left her only once, to go to the lavatory. He was gone perhaps for five minutes. During those five minutes, while she was reading the history of the pop-padom from the back of a packet, a female voice said to her, in a strangled way, "Mrs. Bouverie?"

She looked up. There, poised and trim in a camel jacket (probably Jaeger) and a plaid skirt (undoubtedly The Scotch House), stood Mrs. Richardson. Mrs. Richardson, wife of Colonel Richardson (churchwarden, Diocesan Board of Finance, Red Cross, Council for the Preservation of Rural England) of Quindale House. From her suavely coiffed pearl-grey head to her excellent shoes polished to the gloss of a new conker, Mrs. Richardson radiated amazement.

"Mrs. Bouverie. Anna?"

"Heavens, Marjorie," Anna said, "I quite forgot about you."

"Forgot?"

"Forgot that, occasionally, you shop in Pricewell's."

Mrs. Richardson looked round.

"Are you an *employee*?"

"Yes."

"With your husband's consent?"

"Only reluctant, I'm afraid," Anna said. Tim was coming loping down the aisle. "Needs must where the devil drives, Marjorie. This is my supervisor, Tim. Tim, this is Mrs. Richardson, from Quindale."

"Pleased to meet you," Tim said cheerfully. "Anna's first day."

Marjorie Richardson swung her trolley in a neat, brisk semicircle.

"I shall telephone you," she said to Anna.

Tim watched her walk away from them, upright and outraged.

"She a friend?"

Anna checked her stocklist for the shelf allocation for the poppadoms (plain, spiced, garlic and chilli, ready-cooked) with all the slick professionalism of three hours' experience.

"Not any more, I'm afraid."

"Was it very dull?" Kitty Bouverie asked her daughter-in-law, on the telephone.

"Yes. But quite peacefully so. I am instructed by a boy who is getting married because his girlfriend's mother has told him to."

Kitty Bouverie was not really listening. Since hearing of Anna's job, she had been fired with restiveness, pacing round her small green-and-magnolia sitting-room, peering yearningly out of its single window at the narrow terrace which was all of the outside world that she owned.

"How old," Kitty said, "were the oldest people working at Pricewell's?"

"I should think in their sixties."

"I'm in my sixties!" Kitty cried.

Anna waited.

"There's a branch of Pricewell's here," Kitty said. The flat seemed suddenly as small and confining as a birdcage. "Was it difficult, what you did today?"

"Oh no. And you are helped."

The word "helped" seemed like a balm to Kitty. Nobody helped her beyond the poor sad girl at the library to whom she was kind and who now bounded about the romantic fiction section for her, feverishly pulling down titles she thought Kitty would like. Neither of them cared for the sexually explicit—"Rather like having an operation described to one, don't you think?"

"Do you suppose," Kitty said now, "do you suppose that there is even any point in my going to the manager and asking?"

Anna thought not, and could not say so.

"I would so like it," Kitty said wistfully. "I would so like to be with people."

"Isn't there something gentler?"

"I'm tired of gentleness," Kitty said crossly. "I feel like an old Marie biscuit that someone's left under the sofa."

"Then go to Pricewell's," Anna said, closing her eyes at the thought of telling Peter. "Go and good luck to you."

She had hardly replaced the receiver, when the telephone shrilled again.

"Anna?"

"Yes."

"My dear, it's Harry Richardson here. From Quindale. I wonder if I could just pop over. Have a quick word?"

On the second day, Tim showed Anna the system in the warehouse. On the third, he explained how to use the computer for reordering. On the fourth day he was off sick, and Mr. Mulgrove asked Anna if she thought she could manage, and to ask Heather on flours and dried fruits if she wasn't sure of anything. She said she would be fine. Indeed, to have a whole morning undisturbed by any thoughts profounder than wondering why on earth the people of Woodborough should consume so much tandoori curry powder, while ignoring pesto sauce, was quite luxurious. But Colonel Richardson came between Anna and the tandoori curry powder; personable, kindly, inflexible Colonel Richardson, who had sat in her insufficiently tidy sitting-room in his beautiful old tweed jacket, and had said to her that she was harming her husband, the community and the Church. She had explained to him about Flora, thinking that his undoubtedly benevolent heart would be touched. It was. Harry Richardson appalled Anna by offering to lend her Flora's school fees, interest-free, for as long as she needed them.

"Be glad to," he said.

Anna sat dumbstruck.

"Marjorie mistook you," Colonel Richardson said. "Didn't understand. Thought it was defiance. No idea about Flora. Too bad. Poor girl. Frightful places, these great state schools can be. Such a pity. Noble experiment, state education. Like the welfare state."

Anna said slowly, "You are so kind. But—but I don't think I can accept."

"Nonsense. Who's to know? You, me, Peter and Marjorie. Look," he said, leaning forward and putting a warm, capable hand on her knee. "I know what your financial situation is. Better than anyone. No joke. Don't blame you for earning a bit. Plucky stuff. Admire you for it. But it's out of the question. Completely, utterly. Not to be thought of."

"I want to do it," Anna said.

Colonel Richardson took his hand away.

" 'Course you do. Natural for a mother. Quite right. But you're a rector's wife before you're a mother. Church before children. Setting an example, if you like."

"Oh no," Anna said.

He stared.

In the phrase of twenty years before, Anna said, "I married the man, not the job. I'm not an outboard motor, I'm another boat."

"Don't follow you."

"I am truly grateful to you. You're a kind, dear man. But you are so used to an unquestioned independence that you forget how many people don't have it, people who, in human terms, Christian terms even, have just as much right to it as you do. The Church doesn't understand it either. Lambeth has no idea in the world what it's like for people like us. I'm Peter's wife, not an unpaid curate. And I am Flora's mother, which I rate very highly indeed. I would rather, please, find her school fees myself. It is good for all of us, in this beleaguered little rectory, if I do."

She could see she had made Colonel Richardson very sad indeed. It was not his way to speak sharply—that was his wife's department—but he could not conceal the fact that he thought Anna was both wrong and behaving badly. Her remarks about independence were totally incomprehensible to him. What did she mean? Good God, if you marry a parson, you marry all that goes with it! Like marrying a soldier, as Marjorie had, seventeen moves in twenty-four years of active service and never a bellyache out of her. She knew the terms even before he'd turned to her, by the water jump at a point-to-point in 1949, and said, "I suppose you'd never marry me, would you?" So Anna should have known, indeed she should. What was the use, Colonel Richardson asked himself, what was the use of being such a splendid rector's wife all these years, and then chucking the whole lot out of the window, for a pig-headed whim?

"I suppose," he said to Marjorie later, pouring

whisky for them both, "it's all this women's lib nonsense. Whatever that may mean."

"Too old for that." Privately, Marjorie Richardson had decided in favour of the menopause as the culprit, but not for the world would she say such a thing to Harry. Her own menstrual cycle, including its uncomfortable drawing to a close, had been strictly her own affair. Some things—love, sex, God, bodily functions—were simply not for discussion.

Am I being defiant, Anna thought now, pushing her metal cage of bottles down the aisle towards her allotted shelves, am I simply cocking a snook at Peter? At the Church? Is it because I am consumed with envy when I pass the Woodborough bookshop, and there is Eleanor's newest novel in a special display, and with resentment because I haven't heard from Mary for over a year because she is so busy now, commuting to Brussels being a Euro-lawyer? Is it because I am forty-two? Or is it because I am worn out by passivity, by having to accept and bear and endure, and because I am quite clever and resourceful, I have just turned, like the proverbial worm? If I'm a worm, I'm a fairly angry worm, but then I did not like my interview with Colonel Richardson, and I did not like it because he wasn't angry, he was hurt. I could have coped with his anger, using mine, but not his pain. Colonel Richardson's pain is only the first pain to make me feel dreadful (why, oh why, do women take to guilt like ducks to water?) and most people won't be as nice as he was. It's only the beginning, this arranging of soy sauce, it's only a start. I wonder, she said to herself with a sudden lurch of her heart, I wonder if I'm embarking on something I shall not be able to stop?

"You there?"

Anna turned. Heather from flours and dried fruits was

standing in the gap between two aisles. She was a small, rat-faced girl with a frizz of dry brown hair and a crucifix round her neck. ("They said to me in the shop," she'd said to Anna, "they said did I want the one with a little man on or not. 'Course I did! The plain ones look ever so bare.")

"Yes, of course."

"There's a gentleman looking for you. I thought you were in the warehouse. I'll send him round."

"Thank you—"

A gentleman? Round the corner came a perfectly strange man, a stocky middle-aged man with wire-rimmed spectacles and a shock of greying brown hair. He wore a grey tweed jacket and, oh, damn, Anna thought, a dog collar. Here he comes, sent by the Bishop, at the Richardsons' instigation, via all those labyrinths of diocesan checking-up they call ministerial review, ho ho, here he comes, the official ticker-off. He smiled at Anna. He had a sweet face.

"Yes?" Anna said, unhelpfully. She held a raft of glass jars between them.

"Mrs. Bouverie?"

"Yes."

"I'm so glad," he said, "I'm so glad. I was told I'd find you here." He looked at her burden. "Vegetable ghee. How extraordinary that such a thing should sell in Woodborough." He glanced at her. "Mrs. Bouverie, I am Daniel Byrne. I am to be the new Archdeacon here."

5

❖ ❖ ❖

DANIEL BYRNE DROVE Anna home. He was not, she noticed, a good driver, nor was he at all car-proud. The back seat was strewn with books and newspapers, and the floor was littered with car-park tickets. If Laura had ever owned a car, Anna reflected, this is how it would have looked inside, with the addition of old shoes and chocolate wrappers and squashed hats. Indeed, their own car would probably look like this if left to Anna; but Peter tidied it, because of all the parishioners he gave lifts to. "Oo," they'd say at the merest smear of mud, "you had a pig in here?"

"I saw your husband," Daniel Byrne said. "I found him at Church End. He said I was to talk to you first. He said you had been harder hit than anyone."

Anna said nothing.

"I see," said Daniel Byrne.

"I'm sure you don't."

"But I will," he said equably, "in time."

Anna looked out of the car window. The ploughed field they were passing was speckled with brilliant-green

73

shoots. Damn Peter. Damn him for dissembling; for pretending to Daniel that he wasn't wounded to the core at being passed over, pretending that it was only Anna who was suffering, as if it were she who could not bear the lack of advancement, of increased prosperity. She glanced sideways at Daniel's profile. It looked sturdy and peaceful and good-humoured. Had Peter implied, or worse even, said, that Anna had rushed impetuously to take a job in a supermarket because anything was better than the prospect of an unchanged status quo? Had he— no. She must stop. She must not work herself up into a terrible temper on supposition.

"What are you bursting with?" Daniel Byrne asked.

Anna was so startled by his perception and directness that she said, "I was worrying that you had got the wrong impression, that you—" She stopped, silenced by loyalty.

He changed gear at precisely the wrong moment and the car bucked and complained.

"I'm a mass of impressions," he said, taking no notice and merely raising his voice a little to be heard above the unhappy engine. "I came down from Manchester two days ago, to meet my fellow archdeacons, and the Bishop told me of your husband's application and of course that made me wish to meet him, and to meet you. I had no idea."

"Why should you have? It's hardly your fault."

"That isn't the problem."

"No," Anna said.

"Which is why I came to find you. Why I am driving you home. Why I asked your husband if we could all three meet for a little when I got you home." He swerved without warning to avoid a peaceable bicycle and was hooted at violently by an approaching car. He threw Anna a smile. "If, that is, I do get you home—"

She did not mean to, but she laughed.

The sitting-room at Loxford Rectory was a surprise to Daniel Byrne. It had been a surprise to Loxford for ten years, previously accustomed, as rural communities are, to modesty and neatness in the pastoral dwelling-house. It contained the Knole sofa on which St. Agatha had reclined in West Kensington (too large for Laura's tiny flat), several lowering pieces of reproduction Jacobean furniture donated by Kitty ("Your father loved it but I can't bear it, it's so threatening"), hundreds of books on shelves made by Peter out of bricks and planks, and the unmistakable overlying detritus of family life. Anna, making room for Daniel on the sofa, moved a pile of sheet music, several seed catalogues, a jersey of Luke's, and Flora's latest piece of chain stitch, in which a huge needle glittered.

"How very nice," said Daniel, sitting down. He looked round him. "How comfortable. Tidiness makes me nervous."

"When Peter married me, I was tidy," Anna said, recalling her cardigans with a sudden pang; those emblems of an imagined and ordered future. "I seem to have slumped, as time's gone on."

"Me too," Daniel said. He leaned back among the battered brocade and velvet cushions that the sofa had always owned. "I was a monk until I was thirty-five. One would think that monastic orderliness would be ingrained in one as deep as heart's blood, by thirty-five, but it did not seem so, with me. Perhaps," he said, turning as Peter came in with a tray of tea, "perhaps being a monk is bad training for the handling of possessions.

Not having any for fifteen years means I find them quite arbitrary now, impossible to control. It's as if they have a life of their own.''

Peter put the tea tray down with difficulty on a table already strewn with books and papers.

"You were—" he said. His voice was tight with suppressed curiosity.

"A Benedictine," Daniel said. "I decided, when I was thirty-five, that I was more use out than in. Fifteen years on, I couldn't be sure of that intellectually, but the instinct still says I'm right. We none of us listen to instinct enough."

"Hear, hear," Anna said. She poured tea. Passing Peter to take a cup to Daniel, she tried to catch his eye, to give him a little loving glance, but his expression was withdrawn, his eyes and thoughts elsewhere.

Daniel watched them both. He drank his tea. He noticed how they took chairs at some distance from one another and from him. He debated, within himself, whether to be oblique or direct with Peter, whose face seemed to him both shuttered and vulnerable. He would clearly hate to be patronized; he would smell patronage in any apology, in any request for help made out of desire to soothe sore feelings. Daniel glanced at Anna, upright on her ugly dark chair, her gaze bent on the carpet. They don't talk, Daniel thought. They can't. I smell no honesty here. He sighed. He said, "May I call you Peter?"

Peter jumped. "Of course—"

"We are brothers in this."

Anna wanted to say, I don't think Peter is brother material. That's part of the trouble, part of why he is so lonely, but she just looked at the carpet in silence, at the dark place where Luke had once spilled black coffee.

"I have never been in rural ministry," Daniel said. "I suppose I could learn without you, but I would so much rather learn with you."

"Of course," Peter said again, politely, without warmth.

"One of the useful things you learn, as a monk," Daniel said, putting his empty teacup on the floor by his feet, "is how to gauge character and mood without speaking. I am under no illusion about how difficult my presence here is for you."

"Robert Neville will be a great loss to me," Peter said rapidly, mentioning the last archdeacon.

"And I might be a gain," Daniel said, "if you would let me."

He glanced at Anna. Her head was now so bent that her dark hair had swung forwards so as to obscure her expression. Daniel felt that she was willing Peter to respond, to show himself bruised and in need of comforting, to expose his wound so that it might be healed.

"Of course," Peter said, yet again.

Daniel levered himself out of the sofa and stood up. He took off his spectacles and polished them thoughtfully with a red snuff-handkerchief. He seemed to be weighing up what he should say next when Peter exclaimed, "It's so hard on Anna. And the children. She works too hard in any case, so much parish work, so much—" He stood up. "You should see her vegetables."

"I don't mind," Anna cried, flinging her hair back from her face.

Peter said, "Of course you do."

She said, "I don't mind hard work. All I mind, all I really mind is—" She caught Peter's eye and stopped.

Daniel said, "May I go and see your church?"

"Certainly. Let me show you."

Daniel put his hand on Peter's arm.

"Thank you, but no. I will go alone, if I may." He turned to Anna. "Thank you for tea."

She looked up at him. Her eyes were miserable. "And you, for the lift."

Later she said to Peter, "I think he's a lovely man," and the moment she had spoken, she knew it was a mistake.

Sister Ignatia led Flora down a clean, polished corridor. On one side, the corridor was walled, but on the other it was glass, and through it, Flora could see a very orderly garden with a pink blossomed tree in the middle, and a bird bath. The corridor smelled of polish and Sister Ignatia smelled of cloth and soap. She wore a short grey habit, and behind her glasses, her eyes were as bright and dark as a robin's.

They had left Anna sitting in Sister Ignatia's study, looking at the school prospectus. Sister Ignatia had said that Flora couldn't know whether she wanted to come or not until she had had a sniff of the place, seen some of the other girls.

"Convent schools aren't what they were," Sister Ignatia had said to Anna, "nothing like so enclosed. I like to think our academic standard's gone up, and we know what's what in the world. It wouldn't be much use a modern nun not knowing where to kick a troublesome man, now, would it?"

She led Flora by the hand. She said, "And why aren't you getting on where you are?"

"I'm different," Flora said. "I don't know why, I just am."

Like your mother, Sister Ignatia thought. She opened

a cream-painted door and the smell of school lunch rushed out at them.

"Nobody'll be concentrating," Sister Ignatia said. "They never do, after twelve strikes, all thinking of their tummies. Now, in we go and you'll see the third form."

She knocked on a second door and opened it to reveal twenty children of about Flora's age at old-fashioned desks with inkwells sunk into the top right-hand corners of the lids. There was a youngish nun by the blackboard, drawing a map of the River Nile. Everybody stood up.

"Good afternoon," Sister Ignatia said, "good afternoon, Sister Josephine. This is Flora, girls, this is Flora who may be coming to join us."

Flora looked down. Twenty pairs of eyes stared at Flora. Sister Josephine did, too, and so did Christ, sadly, from his crucifix above the teacher's desk.

"I know her," someone said.

The eyes all swung to the speaker.

"Her father's a vicar," the someone said. She was small and plump and her hair was tied in bunches like spaniel's ears. "Her father's the Rector in our church."

Flora raised her head. It was Emma Maxwell, from Snead. Flora waited, her heart like lead in her chest, for the inevitable reaction to her shameful and laughable parentage.

"Well now," said Sister Ignatia, "isn't Flora the lucky one?"

Emma Maxwell thought that actually Flora's luck lay more in having an older brother. She resolved to tell the others, over lunch, about Luke Bouverie, whose brooding adolescent glamour gave his parents a certain status in the eyes of the parish's girls.

Sister Josephine smiled at Flora. "She is, indeed," said Sister Josephine, with warmth.

"We'll leave you now," Sister Ignatia said. "We've the art room to see, and the music school. What about a kind goodbye to Flora?"

Amid an obedient chorus, Flora followed Sister Ignatia with a bursting heart.

"I don't think you'll feel so different here," Sister Ignatia said. "We're all different in ourselves, but we're all the same family. Now, whose family could that be?"

Back in the study, Flora turned a beseeching face upon Anna. Anna had no need to be besought, for she had done a quick sum on the back of her child benefit book, and had worked out that, if Flora could start at St. Saviour's in the summer term, she would have earned enough to put down at least £100 towards the first term's fees. While she waited, she had rehearsed what she considered a dignified little speech for Sister Ignatia, explaining that, for this first term, it would not be possible for her to pay the fees in advance, as was customary, but that she would . . .

"If it helps to make up your mind," Sister Ignatia said, "I've four places a year to offer without fees. At my discretion. There are only two such girls in the present third year. I'd be happy to suggest such a place for Flora."

Anna said, quite thrown, "Oh, but you see, I can pay, and being Protestant—"

"Please," Flora screeched, not comprehending Sister Ignatia's offer but terrified that Anna would somehow bungle her chance, "please!"

"It's at my discretion," Sister Ignatia said.

"How kind, how nice of you—"

"Talk it over with Flora's father. Talk it over. Then telephone me. I shall reserve a place for Flora from the end of April."

Flora, heavy with adoration and gratitude, but uncertain of the etiquette involved in hugging nuns, stood and yearned towards Sister Ignatia.

"I will telephone," Anna said. "I am so grateful."

Sister Ignatia put her hand on Flora's head.

"God bless you."

Flora closed her eyes in ecstasy. Clearly quite a different and much more glamorous God than the Loxford one lived at St. Saviour's.

Later, while sitting at the kitchen table making a special list of people to help with Easter flowers, and a subsidiary list of those who might be approached to donate Easter lilies, Anna and her conscience had a little tussle. Anna's conscience said that she must report the whole of her interview at St. Saviour's faithfully to Peter, and then they could rejoice together that prayers had been answered, and that Pricewell's could be abandoned. But Anna found herself wholly disinclined to listen to her conscience. She discovered that she had no intention of making Sister Ignatia's offer plain to Peter, and no intention of giving up Pricewell's. Pricewell's, whatever its reality, represented the best taste of independence that Anna could remember since those far-off days in Oxford when Peter was a theology student. Twenty years was a long time to bear dependence if your spirit craved something stronger and your intelligence rebelled at continual submission to powers who neither, Anna felt, knew or cared how she and Peter lived. Pricewell's gave Anna that inch or two of dignity she had felt so sorely in need of and that she now felt she could never again surrender. What Eleanor and Mary took for granted in their lives Anna was just creeping towards, as a novice. If, she said to herself, writing Marjorie Richardson and Lady Mayhew and Miss Dunstable down for Easter lilies, if I do everything in the parish that I should do, and I keep the garden going and the meals and the house (sort of) and the translation, then where can be the harm in doing this other undeniably humble little thing that so curiously makes me feel strong and alive? And if I promise myself that, once Peter has calmed down, I will tell him of Flora's free place, where can be the danger of a little, temporary deception? She waited. Her conscience said nothing, it felt as if it were holding its breath. It was, of course, poor thing, out of practice at making decisions of the kind she had just put to it; it had, Anna considered, been given an easy ride for twenty years. She put her hands over her ears. "That's settled then," Anna said loudly, to whoever was listening.

Peter sat in Celia Hooper's sitting-room in Quindale. Her house was a new one, built of bright reconstituted stone, and her sitting-room was full of blue Dralon armchairs, and occasional tables, each bearing a single china ornament, mostly whimsical animals. Celia Hooper's husband was a bank manager in Woodborough, and it was he who tended so ferociously the disciplined garden beyond the patio doors. Celia, who had trained as a physical education instructor, now ran the Loxford parish Guides, a swimming group for the disabled, and was Peter's Deanery Secretary. She was formidably efficient. Her minutes were works of precise art. She believed— and frequently declared—that the rural deaneries were the grassroots of the Church of England.

Peter sat in one of the blue chairs. At his elbow, a little table bore a cup of coffee and a piece of shortbread on a plate that matched the coffee cup. Celia Hooper— seated opposite him in just such a chair and situation, so that they resembled two bookends without intervening books—was suggesting that she should draw up a basic plan for the annual deanery party, which happened at Loxford Rectory after Easter, a get-together for all the priests of the deanery, eight of them, and their wives.

"If I do the planning, you see," Celia said, turning to a clean page in her notebook, "that will spare Anna." Mindful of the proprieties, Celia was not going to mention Pricewell's.

Peter said quickly, "Anna won't mind. She's so used to it—"

"I thought perhaps this year, if I just rustle up a few quiches, buy some French bread "

"Very kind of you, Celia, but really I think Anna would like to do it."

"She has so much on her plate. We all know that."

"No more than usual," Peter said loudly.

Celia looked at him. Her face was full of sympathy.

"I have no one to talk to," Peter said suddenly, without meaning to.

"I don't think," Celia said softly, "I don't think you ought to assume that the laity doesn't notice. Or understand."

He looked at her, at her neat, gleaming brown bob, at her clear outdoor skin and eyes, her new-looking, well-kept clothes. He said, "Do you know, I sometimes think that the laity are the only people who do understand."

Celia began to write in her notebook.

"Quiche, then. Several varieties. And some nice mixed salads. Mustn't forget, must we, that John Jacobs is a vegetarian—"

"Please," Peter said protestingly, thinking of Anna.

"That's all right," Celia said, thinking of her too, but differently, "I'll ring Anna. Don't you worry." She gave him a little glance of understanding. "You've got enough to worry about. You leave what you can to me."

On the way home, filled with an indigestible mixture of relief and regret, Peter observed that there were removal vans once again outside Loxford Old Rectory. The new owner—a man on his own, gossip said, a wealthy man—was plainly moving in. He would of course require a pastoral call even if he did not—and his car did not bode well—look like the kind of man Peter might hope for, as a breath of fresh air on the PCC; as a possible churchwarden in place of old Sir Francis Mayhew, who said he'd done fifteen years, which was more than enough; or even as a parishioner willing to raise the £25,000 that the diocesan architect had said would have to be spent on Loxford church roof within the next three years. Peter drove slowly past the gates— the dignified gates through which most of his predecessors had stepped on their way to the church—and, as he did so, the new owner came out of the front door and clearly observed the dawdling and curious car.

Peter pulled up. He got out of the car and crossed the deep, luxurious gravel of the Loxford Old Rectory drive. He felt faintly foolish. The man on the steps was middle-aged and authoritative-looking, and wore well-pressed jeans and a brass-buttoned blazer. Peter said, "This isn't really a visit. It's plainly no time for that. I was just passing—"

"Patrick O'Sullivan," the man said, holding out his hand. He smiled.

"Peter Bouverie."

"I've seen your wife."

"Oh?"

"I'd ask you in—"

"No, no," Peter said, "not now. Just passing."

"Lovely place, this," Patrick O'Sullivan said.

"I hope you will be very happy here."

"So do I."

Peter backed away a little. Two removal men came past him carrying a huge painting shrouded in a blanket. "Goodbye," Peter said, "and welcome. I mean, welcome to Loxford."

Patrick O'Sullivan put his hands in his blazer pockets. He was still smiling.

"Thanks," he said.

Peter got back into his car and started the engine. That had not been, on reflection, a successful impulse, nor a socially accomplished two minutes. He thought of his mother-in-law. "What," Laura had said, on her first visit to Loxford, "what! Put you in that—that *kiosk*—and expect your parishioners to admire your humility? Why are you not where you should be? How can you retain any kind of status in that council house? I promise you, the village won't think you're one of them because you aren't in the proper rectory. They'll simply think you haven't any clout."

Patrick O'Sullivan, standing easily on the steps of Loxford Old Rectory, had looked to Peter a man on first-name terms with clout.

Patrick O'Sullivan went back into his house faintly amused. He was not conscious of having had any contact with a clergyman since school, where religion had been regarded as an unavoidable mixed dose of discipline, cissiness and mild buffoonery. In his address, the bishop who had confirmed Patrick and his year had urged compassion in sexual matters upon them, which had decided them all finally that the Church was a refuge for old women, and that Christianity was somehow neutering in its effect. When he left school, he forgot entirely about the whole business, forgot about it for a couple of decades, forgot until this thin, tired fellow, looking so very much like his old school chaplain, came and hovered in the drive, the epitome, it seemed to Patrick, of the doubting kind of modern Anglican clergyman.

He went into the kitchen, where his housekeeper was filling cupboards with pans. "I met the Rector!"

Ella Pringle, who was heavy with misgiving about the move from London, merely grunted. A rector was, in her view, part of the traditional and comic cast list she had expected to find in the country, along with the squire and the village idiot.

"Looks just as I expected," Patrick said, plugging in the kettle. He sounded pleased. "Shall I go to church?"

"You wouldn't know how to behave in church," Ella said from inside her cupboard.

"I could learn."

She came out abruptly. "Learn? Whatever for?"

He was looking out of the window at his lovely new garden, at the exquisite magnolia just breaking into its goblet-like, glowing blooms, which were, since Monday, also his. He had never owned a magnolia before, nor a view. He said, "Because my life is going to be different here. It is why I have come."

Ella thought it was a fad, a passing and Toad-like enthusiasm for something novel. She had been Patrick's housekeeper for fourteen years, through his brief and disastrous marriage, through his long and complicated liaison with a woman who had left a year ago, telling Ella that there was no point in waiting any longer for Patrick to marry her. He never would, she said, because he didn't need to. He only ever did things he needed to do, and someone as economical with their emotions as that was not good lifetime material. Ella liked having Patrick to herself. She treated him as if she were his prep-school matron. When he said he was moving to Loxford to start another life before it was too late, she thought of abandoning him but she did not think it for long. He was, in any case, very persuasive. He needed Ella. He now said, "Where's the tea?"

"Honestly," she said, "honestly. We move in seven hours ago and you expect everything to be in order." She got up from her knees and made shooing gestures. "Get out. Go into your garden. Come back in ten minutes, and there'll be tea."

He went out through the glazed garden door at the back of the hall. There was a terrace outside, with a low balustrade and several graceful lead urns filled with early blue pansies—they don't look right, he thought. Wonder why—and then a great green carpet of lawn, and shrubs and trees, and, way beyond them, the far hills. He stood and breathed a bit, in and out, deeply. Then he went across his terrace and down on to his damp spring lawn.

It was a majestic lawn. It rolled away from the house for a couple of hundred yards, its length deceptively magnified by little outcrops of planting here and there which hid its true limits. To the right, as he walked down it, he could see nothing but the trees of his own orchard and, beyond them, the decorative ridge of a thatched roof, crowned with a squat brick chimney. To the left, he could only at first see his own garden, his tennis court, the old wall that screened his vegetables—to eat what one has grown, actually to eat that!—but then, across a low hedge and a fence that needed repair, he found he could see into the garden of the new Rectory, whose impersonal little back windows faced the same way as his own. He could see grass, and a long dug strip—vegetables, too?—and a few fruit trees. He could also see a line of washing, which included, he realized to his delight, the clerical undergarments. He must be the only person in the village with a view, if he chose to take it, of both vest and surplice. While he looked the back door opened, and a woman came out, calling over her shoulder to someone in the house, as she came. She wore a swirling dress with something bright wrapped round the waist, and she carried a laundry basket. Patrick leaned in satisfaction on a fence post. The Rector's wife.

He watched her. She went over to the vegetable patch and looked at the earth for a while. Then she carried the basket to the washing line and unpegged the clothes rapidly, chucking them down in a windblown tangle (Ella folded things as she took them out of the tumble drier. He would have to train her to a line. In his orchard? He thought of his Jermyn Street shirts blowing in the orchard, with pleasure) and then, for a second or two, she stood quite still, looking down, the back of her hand to her forehead under her dark fringe. When she stooped and retrieved her basket, and went rapidly back to the house with it, Patrick wished he had said something, that he had called out to her.

He went back to the kitchen.

"Now I've seen the Rector's wife. Again, actually."

"Thrills and spills," Ella said, pouring tea into a mug for him. "Now see if you can find the gravedigger. Good game, this. Might even keep you quiet for an hour or two."

Patrick took his tea and went up to the first floor, to the long landing window which looked over the village green. Smoke rose from several chimneys, straight blue columns in the still air, signs of habitation. All those cottages had people in them, Patrick realized, people and televisions and plates of fried fish and dogs and Wellington boots at the back door. He swallowed some tea. He was charmed by his thoughts, charmed by the look of his new village, like a doll's house with the front enticingly shut. And there, if he looked hard to the right, was the tower of the church, like a benevolent old watchdog, keeping an eye on things, protective, changeless. He looked down at his clothes, on an impulse. They looked wrong, suddenly, too blue, too urban. He must buy some corduroys.

6

❖ ❖ ❖

ISOBEL THOMPSON HAD been a missionary in West
Africa for seventeen years before she became a deacon.
She had loved it. She had loved the sense of purpose
and the freedom and most of the Africans, and she had
always supposed that she would stay there all her life,
and finally die there, and be buried, like David Living-
stone's wife, under a baobab tree. She prayed steadily,
all those seventeen years, for guidance, for confirmation
that she was still fulfilling divine purpose, and was only
interrupted at last by her mother's voice, demanding in
a querulous letter that Isobel should come home and
nurse her while she died—as she had been told she soon
would—of cancer.

She took five years to do it, five years of remissions
and declines and suffering borne with no patience whatever. She was furious with Isobel for preferring God to
any man, and thus denying her the status of grandpar-
enthood, and furious with her husband for dying before
her. She lay in her carefully, fustily feminine bedroom
in her little house in Woodborough, and tormented Iso-

bel. Nothing was right, from her physical misfortune through Isobel's appearance to the strength of her early-morning tea. Isobel began to feel that her life had been the wrong way round, that Africa had been no training at all, with its comparatively easy, impersonal requirement of Christian love, for these savagely difficult demands for daughterly love. Praying was ten times as hard as it had ever been in Africa, so was steering clear of hatred, a problem Isobel had never encountered before. She told herself that she must confine herself to anger only, but it was easier said than done. Standing at last in Woodborough parish church—dedicated to St. Paul—watching her mother's coffin being lowered on to trestles below the chancel steps, Isobel was so riven with thankfulness she could hardly keep upright. Her dedication would now be complete, an offering made from a full heart and an intimate knowledge of mental pain. There was to be no more Africa, however much it beckoned. Isobel would enter the Church as a deacon, would tackle the domestic problems of Woodborough. If she had failed to love her mother, she the missionary, what must it be like for people who, without God, had not even got a Christian obligation to try?

Sometimes, in the years that followed, she longed for Africa, like a lost love affair. Yet she also knew that if she had succumbed to her longing she would not have been satisfied, knowing what she now knew of the terrible difficulties of love. She also came to see that, as a woman, she understood the psychology of this difficulty of human love better than most of her male colleagues, who were often, she considered, almost callous in their disinclination to feel the emotional agonies in which some people laboured, shackled to delinquent children or senile parents or destructive marriages. You could not just say, Christ will help you bear it. That was opting out. You had to show that you understood the suffering, knew the price it exacted, as a fellow human being, before you even thought of bringing Christ into it.

It was such a discussion that had first brought Isobel and Anna together. The last Archdeacon of Woodborough, a genial and easy man, had invited all the priests of his eight deaneries to a fork supper laid on with great relish by his wife, a woman whose every fibre rejoiced at being a clergy wife. In the Victorian Woodborough Vicarage, the priests and their wives milled through the ground-floor rooms with plates of cold chicken and ham, and glasses of encouraging German wine. The atmosphere was of an end-of-term party given by a headmaster in his study for the prefects. Anna and Isobel, finding themselves together in front of a bright watercolour of a Cornish harbour painted by Archdeacon Neville on one of his walking holidays, fell into conversation.

It was an easy conversation from the beginning. After a while, they left the watercolour ("Not a very adventurous subject," Isobel said) and found two chairs in a corner. Isobel, who had told nobody about her mother, found herself telling Anna. From there, they progressed to the enthralling problem of human and divine love. Isobel said that, personally, she found the latter much easier, but that she felt that the former was, in every sense, her job.

Anna said, looking round the crowded room whose noise-level had risen considerably with alcohol-released confidence, "Do you think most of the men here feel like that?"

"I do. And what is more, I think most of them give in. How much easier and publicly commendable it is to devote yourself to the parish, however demanding, than to a wife having a nervous breakdown at home.''

"Oh Isobel," Anna said. They looked at each other. "You don't even need to be having a nervous breakdown to become a burden to a priest husband, you know. You simply need to ask to be visible, to be seen as a human being, not an unpaid curate. That's all the amount of nuisance you have to be to drive a man into the arms of his parish.''

Isobel said, "Are you speaking personally?"

Anna felt herself colouring. She had gone too far. "Some husbands," she said, pulling herself together, finishing her wine, "get very disheartened. There are so many demands, so little help. Were you lonely as a missionary?"

"Oh no," Isobel said. "Never. I felt like the nineteenth-century missionary, Annie Taylor, who wrote in her diary on Christmas Day, in a blizzard on a Tibetan mountain surrounded by absolutely untrustworthy tribesmen, 'Quite safe here with Jesus.' Africa was wonderful. It was in every way so much easier than here, but then the love required was simpler, more childlike. It was, looking back, a kind of holiday at times.''

Anna stood up. "Come and see me," she said, "any time. Just come. I could do with a friend.''

Isobel smiled up at her. "So could I.''

It was not a friendship Peter understood. He liked Isobel well enough but she seemed to him to bring, as did most of the other women deacons in the diocese, a fussy, housekeeping approach to Christianity, a domestic preoccupation with women and children and primary schools, that irked him. She did not, in his view, understand ritual and language, she did not speculate about theology, she used her heart too much without her head.

He could not see why Anna did not find her dull. But he could not complain of the unsuitability of the friendship between his wife and Isobel, and at times it was extremely useful. Isobel could be, occasionally, a channel to communicate through, with Anna. It was obvious now that Isobel should be the person to talk to Anna about this job in Pricewell's.

Isobel objected at first. "It seems harmless enough to me."

"In itself, of course it is," Peter said. They were in the sitting-room of Isobel's little house, the house she had inherited from her mother. It looked across the street at one of Woodborough's dental practices, so that people passed the windows all day in various stages of apprehension and relief. "The job itself is innocent. It's the motive, and the effect."

"Ah," said Isobel.

"Anna was terribly shaken by Daniel Byrne's appointment. She couldn't bear to feel helpless, to be passive. But there is nothing I can do, we can do. She has relieved her most understandable feelings by taking this job."

"Do you think she is defying you?"

"Yes," said Peter.

"Oh dear."

"And possibly the parish, too."

"I don't mind so much about them."

"They mind," Peter said. "I can't go anywhere without falling over references to it. I've even had a letter from Lady Mayhew, who, before she realized who it was, found herself asking Anna for the whereabouts of Dijon mustard."

Isobel said, "Bother Lady Mayhew."

"She is my parishioner. I have to live in such a community. You may think Loxford light years behind Woodborough, but it is my patch, where I live and work, however anachronistic. I've just got all the apples into the cart, and it looks as if Anna has upset the lot.''

''Why have you come to me? Why don't you go to our nice new archdeacon?''

''I don't know him. He doesn't know Anna. He doesn't know this area. He said he knows nothing of rural ministry.''

''Typical,'' Isobel said. ''All right. I'll try.''

In the Loxford Rectory garden Anna was in tears. In front of her, close to tears also, stood Luke with his chin thrust out mulishly. She had taken him out into the garden to show him various easy spring tasks that must be done, and for which she would pay him, and he had refused. He didn't want to garden and he didn't want her money. Anna, exhausted by all she was trying to do, plummeted from fury to weeping.

''Don't you understand, you stupid child!'' she screamed at Luke. ''Can't you see? I'm earning to pay you to help me! To save your blasted dignity since you think a supermarket beneath you!''

Luke muttered, ''I don't think that.''

''What then? What do you think?''

Luke shuffled. He put his hands in his jeans pockets and hunched his shoulders.

''You're making Dad look a fool. And me. And Flora. You're making us look pathetic.''

Anna said tiredly, sniffing, ''We are pathetic.''

''Well, you don't have to broadcast it,'' Luke said, gaining courage from her ceasing to shout. ''You don't have to advertise it, do you? Other vicars' families manage, don't they?''

"We aren't other families. We are us."

Luke said in relief, "Here's Isobel."

Anna looked up. There was Isobel, coming up the path in her fawn mackintosh. She waved.

Isobel waved back, all smiles, then saw their faces and said, "Oh dear. I thought I heard shouting."

"You did."

"Will you tell me why?"

"Luke will," Anna said unfairly, turning away and looking at her beautifully dug earth, and thinking how much she would just like to lie down on it and sleep.

Isobel looked at Luke. He wore an expression of the deepest misery. "No," Isobel said, "you will. And Luke can correct you if he needs to."

There was a silence. Then Luke said, "I do want to help. Just not this way."

Anna put a hand out to him. He took it awkwardly. She said, "I'm so sick of being limited, tyrannized. Whenever I turn to try and get out of the cage, someone is offended or upset, says I'm defying them or humiliating them. I have a space to occupy on this earth, you know, I have a space with just as much validity to it as yours or Dad's or—or the Archbishop of Canterbury's. But I don't hedge you about with my objections or complaints, do I? I don't criticize you for enterprise or initiative. Do I? Do I?"

Tears slid down Luke's face. He said with difficulty, "But you've still got the power—"

Anna dropped his hand. "How mistaken you are."

Luke turned and fled. Isobel came over to Anna and said, "I suppose this is all about Pricewell's."

"Of course."

"Peter came to see me."

Anna fumbled about in her pockets for a handkerchief.

"So this is a little pastoral call to dissuade me."

"If it's defiance, yes."

Anna's eyes, visible over the top of her handkerchief,
were enormous. "Defiance?"

Isobel said steadily, "If you are aiming somehow to
shame the Church establishment for what you see as its
treatment of clergy families, and you imagine that this
might be achieved by humiliating Peter, then yes, defiance."

Anna blew her nose ferociously.

"Go away."

"So I am somewhere near the truth?"

"Isobel," Anna said. Her voice was not at all steady.
"Isobel, would you please stop being a deacon and be
a human being for a moment? If I don't do something,
take some action, in our present situation, then I shall
not have one atom of strength left to support Peter. I
want to support him, I am doing so, even if he refuses
to acknowledge that just now because it's easier for him
to bear what has happened if he pretends it is me who
is more broken than he. But I can't just play the pawn
any more. I can't just bear and endure. And don't," she
said with sudden vehemence, "don't tell me that suffering is part of the Almighty package."

"But marriage—"

"What would you know about marriage?"

Isobel turned and began to walk back towards the
house. Anna watched her, tense with the impulse to run
after her, say sorry, throw her arms round her, make up,
be friends again. Isobel did not turn. Anna did not move.
Isobel vanished round the house and after a while Anna

heard the engine of her little car start up and putter away down the drive.

Ella Pringle only let Luke into the Old Rectory because he said he was the Rector's son. He had knocked on the back door while she was kneading the first batch of bread dough she had ever made in her life—something to do, she thought crossly, with coming to the country—and she had gone to answer him with floury hands and a frown. He said could he speak to Mr. O'Sullivan and she said no. He said please, he was Luke Bouverie, he was the Rector's son, and Ella, uncertain of village etiquette, acted out of character on the safe side, and allowed him in. She left him in the kitchen examining the espresso coffee machine with wonder, while she went to Patrick's office.

Patrick had made it a rule that he was never to be disturbed in the mornings, but that she might bring him urgent interruptions in the afternoon. Ella was doubtful of Luke's urgency. She knocked and opened the door and saw Patrick asleep in his wing chair. Ella considered daytime sleeping decadent. She said loudly, "You have a visitor."

He woke calmly. "I do?"

"The Rector's son. Shall I send him in?"

"Of course!"

A minute later, Luke said diffidently, "In here?" His face came round the door.

"The Rector's *big* son, I see. I thought you might be conker-age."

Luke came in and looked round him. "Wow."

"How to run a business at arm's length."

"We do computer courses at school—"

"Would you like tea?" Patrick said. The boy's face looked faintly smeared, as if he had been crying. But of course, boys that size did not cry.

"Oh," Luke said, his face lighting up. "Yeah. I mean, please—"

Patrick went out to the kitchen.

"A vast tea," he said to Ella. "Everything you can think of. Bunter-style."

She looked pointedly at the front curve of his new olive-green Shetland jersey.

"For my guest," Patrick said.

"I see."

Back in the office, Luke was standing in an attitude of longing in front of Patrick's computer.

"Suppose you tell me why you've come, and then we'll enjoy ourselves."

Luke said, going scarlet and looking out of the window, "I wondered if, I mean, do you need, I mean, would you have any job you could give me? Anything, I mean, I don't mind what, logs, digging, you know—"

"A job."

Luke nodded.

"What," said Patrick, "is the basic industrial wage?"

Luke swallowed. "If you're over eighteen, two seventy-five an hour."

"And you?"

"Seventeen," Luke said.

Patrick, who was enjoying himself, eyed his visitor. "And what experience have you?"

"I help Mum and stuff—"

"Yes."

"Garden, firewood—"

There was a pause. Luke spent it wishing he had never

come, dreading tea, dreading having to say he didn't mind, that it was quite OK, he quite saw, shouldn't have asked . . .

"All right," Patrick said. "I'll pay you two fifty an hour for as many hours as you can put in these holidays. Does your mother know you are here?"

Luke gaped.

"I see. Then should we ask her? When we have had tea, I think we should go home together and ask her. Don't you?"

Luke said, "She won't mind—"

"But I might. I'm a newcomer here. Don't know the rules, don't want to tread on any toes. Now, while we wait for tea how would you like to send a fax to New York?"

"It's four afternoons a week," Kitty Bouverie said down the telephone to Anna. "Four, and sometimes five if the owner's busy."

She sounded full of triumph. She had combed the shops of Windsor looking for work, and at last had found some.

"I suppose it's a gift shop really. Birthday cards and little ashtrays with pictures of the castle on them and necklaces and keyrings. That sort of thing."

"Kitty. You're so clever!"

"I know," Kitty said, "but I'd never have thought of it without you, it just wouldn't have crossed my mind. The owner's so nice, another widow. She has a Pekinese. She wants to open a coffee shop next door. If she does, I could make cakes for it, couldn't I, and jam—"

"What about the adding up?"

"I have a calculator," Kitty said proudly, "made in Japan."

"Oh Kitty, I think it's wonderful. I'd get Peter, so you could tell him, but he's out—"

"There's no point telling him, is there? He'll only sniff. No, it was you I wanted to tell. How's Flora?"

"On the verge of seventh heaven. St. Saviour's next term. She's practising for Catholicism. Draws pictures of the Virgin Mary and writes, 'Our Lady' underneath—" Anna broke off. Through the window, she could see Luke coming up the drive accompanied by a strange man to whom he seemed to be talking animatedly. She said, "Kitty, I think I have to go. Luke seems to be bringing a visitor. I'm so pleased for you. And admiring. I'll ring you in a day or two."

"I'm admiring too," Kitty said. "I'm so pleased with myself, you can't think."

The back door opened, and Luke ushered in his companion.

"Mum, this is Mr. O'Sullivan—"

Anna held out her hand.

"Anna Bouverie."

"Yes. I know."

"Welcome to Loxford."

"Thank you."

Anna said, "Come through. Come into the sitting-room. Luke, put the kettle on."

"No. No thank you. We are groaning with tea. Aren't we, Luke?"

Luke looked tremendously happy. "It was brilliant."

Anna looked at them both.

"I don't understand—"

"We have just had tea together," Patrick said. "Luke came to me looking for work, and we sealed the bargain with egg sandwiches. Now we have come to ask if that's all right."

Anna said, startled, "Yes, of course, what kind of work?"

"Gardening, logs, that kind of thing."

Anna looked at Luke. "Gardening?" He blushed.

"Is he no good?"

"Oh, I think he's perfectly good. His goodness seems to depend upon who asks him."

Luke said hurriedly, "I'll go and see to the sitting-room fire."

When he had gone, Patrick said, "Is this all out of order?"

"Not at all. It's very kind of you."

"I felt I should come and ask you—"

"Thank you."

"—but what I really wanted to ask you," said Patrick O'Sullivan, putting his hands in his jacket pockets, "is what is a woman like you doing in a place like this?"

And then Luke came in and said the fire was fine and that he'd bashed the cushions up a bit, to make it all OK for them.

Woodborough Vicarage was the largest space Daniel Byrne had ever occupied. In Manchester, he had shared a simple, newish little house with a succession of curates, and he rather thought, pacing his new Victorian Gothic halls, that he would like a whole army of curates with him now. The last three archdeacons had had sizeable families, so that the Vicarage, though impractical to run, had at least been filled. Yet even though Daniel had spread himself as far as he could, including making himself a primitive chapel out of an east-facing bedroom, there was still a good deal of vicarage left over.

The diocese had found him a housekeeper, a Miss Lambe, who was as small and anxious as a hamster, and who had taken a tiny, remote bedroom as her burrow, and already filled it with crocheted mats and pictures of the Royal Family. Daniel had explained to her that he liked very simple food that he could eat with one hand, because of his inability to eat without reading, and so, for supper his first night, she had brought him scrambled egg on a piece of toast that she had already cut up into precise and helpful squares. He thought, eating it, that he must be careful not to be too metaphorical in his instructions, since, in her anxiety to obey him to the letter, she might feed him a diet of unrelieved soup and rice pudding.

Miss Lambe helped him to unpack his books, holding each one with as much reverence as if it had been the Sacrament. It took for ever. In the middle, she went away to make tea, and brought it back with digestive biscuits she had broken into quarters.

"You will have to get used to my peculiar sense of humour," Daniel said.

Miss Lambe blinked at him. "I quite like a joke," she said bravely.

He pinned a huge map of the diocese on his study wall, and then outlined his own archdeaconry in red. Eight deaneries lay within it, of which only one—Woodborough itself—had any kind of urban character. The rest were a maze of villages with names that sounded like the refrain for a pantomime song, villages whose lives were as far removed from those Manchester lives he had known for so long that it was as if they inhabited another planet. He had wanted this change, not least because he felt that the rural Church was being neglected, that progressive Church thinking was forgetting to take into account that huge section of the population whose rhythms were dictated by quite other influences than urban ones. He had also felt that, contrary to popular supposition, a dangerous loneliness might afflict priests living and working in rural places, however lovely. Looking at his map, and thinking of such men—men who were much less resilient than those to whom a more evangelical and dogmatic faith appealed—Daniel Byrne thought of Peter Bouverie. No doubt, it was for such men as Peter Bouverie that he felt he had been called to come south.

Peter himself, robing in the vestry at Quindale for the last of the special Lent evening services—theme: ''Can there be change without sacrifice in a Christian world?''—was not thinking of Daniel Byrne. He was thinking instead of the twenty minutes he had spent at home between a difficult hour persuading the voluntary organist at New End (a retired primary-school headmistress who felt she was being taken for granted) to continue, at least temporarily, and this service of compline at Quindale. In those twenty minutes, Luke had told him that he had found part-time employment at the Old Rectory, Anna had told him that his mother had found employment at a Windsor gift shop, and his mother-in-law, Laura, had telephoned to say she had landed three lines in a television commercial for an Irish stout, dressed as a pearly queen.

Peter had heard all this, sitting at the kitchen table with a cup of tea and a sandwich made for him by Anna to sustain him to the far side of compline. While he ate and listened, the telephone rang three times on minor parish business and Flora badgered him to read a pious poem she had just written which began:

I love Jesus,
He's my baby brother
I love Mary
She's my Holy Mother.

("Yuk," said Luke with vehemence, "and you aren't even at St. Saviour's yet.")

Peter noticed that Luke and Flora both looked extremely happy, and that Anna looked desperately tired. She had said that Isobel had been to see her, and that she, Anna, had been horrible to her. Peter said nothing. He said nothing for almost the whole of the twenty minutes, until he got up and carried his plate and cup to the sink and then said, as he left the room, "I see. So I am now the only one in the entire family without a job in the real sense. So you can all do without me."

Now, in Quindale vestry, putting on his Lenten stole (regarded as unacceptably High Church by some of his deanery), Peter was full of remorse for his petulance. Yet, at the same time, he could not bear the feeling that, if the career tides were receding from him, then his family's response of withdrawing too, into their own remedies and inevitable independence, might leave him quite beached like an old wreck on the shore.

Celia Hooper's husband, Denis, had fixed up a little mirror for Peter to examine himself in before he emerged into the church. Peering in it now, he thought: How grudging I look, how pinched, how disappointed. He straightened up. I am disappointed, he told himself, and I am quite trapped in it. I can't think what to do next.

He went quietly out through the little vestry door—ancient, ogee, poignant—into the chancel. There were seven people waiting for him, the Richardsons, the

Hoopers, two parishioners from Snead, and Miss Dunstable from Loxford. As he passed her, Celia Hooper raised her head and gave him a look of steady encouragement.

7

❖ ❖ ❖

A̲T THE BEGINNING of Holy Week, Charlotte Bou
verie came home. Term at Edinburgh University had
ended weeks before, but Charlotte had stayed on in order
to try and resuscitate an ailing love affair with a boy in
her year. The attempt had failed, largely because Charlotte had discovered that she was so annoyed by Giles's
apathy and introspection that she could hardly remember
how wildly attractive she had found him only a month
before. She gave him a lecture on his immature short-
comings, during which he lay on his bed with his back
to her and emanated suffering, and then she packed her
black kitbag with the possessions necessary for Easter
at home—Simone de Beauvoir, cigarettes, black socks,
Texas Camp Fire tapes and scent—and caught the overnight bus south.

Like her grandmother, Charlotte was good at bus
travel, making friends and ignoring tedium. She changed
buses in London, and telephoned Loxford to say what
time she would be getting to Woodborough. The telephone wasn't answered. Charlotte, assuming her mother

to be about the parish somewhere with Flora, and Luke to be in his room working, with the music turned up so loud that no telephone stood a chance against it, caught her intended bus anyway. She would ring again from Woodborough.

Now that the Giles question was settled—as much a relief, curiously, as a disappointment—Charlotte was pleased to be going home. She was staunchly fond of her family but, being the eldest, guarded her pioneering independence fiercely, and therefore stayed away from home a good deal in order to train her family to detachment as much as herself. For the same reason, she seldom wrote letters, and for financial reasons, seldom telephoned. But she thought about the Rectory at Loxford a good deal more than its inhabitants supposed, even if being a clergyman's daughter was not something she actually advertised in her socially and politically dogmatic student circles. Being agnostic, as she was, Charlotte couldn't exactly empathize with her father's faith, but she could envisage a time in the future, when she was famous—and she fully intended to be—when admitting to her parentage would be something that could only benefit her image; something indeed rather stylish.

When the bus reached Woodborough, Charlotte again tried to telephone. Again there was no reply. She crossed the bus station to read the timetables—remembering, she thought, an early-afternoon bus to Loxford—and met her mother, burdened with Pricewell's bags and looking quite exhausted, coming towards her. Dropping everything, they embraced each other with enthusiasm, and the lady driver waiting to drive the next Loxford service remarked to her friend, the bus station manager, that there was no mistaking those two being mother and daughter.

"But why didn't you ring?" Anna said. "I'm absolutely enchanted but I'd have hated you to get home and find nobody—"

"Nobody?"

"Oh darling, we're such a hive of industry. Luke is working for the tycoon who's taken the Old Rectory and Flora's gone to play with Emma Maxwell at Snead in the mornings while I work, so that she will have a thorough friend to start St. Saviour's with."

"What?" said Charlotte.

"I wrote. I wrote and told you. About Flora being so miserable and my job and Luke wanting to go to India."

Out of the mists of recollection swam a dim memory of such a letter. Indeed, Charlotte could almost visualize it, on her table, among the dye pots and coffee mugs and edifices of books, most of which she never opened.

"Oh Ma. Sorry, but I've been absolutely frantic—"

"It doesn't matter," Anna said, stooping to pick up the bags again.

It clearly did. Charlotte said, "I really am sorry. I get sort of caught up—"

"I know."

"Remind me about your job," Charlotte said in a small voice.

Anna swung an armful of bags. "Pricewell's."

Charlotte remembered. " 'Course."

"Your turn now," Anna said.

"My turn for what?"

"Your turn to say that I am defying Daddy and humiliating us all and failing the parish."

"Who says that?"

"Everyone. Everyone except the grannies, who are wonderful."

Charlotte said, "I join the grannies."

Anna looked at her. Charlotte's expression was determined.

"Darling. Do you?"

"Of course. It's great of you. I just wish—"

"What do you wish?"

"I just wish," said Charlotte, "that you could do something that exercised your intelligence more."

Loxford church was in a ferment. The new Archdeacon was coming to celebrate an Easter eucharist there, before driving back to St. Paul's, Woodborough, for family matins. This had thrown the flower ladies into a competitive frenzy. Loxford must surely outdo St. Paul's in Paschal floral glory, so that the Archdeacon would have his eyes quite dazzled by their achievements and in consequence be almost blind to anyone else's, all Easter Day. To Loxford's intense satisfaction it started with two tremendous advantages, Loxford church was stone, and fourteenth century, St. Paul's was brick, and Victorian. In Miss Dunstable and Lady Mayhew, Loxford possessed flower arrangers of an almost poetic ability. St. Paul's, dominated as it was by the diocesan Mothers' Union, could hope for nothing so elevated.

The only drawback was that no plans could be put into action until after the three-hour service on Good Friday, when Peter liked the church quite unadorned, with the crucifix above the altar shrouded in black. Even so, on Maundy Thursday evening, special long-spouted watering cans appeared in the vestry, along with new rolls of wire netting and blocks of flower arranger's foam.

Anna, who had had a grim time persuading anyone to give Easter lilies—"Considering what she is doing to the parish," Lady Mayhew had remarked to Miss Dunstable, "I think she has a nerve to ask"—found herself suddenly inundated with offers. What might not be given to God in the name of His risen Son most certainly could be given to the Archdeacon in the cause of snubbing St. Paul's. The flower ladies, those obliging people like Elaine Dodswell, found themselves issued with instructions, in Miss Dunstable's large, old-fashioned hand, run off on the copier in the village post office. Anna said to Elaine Dodswell, in the shop, "I'm so sorry. It all seems to have got out of hand," and Elaine, who had spent the last weeks quite stunned with horrified pity that Anna should be reduced to taking a job in a supermarket, said quickly, oh, it didn't matter, you just had to humour people sometimes, didn't you?

There was, Anna discovered, to be no place for her in these arrangements. She had done twenty-two Easters at Peter's side, but she was plainly not going to be allowed to do this one. Whether the parish wished to punish her or cherish her—and she strongly inclined to the former view—hardly mattered; the exclusion was frightfully annoying.

"The small-mindedness of the Christian community when seen at close quarters," she said angrily to Peter, "beggars belief."

Peter thought he would not mention Celia Hooper's competent plans for the deanery supper. He thought also that he was not, just now, very sympathetic to Anna's temper. He had even allowed Lady Mayhew to be loudly sorry for him in front of Marjorie Richardson, and although he was later ashamed, he knew he was not ashamed enough.

Anna went down to the church alone on the evening of Good Friday. Flora had wanted to come—"I must *practise* my prayers!"—but had been deflected by the lure of being allowed to dress up in Charlotte's clothes. Luke was, as usual, over at the Old Rectory, and would return at supper-time with the air of small superiority he had adopted for his family after ten days' association with the way of life of Patrick O'Sullivan. Peter was at Snead, taking evening prayer. The flower ladies, Anna thought with some savagery, would be at home, down on their marks for an early night before the onslaught on the church in the morning. But for now, in the quiet early evening, the church was to be hers and she could explain to it how the unseemly exhibitionism that was about to overtake it was nothing to do with her and that she quite understood its distaste.

The church, however, was not empty. Standing in front of the altar and looking up at the west window— the original glass regrettably replaced by a Victorian riot of red and blue with a voluminously robed Christ presiding in the centre—was Daniel Byrne. He was dressed as he had been dressed on the day she met him, and he had his hands in his pockets.

He glanced round at Anna's step, and said, "I suppose it's unrealistic of me to expect a late-nineteenth-century craftsman to have any understanding of humility."

Anna came to stand beside him. She regarded the glassy Christ.

"Wouldn't you say He looked serene?"

"No," said Daniel Byrne, "I'd say He looked smug."

Anna laughed. "I've come in here to work off temper."

"And I've come in to make sure I know the lay of

the land before Sunday. I'm always thrown by strange churches. Can't concentrate if I think I'm going to miss steps.''

"Are you settling in?" Anna said politely.

"Ask me in six months."

"Mr. Byrne—"

"Daniel."

"Daniel," Anna said. She paused. "May I tell you something?"

"I wish you would."

"I have been given a pay-rise."

He said gravely, "At your supermarket."

"Yes. And a recommendation to apply for a management course. I shan't, of course."

"No?"

She looked at him. He said, still gazing up at the window, "I congratulate you."

"Heavens!"

"I expect you haven't told your family."

"Oh no."

He looked at her. "Won't you try?"

"No," she said, "I don't think so."

He turned to face her. His eyes, enlarged by his spectacles, were the same grey as the tweed of his jacket.

"If you have the courage to do what you are doing, why don't you have the courage to speak to them?"

"Courage!" Anna said. "Courage! Round here it's called defiance."

"Then round here is wrong."

She would, she suddenly discovered, have given a good deal to step forward and put her head down on his sturdy shoulder. Had anyone ever done that? Did monks, even ex-monks, get touched?

"I think," Daniel said, taking her hand in a firm

grasp, "I think we will sit down and talk."

He led her to one of the front pews, to the carved and throne-like seat where Sir Francis Mayhew led his lady with no small pomp and circumstance on Sundays.

"You can't do this," Anna said. "You can't give time to this. You're an archdeacon, you've got rectories and churchwardens and bridges to build to Methodism to think of, you can't—"

"Yes, I can."

He sat down beside her on the flat red-velvet cushions.

"If I hadn't liked humanity, I'd still be a monk. My brother says I am still a monk, only now in high-street clothing; a voyeur monk, he says. You will meet him on Sunday. He's coming to church here. He is younger than me and very clever and difficult. I suppose," Daniel said thoughtfully, "I suppose Jonathan is really my private life. And of course you"—he turned to Anna— "you can't have one. Can you?"

She gazed at him.

"Or is it more accurate to say that you could have a private life, but that you don't happen to?"

"I truly don't know, I've changed so, things haven't turned out as we hoped. Everyone underestimates the effect of disappointment, of prolonged disappointment. Poor Peter," Anna said suddenly, putting her hands over her face.

"The parish needs him for what they need—"

"Yes."

"And you, similarly."

"Yes."

"Odd," said Daniel reflectively, "so odd that humanity declines, on the whole, to think that other people are as human as itself." He was silent for a moment. "I don't know what I can do to help you. If anything. Is it enough to know for the moment that I understand?''

She nodded. He stood up. ''I must get back. Jonathan is arriving, and I'm afraid he will alarm Miss Lambe if I'm not there to restrain him.''

''Is your brother a priest?''

''No indeed. He's an academic, a philosopher. He is taking a sabbatical term and will live with me while he writes a book.''

''Does he—'' Anna began doubtfully, uncertain as to how to ask if Jonathan Byrne shared his brother's faith.

''Lord, no,'' Daniel said. ''Thinks the whole thing is a fairy story devised to keep the peasants quiet.''

''A plot?''

''Yes—''

''I shall like your brother,'' Anna said robustly. ''I think a lot of it's a plot, too.''

''We played nuns at Emma's,'' Flora said. She threaded tubes of macaroni cheese on to her fork. ''I was Mother Superior.''

Everyone ignored her.

''I did chanting. I went, 'Ho-o-o-oly, ho-o-oly, ho-o-oly is His Na-a-ame.' ''

''Shut up.''

''I did it in the bathroom, because it echoes. They've got a shower curtain with flowers on. I sent Emma behind it to confess. She had to confess her sins.''

''What sins?''

''She lied,'' Flora said complacently.

''Flora!''

''She did. She told her mother she hadn't had a biscuit when there was one in her hand.''

''Flora,'' Peter said, ''any more of this and you will not go to St. Saviour's.''

Flora, secure in the knowledge of the division between her parents on this subject, merely looked smug. She had made Emma wail, "Oh woe, oh woe, oh woe is me," behind the shower curtain, and tug at her fat bunches of hair in an agony of remorse. The memory of this was very satisfying.

"I do hope," Charlotte said seriously, "that St. Saviour's is going to be intellectually up to Flora."

Luke said, "God, don't egg her on—"

"Don't say God like that."

"Charlotte, must you put spanners in the works?"

"In my view, Anna, Charlotte has a perfect right to ask, and I think has a very valid point."

"But you are actually trying to make quite a different point."

"This," Peter said repressively, "is no moment for such a discussion."

Anna leaned forward. The children stopped eating and waited. "Look," Anna said to Peter, trying to make him meet her eyes. The telephone rang. "Damn," Anna said.

Luke got up. "I'll go."

Anna hissed at Peter, "If you think I'm going to dodge crucial issues because of your notions of what is seemly and what—"

"It's for you," Luke said, holding out the telephone. "It's Celia Hooper."

Anna got up. Peter's heart sank. He pushed his macaroni to the side of his plate and looked without much hope at Charlotte. She was gazing away from him at some spot on the kitchen floor, and her mind had left Flora and her family and had alighted upon Patrick O'Sullivan, whom she had met that afternoon. He represented, Charlotte reflected, absolutely everything she despised, and she had found him hugely attractive. He had been dressed in that terrible affluent middle-class uniform of corduroy trousers and striped shirt and heavy jersey, and he had simply exuded confidence. Charlotte very much hoped she hadn't flirted with him, but she was anxiously afraid that she had.

"No," Anna said loudly into the telephone. "No, thank you. Of course I can't forbid you, Celia, I wouldn't be so stupid, but I can make it plain that I would so much rather you didn't. When I want help, I'll ask for it. What do you mean? What do you mean, I need it? Need what? To be bossed about and organized by people who think they can do my job for me better than I can? Celia, I am sure you mean well—or am I?—but I will organize the deanery supper as I have done, thank you, in the past. And I won't be patronized. Do you hear me? Thank you for ringing. Not at all. Good night."

She put the telephone down and turned to Peter.

"You knew about this."

He said nothing.

"You not only knew, you encouraged her."

"I tried to stop her—"

"Huh!" Anna shouted. Flora wondered whether to cry and decided not yet.

Peter stood up. "You drove me to this," he said furiously, "and Celia. You are deliberately pushing the whole parish to take stands against you so that you can be the victim, you can feel you are in no way to blame. If you refuse to do what it is your duty to do, then no-one is to be blamed for generously doing it for you."

Anna stared. Luke and Charlotte watched, breaths held. Flora let out a loud wail and rushed to her father, and over the top of her head, Peter glared accusingly at Anna. She said nothing. Her anger had died out of her like a blown flame. She made some small clumsy gesture with her hands towards Peter, and then she turned and went out of the kitchen door into the garden.

It was dusk-dark. The black silhouettes of trees stood against a sky still lit by a dramatic glow from the western horizon, and faint mutterings from the branches indicated that it was not quite yet night. Anna walked carefully along the slippery path to the garage and unhooked, from a nail inside the door, the elderly mackintosh she used for winter gardening. Like so much they possessed, it had been left behind at the end of a jumble sale, a waif and stray nobody wanted, despite the faded Burberry label at the back of the neck. Anna put it on. It smelled of earth and its pockets rustled with garden tags and toffee papers and torn seed packets. Anna put her hands down into the comforting rubbish and simply let the tears slide.

It was easier to cry if she walked. She went across the patch of lawn in front of the house, and down the drive beside the churchyard wall. The sight of the bulk of the church was comforting, and for a moment she thought of going in and sitting where she had sat, only hours before, with Daniel, and talking to his imaginary presence. But then she remembered that Peter would have locked the church on his way home from Snead, because he was afraid that the chalice would be stolen from its safe in the vestry, or that vandals would deface the altar, or the huge bible that rested on a lectern carved into an eagle with its wings outspread. So she turned into the lane, and walked slowly past the high garden wall of the Old Rectory, blowing her nose fiercely on a crumpled paper handkerchief from one of the pockets of the Burberry.

From behind the wall, Patrick O'Sullivan heard her.

He had been lured out by the gleaming spring night to see if—as one of his newly acquired gardening books promised him—his *Magnolia stellata* actually glowed in the dim light. It didn't; but, while he peered at it, willing it to enchant him all the same, he heard the sound of someone coming crying along the lane; and then he heard them stop, and sigh, and then whoever it was blew their nose, and he could tell that it was a woman. He straightened up. He thought of rural tragedy, of abandoned girls in ballads. Then he thought of Anna Bouverie. He moved quietly away from the magnolia, on to the rim of grass that edged the gravel of the drive, and, as Anna's figure passed the open gateway, he said, "Good evening."

She gave a little cry.

"I'm so sorry to startle you," Patrick said, "but I couldn't help hearing. And having heard, I couldn't ignore you."

Anna did not turn. She simply said, "I think you'd better."

"Ignore you? Certainly not. Unless of course you want me to."

She stopped walking. He couldn't see her face in the darkness, but he could tell she had also stopped crying. She said, "I wish you hadn't heard me, of course, but now that you have it would be melodramatic to demand that you pretend you never heard a thing."

He stepped on to the gravel.

"Will you come in?"

She hesitated.

"Please," he said, "I'd like to give you some brandy."

The thought of brandy suddenly seemed heaven-sent. Anna said, "Oh! Oh, thank you," and moved forward.

He grasped her arm firmly and led her up the steps into what seemed the exaggerated brilliance of his lighted hall. He looked at her. She was wearing a tramp's mackintosh and her face was absolutely forlorn. He said gently, "This is rather an honour. For me."

She gave a little smile. She let him take off the Burberry and lay it on a chair, and then lead her into the room that Susie Smallwood had painted dull red, and then hated, and which Patrick had lined with handsome books and careful pictures. There was a blazing fire. Patrick put Anna into a fat chair. He said, "Perhaps you'd rather have whisky?"

She shut her eyes and put her head back into the cushions. She said, "I think brandy. I don't know. I'm hopeless at drink. Not enough practice."

He went across the room to a tray of decanters and bottles on a table made of beautiful, rich, red-brown wood. The cushion under Anna's head was beautiful and rich too, and so was the carpet in which her feet were now sunk, feet encased in shoes that had no business, she dreamily felt, to consort with such a carpet.

"I don't quite know," Patrick said, coming back with a tumbler and a dark bottle, "having had so little practice myself, if there are special rules of conduct for talking to rectors' wives."

"Oh, please," Anna said faintly.

"Please what?"

"Don't make a category. I live in one all the time. You're a newcomer. You start new."

"Right," he said. He poured brandy into the tumbler, a lot of brandy.

She eyed it. "I think you should dilute that. And halve it."

"If I dilute it, you'll feel drunker quicker."

She looked pleased. "Will I?"

He put the tumbler on the shining wood at her elbow, beside a small bronze racehorse on a little podium.

"Everything here is so new—"

"I know. Nothing I can do about it. You can't hurry ageing, except in people, where you don't want to."

He sat down opposite her and crossed his legs. His shoes were suede. Anna took a swallow of her brandy and said, "I wonder if anyone saw me come in."

"Does it matter?"

"Yes."

"Is that why you were crying?"

"Among other things."

"Such as?"

Anna said primly, "I don't know you well enough for this kind of conversation."

"You won't get to know me better any other way. Nor I you."

"Does that matter?"

"The very fact," Patrick said, "that you made that last remark a question not a statement shows that you are enjoying yourself."

"Oh dear," Anna said, bending her head to hide her smile.

He watched her. She was staring down into the brandy glass she held between her hands, in her lap, and she was plainly doing a lot of thinking. He realized, with no small *frisson* of pleasure, that she was not used to being flirted with, that men did not flirt with priests' wives, whom they put into a special social category that made them, in the public view, virtually sexless. Patrick looked at Anna's legs. Nothing wrong with those. He saw her suddenly at twenty, at the age of the pretty daughter he had met that afternoon, full of promise and enthusiasm. He was very touched—touched and excited.

He said, "There's no need to be so lonely, you know."

She put her brandy glass down with a bang.

"I don't want this kind of thing," Anna said, struggling out of her chair.

He stood up to help her, but she shook him off.

"I'm so sorry. Clumsy—"

"I'm not a toy," Anna said. "I may be naïve but I am not a plaything."

"I wouldn't dream—"

"People assume," Anna said angrily, "that priests are quite inexperienced, that they know nothing of the world. It's so patronizing and ignorant. Who else, if not priests, see humanity at its very worst?"

Patrick put his hand on her arm. With her free hand, Anna picked it off.

"Won't you even let me apologize?"

She looked at him.

"Of course."

"I am really sorry," Patrick said, "to have behaved like a bad cliché, to have been so arrogant."

She managed a faint smile.

"But I would like us to make friends."

Her smile faded. She said, "You'll see, after a month or two, how difficult that would be."

He opened his mouth to say that he would like a challenge, then shut it again prudently. Her expression was not encouraging. She crossed the creamy carpet to the door.

"Won't you even finish your brandy?"

"No, thank you."

"When will I see you—"

"In church. On Easter Day."

He reached in front of her to prevent her turning the door handle.

"Look. You are a prisoner and you hate it but you refuse to be released!"

Anna looked at him again. She said, "It isn't as simple as that," and then she looked pointedly at the door handle.

When she had gone—she declined to let him see her home—he poured his remaining brandy into hers and took her tumbler back to his armchair. He held it up. There was no trace of lipstick on the glass, no fingerprints, nothing. Her hands must have been very cold. He closed his eyes and thought of them, of warming them. He said to himself sternly, "This must not be a game." It did not strike him that there was any doubt of his both having and keeping the upper hand.

"Where've you been?" Luke demanded. He was making himself a mug of hot chocolate.

"Drinking brandy with your boss," Anna said.

Luke whirled round from the cooker. "You can't mean you just went and asked—"

"Of course not. He was skulking about in the garden as I went by, and then he asked me in."

"Brandy!" Luke said.

"Yes. All of three swallows."

"What was he doing in the garden?" Luke was aggrieved. Patrick was his. It was bad enough having to introduce him to Charlotte, who had, of course, gone straight into the blatant routine Luke knew she would, but Mum . . .

"I couldn't tell you. Where's Flora? In bed?"

"Watching telly. Dad's in his study."

"I'll go in to him."

125

Peter was at his desk, bent over the foolscap pad in which he wrote his sermons. He said, without looking up, "Celia telephoned. To apologize for upsetting you."

"That was nice of her," Anna said, "but she doesn't understand."

Peter ruled a neat underlining.

"Nor do I."

"I think you do," Anna said, "if you really think about it. If you're honest. As honest as you once were."

"Thank you."

"Please—"

Peter said, "We are committed to God. Both of us. With all that that entails."

She came and sat in a chair beside the desk so that she could see his face.

"Are you saying, or implying, that only sacrifice counts? That unless we sort—sort of immolate ourselves, there's no point in it?"

"You are so melodramatic."

She put a hand out to him. He ignored her.

"Do you love me?"

"Of course," he said, not turning.

"That's no answer."

"There isn't an answer that would satisfy you. Not in your present frame of mind."

"Peter," Anna said desperately, "Peter, what do you want of me?"

He turned then. He looked at her gravely.

"You know perfectly well."

"Can we talk about it? Can I tell you how I feel?"

The telephone rang. Peter picked it up at once, and then handed it to Anna.

"Trish Pardoe. For you."

"Yes," Anna said. She took the receiver. "Trish.

Yes. No, I haven't forgotten. I'll be there. Two o'clock. Yes. Goodbye.'' She put the telephone back on its cradle. ''The Brownies' Easter Cake Bake. I had forgotten, actually.'' She stood up. ''I'd better make something now.''

''Right.''

''Could we talk? Will you come into the kitchen while I make a cake?''

Peter said doggedly, ''There is no more to say. You know what the situation is as well as I do. And Sunday is Easter Day and I have a sermon—''

''But Daniel Byrne is coming!''

Peter put down his pencil. His shoulders sagged.

''Of course,'' he said, ''of course. He will preach, not me. I forgot,'' and then he turned away from her completely, so that he might not be comforted.

8

❖ ❖ ❖

COLONEL AND MRS. Richardson came to Loxford church on Easter morning, on account of the Archdeacon. Colonel Richardson always made a point of saying that he did not like to worship outside his own parish, which remark roughly translated as meaning that he did not like to be upstaged at Loxford by Sir Francis and Lady Mayhew, who had an unwritten tenancy of the best pew (front, left-hand side). Also, if you were churchwarden on your own territory, it was hard, he found, to submit to sitting in a pew which wasn't guarded by your official wand. All these feelings, which he would not have dreamt of revealing to Marjorie, made him gruff at breakfast, sharp with the dogs and moved to say, as he entered Loxford church in all its floral abundance, "Good God. Looks like the flower tent at the County Show."

Marjorie Richardson, who knew exactly what he was thinking, moved ahead of him up the aisle, graciously greeting people. She made a point of not discriminating socially. She could see Anna's back, upright in the Rectory pew, beside her untidy children, and she planned, if Anna turned, to give her just a little nod of greeting, a nod that acknowledged her—as was proper—and no more. But, before she reached the pew they had decided upon, the Archdeacon himself, still simply in his cassock, and accompanied by Peter, came out from the vestry and walked briskly across to the Rectory pew and shook hands warmly with them all, smiling down at them as he did so.

Thrown, Marjorie Richardson halted. The Archdeacon was stooping over Flora, who had been allowed to come to church with her hair apparently screwed up in coloured rags.

Behind her, Harry hissed, "Sit down! We'll miss him."

Startled, Marjorie shot into the pew and dropped her immaculate navy-blue handbag. Somebody sniggered. By the time she had retrieved it, and briefly and uncharacteristically hovered over the choice between a quick mannerly prayer or immediately standing up again, Peter Bouverie was by their pew saying, "And this is Colonel and Mrs. Richardson of Quindale. Colonel Richardson is churchwarden."

"How do you do," Daniel said, taking Marjorie's hand in a firm grasp.

She could not think of a fitting reply. She opened her mouth, but no sound came.

Daniel looked at her for a second, and then shook Harry's hand and said, "Ah. Diocesan Board of Finance couldn't do without you, I hear, Colonel Richardson," and Harry said, as she knew he would, "It's nothing. Nothing at all. Like to do my bit."

Then the Archdeacon smiled, and moved on, and Marjorie fell to her knees, ignoring Harry's pleased whisper of, "Very civil. Wonder how he knew? Like a chap who does his homework."

Marjorie was uncertain she liked this chap at all. She was even more uncertain when, at the end of his thorough and genial circuit, he paused by the Rectory pew for a second time and definitely, quite definitely, said something more to Anna.

What he said was, "I have persuaded my brother to come. Quite an achievement." He did not add that Jonathan had come purely to escort Miss Lambe, for whom he had conceived an arcane enthusiasm—an enthusiasm Daniel suspected. "You must not make a fool of Miss Lambe," Daniel had said to Jonathan. "She is easily alarmed." Jonathan had looked mildly affronted. Miss Lambe had dressed for Easter Day at church in a grey-flannel spring coat and a matching beret to which she had rakishly pinned a bunch of artificial daisies. As she knelt beside Jonathan, the flamboyance of the daisies troubled her sense of what was fitting. She was glad that they were on the opposite side of her head to Mr. Byrne.

Jonathan Byrne was not thinking about Miss Lambe or her daisies. He was contemplating, all around him, the seemly manifestations of the rural Church of England; the well-groomed plaster and stone of the church, the flowers, the brushed heads and shoulders ahead of him, the decent sunlight falling through old glass on to the decorous whole. He remembered Daniel's Manchester parish, the church of red- and blue- and yellow-diapered Victorian brick, the energetic and disparate congregation, the bursts of rowdy evangelism. Of course, the Church itself had been ever thus, traditional, tolerant and restrained on the one hand, sectarian, noisy and doctrinaire on the other, and Daniel was, by temperament, the kind of man who could understand both.

He was, Jonathan thought with the strong affection for his brother that he seldom gave voice to, the kind of man who might, by this very perceptive intelligence, thoroughly disconcert such a congregation as now knelt before him, intoning the confession without, Jonathan observed, much anguish of guilt. ''We have left undone those things which we ought to have done, and we have done those things which we ought not to have done, and there is no health in us.'' Sins of omission and commission. What exactly did such sins consist of in a place like this?

Beside him, Miss Lambe and her daisies trembled a little. The general confession, with its dark hints at the opportunities for sin, always made her flinch.

After the service, Anna was amazed to find herself greeted with smiles. Bruised by a difficult weekend with Peter and excluded from the decoration of the church, she turned from her pew, chin high, keeping the children close to her, and expected to be confronted with no more than formality from the congregation. But she had not reckoned on Daniel's influence, his deliberate friendliness to the Rectory pew.

''I must congratulate you on the flowers,'' Marjorie Richardson said.

''Oh, not me, Lady Mayhew—''

''A Happy Easter, my dear.''

''Oh Harry. Thank you.''

''Nice to see the children in church, Mrs. B.''

''Yes—''

''What a lovely morning, Anna, so perfect for Easter.''

''Isn't it—''

"My dear, you look tired. So does Peter. Of course Easter is such a thing—"

"Rather—"

"I wonder if we could have a quick word about the Evergreen Club's spring outing?"

"Oh Elaine, of course, could you ring me?"

"Ah. Little Flora. I hear we are going to a lovely new school?"

"Yes, she is. (Don't scowl, Flora.) Next term—"

"Mrs. Bouverie. Good morning. We seem to have struck lucky with our new Archdeacon, don't you think?"

"Oh, I do—"

"Anna," Daniel Byrne said as the press bearing her along bore her to him where he stood shaking hands in the porch, "Anna, I would like you to meet my brother, Jonathan."

Jonathan Byrne was taller than his brother, less sturdy, and without spectacles. He held out his hand to Anna. "How do you do."

"Welcome to Loxford," she said automatically.

"Your brother took the service beautifully," Anna continued in her parish voice.

"Did he? Should that matter? Is it like comparative performances of *Hamlet*?"

The children, who detested their visibility at such moments, hissed at Anna that they were going, *now,* and went, ostentatiously.

"Yours?" Jonathan Byrne said.

Anna watched them. Charlotte was actually running, which seemed exaggerated of her.

"Mine."

"What is it like, being a rectory child?"

Anna gave him a quick glance.

"I expect you can imagine it. What is it like, being an archdeacon's brother?"

"Touché," he said.

"Forgive me, Mr. Byrne, but I ought to—speak to people."

He stood aside and sketched a little bow.

"Of course."

She hesitated. She wanted to say something grateful about Daniel, something that his brother could pass on over the fraternal lunch-table, but could think of nothing quite right. So she simply said, rather uncertainly, "Goodbye then," and felt foolish.

By the lich-gate a few minutes later, she met Patrick O'Sullivan. He wore a blue blazer with brass buttons and a boldly striped shirt which had been ironed with visibly professional skill. He said, "I hope I look quite different. That's the first time I have darkened church doors except for weddings and funerals since I was at school."

Anna resisted saying, But do you feel different? and merely said, "Well, you were lucky. Because of the Archdeacon, I mean," and then hurried away from him to catch up with Trish Pardoe and ask how much the Brownies' Easter Cake Bake had made.

"Twenty-three pounds! But that's marvellous!" It was necessary to say that, whatever the sum. Brownies, like rectors and mothers-in-law and Flora, and probably archbishops as well, always needed encouragement.

"They were ever so disappointed," Trish Pardoe said, ignoring her, "broke their hearts, really. The Quindale troop made twenty-seven pounds and forty pence." She looked round her. "But what can you expect, from this village?"

On Easter Monday, Patrick O'Sullivan took Charlotte and Luke to a point-to-point. Charlotte, disapproving of such events on social grounds, was poised to decline the invitation, even to the extent of preparing a little speech in her mind, to that effect, to make to Patrick; but Anna and Peter had a quarrel at breakfast, and Charlotte's antipathy to seeing the braying classes at play was dwarfed by her antipathy to the atmosphere in the Rectory. When Patrick manocuvred his gleaming car up the Rectory drive, both Luke and Charlotte—carefully attired to stand out from the green-gumbooted crowd—were actually ready and waiting.

Patrick got out of the car and looked hopefully about for Anna. He was pleased to be taking these attractive children out, but the splendid picnic that lay shrouded in napkins in the boot had unquestionably been ordered with a view to good reports being made of it later. He said, "Right then. Should you sign off before we go?"

"She's gardening," Luke said. She was, furiously, digging the main-crop potato bed as if her life depended upon it.

"Shouldn't you—"

"No," Charlotte said. She eyed the car. The windows had mysteriously tinted glass.

"Sorry," Patrick said, opening the door for her, "habit. I have to tell Ella if I'm even going to post a letter—"

"Hang on," Luke said. He turned and dashed round the house to the vegetable garden. Anna had her back to him, her hair held off her face with a red handkerchief.

"Mum—"

She stopped digging, and turned.

"We're off," Luke said lamely.

"Have a good day. Win lots of money."

"Mum—"

Anna waited.

"Sorry," Luke said. He gestured at the potato bed. "I mean, sorry to go out, not to—"

"You go," Anna said. "I'm not fit for anything but digging, not today."

Luke hovered. He wished very much to make it plain that he loved her, but found himself quite unable to think how. After a long pause he said, "OK then," and she said, "Go on. Don't keep Mr. O'Sullivan waiting," so he went. When he reached the car, Patrick and Charlotte were sitting in the front together, and laughing.

Anna stuck her spade in the earth and went down to the end of the garden, to the rough patch where cow parsley bloomed profusely in May and dandelions flourished their downy clocks about, unchecked. In one corner of this little wilderness was Anna's compost heap and beside it was a low wooden gate, leading into the pasture beyond, a gate Anna had imagined herself using every day for regular, healing country walks. Reality had, of course, proved quite the opposite. She had scarcely opened the gate in ten years and an annual growth of convolvulus knitted itself round the latch. The nearest she ever got to a walk was—as now—to lean briefly on the gate's splintering top bar and gaze at the dark copse on the furthest hill and try to recapture that feeling of combined serenity and adventure that the view had first inspired in her.

Today, however, it inspired nothing. The view lay in all its pretty layers of green like some ingenious tapestry done by the Women's Institute—decorative, controlled, passionless—and had no message. Above it, the sky

136

hung in a tranquil perfection of pale-blue and white. Around her, birds sang casually of this and that, and from the village came the occasional and distant shout of a child. It was all in order and quite remote.

In the house behind her, she had left Flora inventing a newspaper at the kitchen table—*The Loxford Post;* editor, Flora Bouverie; reporter, Flora Bouverie; cartoonist, Flora Bouverie; nature notes, Flora Bouverie; assistant, Emma Maxwell—and in his study, Peter and his sore feelings would be plunged in deanery files. Even if, by going in to him and putting her arms round him and suggesting that they were reconciled, she might have made things better, Anna had no heart for it. She had felt not just anger at breakfast, but dislike; sudden, fierce dislike for Peter's unsmiling, shuttered face, his refusal to look at her, his adamant insistence that, while he was not free to choose how to act, she was—and had chosen to oppose him.

He had, it seemed to her now, leaning on her gate, rejected her. All those years of defending him, of understanding him, of trying to interpose herself as an insulating layer between him and his disappointment, appeared to have gone for nothing. He had made it plain over the debris of breakfast that not only did he feel betrayed by her—and after all she'd done!—but that he did not really want her near him. She had tried to touch him at the end of the quarrel, but he had shied away from her, folding himself into himself like the spines of a rolled umbrella.

I am lonely, Anna thought. An exploring tendril of ivy was growing along the gate, and she began to rip it up, in little bursts, tearing its dry brown suckers from the wood. I am, in all essential senses, alone, because it would be wrong, or unfair, to burden anyone close to me with my isolation and my frustration. And it is more than that; it is that Mrs. Bouverie is taking over from Anna, and, if even Peter does not want Anna any more, then what is to become of her? Is she to become just a competent Pricewell's worker with a blue overall and a jolly plastic badge? Is that to be Anna? She looked up at the innocent sky. "Do you want Anna?" she demanded. The sky smiled on, not heeding her. God was probably as little inclined to indulge such silliness as Peter had been. Why was it that she was made to feel that her claims had no validity, that her existence was only permitted by everyone as long as it remained relative? How did people, Anna cried to herself, how did people get to be primary people—the ones who made others relative? And why, if you picked up a different burden, was it then assumed that you loved your burden and would gladly carry it for ever and ever . . .

"Anna!"

She turned. Peter was standing by the potato bed.

"Yes?"

He made no move to come forward. He called, "You have visitors."

"Who?"

He called again, without answering her, "I think you should come," and then he turned and went back to the house. Glaring at his grey-wool back with something approaching loathing, Anna followed him.

In the sitting-room, Celia Hooper and Elaine Dodswell were standing together on the hearthrug. Peter had invited them to sit down, but had not observed that, unless he did some preliminary clearance, there was nowhere for them to sit. Five people over the Easter weekend had left the Rectory deep in the litter of family living.

Anna appeared shoeless in the doorway.

"Do forgive us, Anna, on a Bank Holiday Monday too, but we knew we'd find you in—"

Anna said, "That's perfectly all right." She moved to the sofa and began to subdue billows of discarded Sunday newspapers. "Would you like coffee?"

"We'd hate to put you to any trouble," Elaine said.

Anna said briefly, "No trouble." She collected Charlotte's ostentatious scatter of books from an armchair. "Please sit down."

"So naughty to interrupt your gardening."

"I'd stopped."

"Robert's hard at it too," Celia said cosily. "First cut of the year. He's fanatical about his edges."

Anna went out to the kitchen.

"Ought my cartoon to be political?" Flora said.

"I think that would be terribly difficult. A political joke—"

"Perhaps I could do something a little bit rude about the Queen—"

"She's certainly easier. If I put all these things on a tray, will you make coffee when the kettle's boiled and bring it in?"

Flora didn't look up. "Who's there?"

"Mrs. Hooper and Mrs. Dodswell."

"Pooper and Plodswell."

"Yes. Shh."

"Mummy," Flora said, "Emma's mother plays golf."

"Does she?"

"Lots of mothers do. Emma's mother said would you like to but I said you spent all your time doing Pricewell's or the garden or German."

139

"What a help to my image you are," Anna said. "Don't forget the kettle."

In the sitting-room, Celia and Elaine were having a carefully anodyne conversation about the church fête. When Anna came in, Elaine was saying, "Well, you can't ask Mrs. Berridge to do teas again, not after last year, with the tea stone cold and flies on the rock buns—"

"Flora's bringing coffee in a minute," Anna said. She sat down on the sofa and looked at Celia. "How can I help you?"

Celia leaned forward. "Oh no. It's quite the other way about. We've come to ask how we can help you."

Anna stared at her. She stared at her blue-and-white weekend jersey and her matching blue weekend trousers.

Elaine, who was genuinely fond of Anna and was disconcerted by her expression, said hastily, "It isn't interference, Anna, really it isn't. It's a Christian helping hand."

Anna turned. "In what way?"

"There's so much for you to do, you see—"

"The cleaning rota, the flower rota—"

"Attending all the parish clubs and services—"

"The parish magazine—"

"And I expect the telephone never stops!"

"And then, of course, the deanery entertaining responsibilities—"

"And your own life—"

"Oh yes, Anna, your own life."

"We just thought," Celia said, never allowing her smile to slip, "we just thought it was all too much for one—for one *busy* person like yourself, so we have come to offer ourselves as—as your deputies."

The door opened uncertainly and Flora wavered in with the coffee tray. Anna got up.

"Thank you, darling."

"I spilled a bit—"

"It doesn't matter."

"Thank you, dear," said Celia Hooper. "What a helpful girl."

Flora, who had abandoned the Loxford Brownie troop after two sessions because of what she termed all the icky *helping*, looked lofty.

"You will excuse me," Flora said firmly, and returned to the kitchen.

Anna, whose hands did not seem as steady as she could have wished them, handed round the cups of coffee. She said, offering Elaine sugar, "Did I hear you right? Are you offering yourselves as deputy rector's wives?"

Elaine looked at her with great earnestness. "Yes."

A mild hysteria seized Anna. She fought with the urge to say, In every sense? and won, by the simple expedient of remembering that, for the last eighteen months, her and Peter's nights had been purely for sleeping.

"Have you spoken to Peter of this?"

Celia looked shocked, largely because she had wished to, and Elaine had prevented her. "Of course not."

Anna returned to the sofa. A dull misery was settling on her like fog. "What exactly do you propose?"

"Well," Celia said. She leaned forward and looked very, very caring. "We thought we could relieve you of all the mundane things—cleaning, flowers, magazines, etcetera—and perhaps some organizational things too, like the nuts and bolts of deanery entertaining, and leave you, as is only proper, the public roles. Being in church, visitors, attending functions. That sort of thing. We have a little team in mind, seven ladies—''

Anna closed her eyes.

''Are you all right?'' Elaine said anxiously.

''Yes. Yes, I'm fine—''

''There you are. Worn out—''

''Please,'' Anna said.

Elaine stood up. ''I think we should go. You think about it.''

When they had gone, Anna went back to the sofa and lay on it, in a stupor.

After a while, Flora came in and said, ''Why are you lying down?''

''Because I'm tired.''

''Why are you tired?''

''Because I think I'm vanishing,'' Anna said.

Flora looked at her, up and down. ''Emma's mother,'' Flora said, ''would think that was a very silly way to talk.''

Later that day, Anna tried to explain to Charlotte. Charlotte had enjoyed the point-to-point, to her amazement, and had won £6. Luke had been allowed to drive the Daimler on a quiet side road, and they were both rather anxious everyone should know that they had been given smoked salmon sandwiches, and then sloe gin to wash down fruit cake. After supper at the Rectory, Luke returned to the Old Rectory to sluice the day's mud off the Daimler, and Charlotte said she would wash up. Anna said they would do it together then, and, when Charlotte protested, explained that she wanted to talk.

Charlotte, however, did not want to talk—or at least, not in the way Anna wanted to. Anna wanted to describe the morning, and her visit, and to attempt to decide, by thinking out loud, why this offer of apparent help should seem to her so deeply depressing, almost offensive. The two women had, after all, proposed to lift chores from her shoulders, but they were chores which, in a curious way, gave her an identity, and at the moment she was truly afraid of having no identity at all. She tried to explain this to Charlotte, to explain her sense of isolation and of losing what little control was left to her. She said, "You see, being married to a priest means such a different kind of marriage to a secular one. It is rather like having a crucial relationship with someone who is always half turned away from you."

Charlotte listened, sloshing soapy water about the sink, but she didn't reply. It seemed to her that her mother was being relieved of all the most demeaning parish duties and that she ought to be absolutely thankful, and accept at once, and go out and find a decent teaching job instead of this obscene supermarket one. She had quite a lot of sympathy for her mother—she found her father impossible just now, quite unapproachable—but she couldn't see why Anna clung to just that society-enforced female stereotyping that Charlotte and her friends were staking their lives upon overturning. She also, at bottom, was not deeply interested. After two weeks at home, she was beginning to feel stifled, and to need the reassurance of her friends that she was independent and free-thinking. She lifted a bunch of knives and forks out of the water and dumped them, clattering, on the draining board.

"You must just do what you want, Mum. You're in charge."

Anna said, "Luke says that. But it isn't true. The constraints may be invisible, but they are very strong."

Charlotte began to dry her hands very carefully, before fitting back on to her fingers her armoury of Indian silver rings. "It's no good, being passive—"

"I know that. But being trapped is different."

"Look, Mum," Charlotte said, "I'd accept if I were you. And get a decent job. What's going on just now is pretty silly—"

"Silly?"

"In all honesty," Charlotte said, "I can't support this supermarket."

Anna turned away and began to stack the clean plates in cupboards. Charlotte watched her for a while and then she said, almost without meaning to, "Sorry—"

"That's all right," Anna said. They did not look at one another. "You go off now—"

Charlotte sidled round to the back door.

"Patrick said to join him and Luke for a drink after Luke had washed the car—"

" 'Course—"

"Won't be late."

"Doesn't matter."

Cold air rushed in with the opening door. "Night," Charlotte said, in a voice rich with relief, and vanished.

On the first morning of the summer term, Peter elected to take Flora to St. Saviour's. This meant that they all drove into Woodborough together, and, after Luke had been dropped at the sixth-form college gates, Anna was let out, with elaborate lack of comment, at the staff door of Pricewell's. Peter then escorted an extremely over-excited Flora to St. Saviour's.

He was slightly defiant about doing this. He was genuinely abashed at his opposition to a move which was very likely to benefit Flora, while at the same time feeling that Anna, by taking charge, had not only made him look weak, but had meant to. She had also said that morning, while they were dressing, "I suppose you aren't trying to impress the nuns, are you? Taking Flora on her first morning when I can't remember you ever taking any of them to school before—"

He said, "I'm trying to make amends."

She had looked at him, with a look that wasn't unkind but wasn't particularly loving either, and then had gone downstairs to find that a radiant Flora, flawless in her new uniform, had already laid breakfast (unheard of) and was slicing bread for toast with a fine disregard for symmetry. Breakfast had been quite cheerful, with Flora so exuberant and Luke able to face a new term and old friends with the dignity of actually, for the first time in his life, being in funds. Charlotte had gone back to Edinburgh on her bus three days before, kissing everyone goodbye with a fervour born of relief. She had left Anna a postcard on her pillow, a reproduction of a Klimt, with, written on the back, "Dearest Mum. Women are no longer victims of circumstance. You have to believe that. Love, Charlotte." Anna had been very touched. The card—an erotic, exotic painting of Judith—was in her bag now.

When he had dropped Flora—"Ah," Sister Ignatia had said, clasping his hands in both her faintly damp ones, "now here's a very special little newcomer"— Peter drove back into the marketplace, and managed to park in the double file of spaces in the centre. He got out, locked the car carefully, and crossed to the pavement that led down to Pricewell's, at the point where the market-place narrowed into the High Street. He walked against the buildings, slightly sideways as if trying not to be conspicuous, and, when he reached the great blank windows of the supermarket, he stopped, and peered in at an angle. The inside was brightly lit, but his view was half obscured by the row of tills against the window. He began to sidle along the glass, gazing up the aisles between the rows of tins and packets and bottles. From half-way along one, standing on a small stepladder, Anna watched him. She watched him reach the door, hesitate, and turn away. He walked back, more briskly, the way he had come. Anna looked for a while at the point at which he had vanished and then shook herself, and turned back to her shelves.

9

❖ ❖ ❖

JONATHAN BYRNE MADE himself a study in Woodborough Vicarage. He spent a happy afternoon roaming
through the unused upper rooms, and chose one with an
elaborate stone-mullioned Gothic window surmounted
by trefoils filled with coloured glass. The diocese was,
of course, agitating to sell the Vicarage and erect the
usual sensible, faceless, mediocre building instead, so
perhaps within years this room and its splendid window
would be taken over as a dormitory by boys from The
King's School, an undistinguished private establishment
currently benefiting from parental anxiety about the un-
reliability of state education, and needing to expand.

In the meantime, Jonathan decided, it would serve him
excellently. He retrieved various pieces of furniture from
around the Vicarage—a table, some tremendously heavy
pitch-pine shelves, several chairs and a spectacularly
morbid Piranesi print of dungeons—and arranged these
to his satisfaction. Miss Lambe, luckily, had no notion
of how to interfere or domesticate, so he was not burdened with curtains or cushions or unwanted strips of

comforting carpet. The uncompromising angularity of the room, when he had finished, pleased him very much. He went down to Daniel's study to summon him on a little tour of appreciation, but Daniel was not there. He was, said Miss Lambe, out in the combined parish of Great and Little Blessington with Mumford Orchus, swearing in a new churchwarden.

Jonathan felt the need of company. Miss Lambe, for all her hamster-like charm, was not much good for conversation on account of her powerful sense of anxious inadequacy, and in any case, she was doing the ironing and, whenever addressed, gave a little start and put the iron down in order to attend respectfully to whatever was being said to her. It was clearly both kinder and more practical not to say anything. Jonathan collected his jacket and a handful of change and said he was going out for an hour. Miss Lambe stopped ironing to say it looked like rain.

Woodborough Vicarage opened straight on to a cobbled lane that ran down to the High Street. It was a neglected lane, too narrow for all but the smallest cars, and dank weeds and mosses grew sadly between the cobbles. It was closed at one end by a small lich-gate to the churchyard intended by the Victorians for the Vicar's private access, and opened at the other on to the pavement opposite Woolworth's. As Jonathan turned away from the church, its clock announced that it was five— time, he considered, for a cup of something to reward his scene-shifting efforts.

The pavements were quite full. Jonathan threaded his way along, thinking how aggressive and proprietorial of pavement space the possession of a pushchair made most women. He passed a newsagent and an electrical goods shop and a window full of women's clothes—

Jonathan had never known how to look at their clothes, but this riotous assembly of floral patterns struck him as quite inappropriate (except, of course, if you were a flower)—and then he came to Pricewell's. Pricewell's. He remembered. He stopped. In Pricewell's worked the interesting Mrs. Bouverie who had, Daniel said, caused such fluttering in her parish hen coop by her small, brave show of independence. Jonathan had seen her on Easter Sunday, but she had been harassed and tense, in no mood to be interesting. He thought he would go in and spy on her, just briefly. He pushed open the door.

Pricewell's was almost empty. In ten minutes, it would be full of people released from their offices, but for now it felt calm and spacious. Jonathan walked up and down the aisles, marvelling at the extraordinary things the public seemed to have a taste for, and looking for Anna. She was nowhere to be seen. Perhaps Thursday was not her day. He stopped a plump woman patting packets of paper towels into order and asked her where Anna was. In the warehouse, she said. Could you . . . She looked at him. He smiled. "All right," she said, but she sighed.

He waited for what seemed a long time among the quiet columns of lavatory paper. When she came down, Anna was wearing a blue overall over much longer clothes, and looked anxious.

"Mr. Byrne, is anything the matter, has your brother—"

"No," Jonathan said, "I just wanted someone to have some coffee with. To talk to. I came in here to have a snoop at you going about your tasks, but then I thought I'd much rather take you out and talk to you."

She looked flustered. "I can't leave until five-thirty—"

He held out his wrist. "Twenty minutes."

"Then I catch the bus to Loxford—"

"I'll drive you."

"Mr. Byrne—"

"Jonathan."

"I'm afraid," Anna said primly, "that my life doesn't allow for impulses."

He stared at her. She looked down.

"Tomorrow," he said, "what hours do you work tomorrow?"

"Until three. Then I collect Flora at four."

"Three o'clock tomorrow then."

She looked up again. "Is there something specific? That you want to talk about?"

"No," he said, "should there be?" Then he said, to help her, "I'm a total stranger here, you see. Daniel's very busy."

"But you are writing a book—"

"Not all the time."

She seemed to give herself a little shake. "Tomorrow then. Thank you."

He nodded and turned away and, on the way out, bought himself a loaf which called itself Lincolnshire Plum Bread, from the bakery section, because it reminded him of the poacher's song he had so loved when he was small.

Long before, Jonathan Byrne had married a fellow undergraduate, the moment he came down from Cambridge. She was ferociously clever, cleverer, he knew, than he, and with a singleness of purpose that he had imagined would give them both freedom. In fact, it gave them no shared goal since Jonathan was not sufficiently emotionally mature to understand the necessity for his own contribution. They had stayed married for three years, and had divorced with brisk friendliness, acknowledging that there was no point to their shared existence because they did not, in fact, share it or wish to. Stephanie had gone to America and a distinguished academic life, which now included, Jonathan heard, a veteran Hollywood actor old enough to be virtually her grandfather. After a few cursory and reactive affairs, Jonathan grew out of the habit of full-time women, assuming, with a certain resignation, that he had not much aptitude for them. When Daniel came out of his monastery and looked about at life, he had asked Jonathan why he hadn't married again and Jonathan had said because he hadn't wanted to. Now, both brothers were conscious of the unmistakable companionable warmth of having one another in Woodborough Vicarage.

Miss Lambe laid supper for them each night at the inadequate dining-room table—inadequate, that is, for the proportions of the room. They ate early, to allow her to escape to her burrow and her wireless—she was disconcerted by television. She left covered dishes and plates on the sideboard, and then hovered in the kitchen until they had eaten because it would have distressed her immeasurably to think of an archdeacon—even a modern archdeacon—washing up. She cooked safe, dull food, but at least Jonathan's presence had broken her habit of cutting up Daniel's meals as if he were a toothless invalid. To be obliging, they ate their chops or ham or sausages at breakneck speed, and then took cups of coffee into Daniel's study. Behind them, in the dining-room, Miss Lambe mourned over an abandoned potato, a half-finished apple crumble. Anything left could only mean that there had been something the matter with it.

The telephone in Daniel's study constantly interrupted

them. Jonathan wondered if the Church of England and City of London foreign-exchange dealers had almost comparable telephone bills. The interruptions made sustained conversation difficult, but there was at least time to tell Daniel about his foray into Pricewell's and his stiff little interview with Anna.

"She was very disapproving. I felt I was behaving improperly. It was only an impulse."

Daniel said, spooning far too much sugar into his coffee, "It was improper. For her, I mean. It isn't the kind of thing that happens to her."

"Why not?"

"Because almost no-one treats clergy wives as if they were human beings."

"Rubbish."

"Not at all rubbish. I didn't see it so much in Manchester because I think cities are much more socially liberal and the hierarchy doesn't exist to the same extent. But out in the country, the vicar's wife is the vicar's wife, and she is required to remember that."

"That's status—"

"No," Daniel said, "it is not. It is an assumption— and not a generous assumption—that not only is a clergy wife expected to live by almost exaggerated standards of rectitude, but that she is somehow immune to the devices and desires of all other human hearts. It isn't just Anna Bouverie. The wife of the priest out at Mumford Orchus was shut in her sitting-room this afternoon with the curtains drawn and the television on. The husband made me a cup of tea in the kitchen and I couldn't help noticing a whole basket of pill bottles on the table. Nice fellow, bit smug, but I don't suppose he knows what on earth is the matter, or why it has come to be the matter."

"Doesn't all this apply to men?"

Daniel drank his coffee.

"Oh yes."

"Well then?"

"The men have chosen God."

"Haven't their wives?"

"A great many of them have. They aren't the problem. The problem lies with the wives who discover, quite legitimately, that, although bowing to the will of God of your own free will is one thing, bowing to it as translated to you by your husband, who has somehow assumed a monopoly on the first place with God, is quite another. This is not pure Christianity, I know, but it is pure human observation."

The telephone began. Jonathan got up to answer it. "Yes? I think so. Who is it speaking?" He put his hand over the mouthpiece. "Terry Bailey. From Dummerford."

Daniel looked pleased. "Ah," he said, "my pet misfit. A full-blooded evangelical who preaches like a Welsh Baptist, stuck in a village made up entirely of retired admirals and genteel widows." He seized the receiver. "Terry? What can I do for you?"

Jonathan went out of the room and quietly closed the door. He crossed the hall, and climbed the stairs, past Miss Lambe's shut door, through which the wireless clucked comfortingly, and up to his new study. Before he went to bed, he would fill the shelves with books.

Anna led Jonathan to a coffee shop attached to a delicatessen whose window was full of ostentatious Italian machines for making pasta. This was not because it crossed her mind as being more suitable for his mildly eccentric appearance, but because she knew that the inhabitants of Loxford, when they came into Woodborough to shop, preferred their refreshment (according to class) at either the jolly red plastic hamburger joint in the market-place, or the Country Kitchen, whose decor was refined rural and whose motto was "home-made." The delicatessen coffee shop was used chiefly by the younger bookbinders and jewellers and leathersmiths who rented workshops in Woodborough's former brewery. It was evident at once that Jonathan only noticed his surroundings if that was what he happened to be concentrating on at the time, which was not, at this moment, the case. He collected coffee for Anna and himself, and then pulled an ancient paperback copy of André Maurois' *Ariel* out of his pocket and laid it beside her cup.

"Have you read that? It's about Shelley."

"No."

"Do. It's dated, but there's something there. And it's relevant. To what I want to talk to you about."

"Oh," Anna said, relieved. "So there is something."

"I want to talk to you about subversion."

"Heavens—"

"Does that interest you?"

She spread her hands. "I don't know. I'm not quite sure of the rules of this kind of conversation—"

"You mean because it isn't orthodox. Or shows signs of becoming unorthodox."

She said, looking straight at him, "I imagine, I can't be sure, being rather out of practice at talking like this, but I imagine it is perfectly possible to long for and dread the same thing."

"Like unorthodoxy?"

"Yes."

"Oh good," he said, "this is exactly what I was hoping for. Are you hungry?"

"No," she said.

He settled himself over his coffee cup. "Don't you think," he said, "that it would be exhilarating to feel a rush of liberating energy?"

"What has that to do with subversion?"

"Aren't they linked? Isn't the desire to undermine the status quo and to mock pretension and apparent unassailability tied up with feeling that after they are overthrown there will be a wonderful, energetic freedom?"

She drank her coffee. She looked at him. She said boldly, "Are we—you—talking about me?"

He smiled. Like his brother, he had a charming smile. "I am absolutely fascinated by your situation." He waited for her to reply that he wouldn't be if he was in it but she said, without heat, "I'm not up for discussion, Mr. Byrne."

"Jonathan. Haven't you talked to Daniel?"

She looked indignant but said, "That's quite different."

"Because he's a priest?"

"Because," she said, her face softening, "because he really does understand the dilemma."

"How do you know I don't?"

Anna thought, briefly, of Patrick O'Sullivan. "You are a man, but not a priest, so I don't trust you."

"What!"

"I can't," she said candidly. "You can't imagine how little chance I have had to form close relationships outside my family. I have seen how people behave, but I haven't experienced it. I've experienced a lot of very unpleasant things that I don't suppose will ever come your way, but I haven't, personally, intimately, been in the thick of human things because, as a priest's wife, I can't be. Are you married?''

"Not now," he said. He wanted to look at her with admiration, but controlled himself.

"In that case," she said unexpectedly, "I assume you know a good deal more at first-hand about women than I know about men. You've probably noticed that there is often a kind of aura of—of unworldliness, almost innocence, about clergymen and their wives. I suppose it is partly lack of money but I think it's partly what I've been saying, too.'' She stopped.

"Go on," he said.

She shook her head. "I never talk like this," she said severely.

"I want to know more about this detachment, this sensation of being in a separate category—''

"I have to go. I have to collect Flora.''

"Don't you like this? Don't you like a little mental exercise? Don't you want to be talked to as if you had never heard of the Church of England?''

She looked up again. She looked quite distraught. He was horrified, remorseful.

"Oh my dear girl, I'm so sorry, I'm so clumsy—'' He pulled a huge navy-blue handkerchief out of his pocket and proffered it. "I meant to be sympathetic, not challenging, I meant to be generous, if that doesn't sound patronizing.''

She nodded, round the handkerchief. "I know—''

He said, "I was too sudden.''

"I think I was rather priggish—''

He leaned across the table towards her. "Is it very imprudent to ask if you believe in God?''

"I think I do. Very occasionally I am almost sure I

do. But it is not a God who seems to bear much relation to—" She stopped. She had been going to say, Peter's God.

Jonathan stood up and came round the little white table to help her up, as if she were ill.

"If I'm very careful, will you talk to me again?"

"Of course," she said crossly. "I don't have to be humoured."

"I didn't mean that. I meant if I wasn't so rough and unimaginative."

She said, "I'll wash your handkerchief."

"And read the Maurois?"

"Why?"

"For a portrait of a particular kind of rebelliousness. Just for discussion."

"I see." She smiled at him.

He said, "Until the next time then," and they went out into the street.

"You're late," Flora said.

"Darling, only five minutes—"

"Five minutes late. That was all very well at Woodborough Junior but here, I can tell you, the mothers are a very different kettle of fish. Where have you been anyway?"

"Sitting in a coffee shop talking about myself with the Archdeacon's brother."

Flora wasn't interested. "I got *another* merit star. In English."

Anna took her hand to draw her down the steps on the way to the bus stop. "Well done. What for?"

"A self-portrait in fifty words. Mine began, 'I am not strong but I am tall and sensitive.' "

Anna suppressed a smile. "I see."

"Sister Josephine thinks I might be quite a spiritual child."

"Oh?"

"But I'm not sure I'd have the *patience* for it."

"Flora," Anna said, suddenly glowing with delayed benevolence from her conversation with Jonathan Byrne, "Flora, do you like St. Saviour's?"

Flora said seriously, "I am absolutely blissful."

"Oh, good," Anna said, squeezing Flora's hand too hard in her emotion. "Oh darling, I'm so pleased."

"But it is *not* blissful," said Flora, seizing her opportunity, "to be the only child at St. Saviour's with a mother who is *late*."

A miasma of elaborate tactfulness hung over Loxford on the subject of the deanery supper. It was known throughout the parish—Celia Hooper felt it was her duty in supporting Anna to disseminate this knowledge—that Anna would be very upset if it was even hinted at that she could not manage it this year. It was not, Celia said seriously to people, as if it was a parish affair involving the laity: no, it was strictly Church business, a little party for the deanery priests and their wives, and Anna must not be made to feel that the laity was in any way butting in. Talking about the deanery supper gave Celia Hooper an excellent chance to moot her idea of a little parish support-group for Anna. Most people were very sympathetic, and eager to help; only Lady Mayhew and Marjorie Richardson indicated that they thought Anna needed a spank rather than support. Celia had said to Elaine that they wouldn't push the matter any further just now, they'd let Anna get her party over.

The pattern of the deanery supper had set itself in

amber some years before, not particularly by Anna's wish, but more by the prevailing wish of her guests, most of whom knew what they expected of a rural dean. They knew, for instance, that he had no extra income from the position, and only a small entertainment allowance. This meant that they wished to be entertained with a delicate balance between modesty and generosity. Cider would be an insult, but anything better than *vin de table* would be improper. The food Anna had learned to provide—cheeses and salads, cold meats and rolls, followed by slightly childish puddings—was always much appreciated. They all ate with an old-fashioned gusto. It was one of the aspects Anna liked best, this unaffected, unspoiled pleasure at greedy eating in a party atmosphere.

The day of the party, she got up at six and moved the furniture in the sitting-room back against the walls. She then collected all the chairs round the house and arranged them in conversational groups. After that, she made three pints of custard for the trifles, washed four lettuces, counted out seventeen plates (mostly odd), seventeen pudding bowls, and arranged them in the sitting-room between fans of paper napkins. When it was properly light, she went out into the garden and brought in armfuls of the last daffodils, and some branches of new willow. Then she got breakfast. In the middle of breakfast Peter said had she remembered that John Jacobs from Dinsbury was a vegetarian and she said thank you, she'd remembered everything. Should he pick up the wine? No need, thank you, she had asked Mike Vinson to bring it home with him. And glasses? We don't need them, there are enough at the village hall.

"Then," said Peter, "what is there I can do to help?"

Anna began marshalling jars and cereal boxes on the table prior to putting them away. "I don't honestly know."

Luke tried to catch his father's eye for a wink of complicity, but it was not to be done. Peter folded up the newspaper with elaborate precision and carried it out of the kitchen.

"No need, really, Mum," Luke said, "to give him a hard time. He was only offering—"

"He doesn't want me to do it. He doesn't think I can do it."

"I think he just feels a bit guilty that you have to do it."

Anna turned from the cupboard where she was stowing things away. "Do you?"

Luke nodded. Anna looked at the clock. "Oh Lord. Ten to. I haven't time to sort it out now. Get your stuff, will you? And shout for Flora." She ran out of the room and up the stairs. Peter was locked in the lavatory. She called, "I'm sorry. Sorry to be disagreeable." He said nothing. "I'll see you later," Anna called. "Will you open some beans for lunch?" She stopped herself from apologizing for the beans. Flora came out of her bedroom.

"Come on," Flora said, sensing drama. "Come on, come on, come on or we'll miss the bus and it will be *utter* disaster."

The guests arrived exactly when they had been asked, at seven-fifteen. Anna felt relief at the sight of them, at their familiarity, reassured by their kind little questions as they came in and by their exclamations of enthusiasm at the sight of the daffodils, of Flora in her green school uniform, of the sherry trifle. They would remain docilely in their couples until, emboldened by a glass or two of wine, they would bravely separate into sexes and get down to the business of the evening which was, of course, diocesan gossip. The priests would compare the impossibleness of their parishes and speak of job opportunities; their wives would talk personalities. Two of them had recently had tea with the Bishop's wife; the rest were burning to hear about it.

The last to come was Isobel Thompson. She had taken to coming several years before, to help Anna dole out supper, and then to wash up. This year she came with a certain amount of trepidation, but Anna seemed only pleased to see her, not surprised and not touchy. She looked, Isobel thought, strained and tired, but she was smiling, and the house and the supper-table looked lovely. Accepting a glass of white wine, Isobel decided that Anna must have come to some kind of reconciliation with herself, and her role, and that the effort she had clearly made for the party was the first step in a new determination. She said to Daphne Jacobs, "Hasn't Anna done us proud?"

Daphne Jacobs had brought up five children in three rectories and, in between, had taken a quiet pride in her parish work. She had seen Anna in Pricewell's, and had heard from Mary Marshall at Crowthorne End that she had taken the job out of disappointment when Peter failed to get his promotion. Later in the evening, she intended to discuss it further (covertly) with Mary, who was busy, just now, putting something of everything available on to her plate. In the meantime, she said quellingly to Isobel, "Lovely daffodils. Ours are all over."

Sighing, Isobel went across the room to talk to Marion Taylor from Mumford Orchus, whose husband had become a priest when he was fifty-five, to her abiding dismay. He had been an accountant before; they'd had a nice house in Lichfield and she had never wanted life to be any different from the uneventful regularity she had known then. Her secret afternoons with old movies on television were not so much a consolation as a lifeline. She told her daughter that the pills she took were vitamin supplements and iron, for her anaemia. She made a place for Isobel beside her on the Knole sofa.

"Anna looks tired."

"She's made such an effort for us," Isobel said. "How's your Sunday school?"

"Folded. Hopeless. They all just used it as somewhere to dump the children for an hour. And I'm no teacher."

"You should learn to play the guitar. It's such a help, a little music, with children."

Marion Taylor leaned closer. "I don't blame Anna, you know. I admire her. I seem to have lost the will to do much, but it doesn't mean I don't sympathize."

Isobel said stoutly, "We have all been praying for her."

Marion Taylor gave a little snort and her wineglass shook in her hand, spilling some into her beige, pin-spotted lap. She mopped at it fiercely with a paper napkin. "Prayer!" she said. "I don't know I've much use for it. But I do know that, if anyone mentions waves of prayer to me again in that awful sanctimonious way they have, I shall be sick."

The party swelled steadily in volume. An animated discussion of Daniel Byrne in one corner was balanced by a debate on the ineffectiveness of synods in another, while in between the subjects of children and villages and the Bishop's wife (a dear, but not really in touch, somehow) ebbed and flowed. Peter toured the clumps of people dutifully with bottles of *vin de pays* and tried to look as he had felt at all previous deanery suppers—like a man with something of a future. They were all extremely nice to him, a little hearty, a shade solicitous, and he began to feel a revived gratitude towards Anna, mixed with a new relief that she might be, somehow, coming through a difficult phase (most natural after such a blow, after all) and that this party was a token of a new leaf turned. He emptied the last of the bottles he had in either hand into the glasses held out to him by Colin Taylor and John Jacobs (vegetarianism, he couldn't help noticing, seemed to be no dampener of enthusiasm for drink) and went out to the kitchen in search of what he was afraid was probably the last of the wine.

Anna was sitting at the kitchen table with her face in her hands, racked with sobs. He said, *"Anna."*

She did not look at him. He put the empty bottles down among the piles of dirty plates and bent over her, putting his arm around her shoulders.

"What is it? Anna, tell me, what is it?"

She hardly could. She said something incoherent, something about its being no good, it all being a sham, and then the tears took over again.

Peter said, "Hold on. Wait a minute," and went back into the sitting-room. Isobel was in the middle of the synod debate, saying with some firmness that the laity didn't contribute more because they were never allowed to know better than the Church. Peter went up to her and whispered, "Can you come? Anna's in the kitchen in an awful state and I can't tell what's the matter."

When Isobel reached the kitchen, Anna was stooped over the sink splashing cold water on to her face.

"My dear, Peter said you were terribly upset—"

Anna turned round, reaching blindly for something to

dry her face on. Isobel handed her a tea towel.

"Thank you. Yes. I'm sorry he found me."

"What is it? What *is* the matter?"

"I don't belong, Isobel. I'm out of it, apart."

"Oh my dear—"

"Don't talk Church to me, Isobel," Anna said, interrupting. "Don't talk about Christian love, I beg of you. It isn't just that I don't belong, but I don't *want* to belong. I feel as if I've been in some school crocodile for twenty years and if I don't break ranks I'll suffocate."

Isobel regarded her. Words like tired and overwrought presented themselves to her. In Isobel's experience, a change of scene was often the best possible medicine for such cases as these. She wondered where Anna could go? She would ask Peter. She went across to Anna and took the tea towel away gently.

"I'm going to get you up to bed. Cup of tea and some aspirin. You're worn out."

"I'm sorry," Anna said, "I'm sorry."

"For what?"

"Breaking down, not being able to cope—"

"Once," Isobel said, "when I suddenly felt I couldn't cope another moment with my mother, I hit her with *The Oxford Companion to Music*. It was lying on the floor, propping the door open."

Anna began to giggle weakly.

"And then," said Isobel, "realizing I had given her a lifelong stick to beat me with morally, I thought I hadn't hit her nearly hard enough. Come on, upstairs with you."

"The party—"

"It's running itself. I'll tell them you've got a blinding headache. It was a splendid supper."

"I bought nearly all of it. I only made the trifles."

"So?"

"Oh, Isobel," Anna said, "you know. Could I buy things if I wasn't earning?"

"Up," Isobel said, "shoo. I'll bring you tea in two ticks."

In the morning, Patrick O'Sullivan went into the Loxford shop to buy tonic water and peppermints, and heard that Mrs. Bouverie had been taken very ill in the middle of a big function, and although she wasn't in hospital, it was touch and go. So he drove into Woodborough and ordered her a basket of lily of the valley, and wrote a card to be dispatched with it.

The flowers arrived and were brought up to Anna by Luke, who had decided on a day off school to look after her and/or revise.

"Heavens," Anna said.

"D'you like them?"

"I like the *flowers*—"

"Yeah," Luke said, "you can't blame the flowers. But doesn't sending them strike you as pretty obscene?"

10

❖　❖　❖

ELEANOR RAMSAY, ALERTED by Peter, telephoned Anna and asked her to come and stay in Oxford. Anna demurred, thinking of the administrative complications. Isobel, however, was ahead of her in this, and said that she would have Flora to stay for a week, and that Luke could spend the week with his friend Barnaby, whose mother liked Luke because she believed he was a sobering influence.

"Don't you want to go?" Peter said.

She was stirring a cup of tea, round and round, pointlessly, since she never had sugar. "Yes, I want to go. But I don't want to have to go."

"Things have got too much for you before, you know," he said, unwisely, thinking of her frantic outbursts at St. Andrew's, all those years before.

She glared at him. "You too," she said, quick as a flash.

He got up and poured more hot water into the teapot.

"I suppose I might get some translation done in Oxford. I've neglected it. I couldn't somehow face it recently, it seemed both inexorable and insultingly second-rate.''

"Even compared with loading shelves in a supermarket?''

"Even,'' said Anna in a dead level voice, ''with that.''

"Perhaps now's the moment to give that up—''

"And perhaps it isn't. I'm only away a week. You forget I'm a star employee. Nice Mr. S. Mulgrove is a man of sympathy and flexibility. I'll work longer hours the week after.''

"And collapse again.''

"I expect so,'' she said. She was beginning to seethe with rage. ''You would like that, wouldn't you?''

"No,'' he said maddeningly, ''it is a great inconvenicncc to me.''

She closed her eyes. She heard him refill her cup. She did not want her cup refilled. She said, hardly caring, ''Will you be all right on your own?''

"Oh yes,'' he said. His voice was faintly complacent.

"The groupies. Of course.''

"Don't be cheap, Anna.''

She picked up her teacup and flung the contents at him. They hit his chest, just below his dog collar, across the triangle of grey-polyester clerical shirt-front that showed above the V-neck of his grey clerical jersey. Then she got up and walked out of the kitchen into the garden, closing the back door behind her with tremendous care.

Eleanor's husband, Robert, met her at Oxford station. It was, he said, perfect timing for an arrival, just after the afternoon batch of tutorials, and before a senior common-room meeting. He was a tall, thin, awkward man with the face of a kindly rabbit. He seized Anna's case and took her arm solicitously.

"Eleanor and I were saying we don't think we've seen you, actually seen you, for over ten years. Certainly not since Ptolemy was born. These parenthood years are simply extraordinary, aren't they? One spends all this time and emotional energy developing a great supporting muscle, and then at sixteen they turn round and say they are living their own lives now, thank you, and simply hack it through. I'm afraid Eleanor has spoiled Ptolemy, being the youngest and unquestionably our most able child. That's why she couldn't meet you. Your train didn't tie in with his violin lesson."

He stowed Anna away in an estate car consolingly strewn with crumbs and discarded lists, and drove her round the city centre, past the Ashmolean Museum, to a large and startling house off Norham Gardens. It was redbrick, its rearing walls irregularly pierced by fantastic windows, and it was crowned at its two front corners with turrets capped in pinnacles of green copper surmounted by Maltese crosses. It was clearly, from the state of the gardens, and the condition of the paintwork, divided into two. Robert Ramsay pulled into the tidier half. His rabbity face glowed with pride.

"Bought this six years ago. After Eleanor won that great prize for *No Joking Matter*. Wonderful family house. We love it."

He took Anna up the steep front steps to a tall door under a fretted canopy. The hall inside was floored with lozenges of black and ochre and russet. Doors were open everywhere and the glimpses of the rooms beyond them gave an impression of vigorous life—tables piled with books, musical instruments propped against armchairs full of papers and cats, wine bottles and bowls of fruit, shawls and jackets thrown about, strong colours, cascading curtains. Robert led Anna up a great wide red wooden staircase, past long windows with occasional idiosyncratic patches of chequered glass in blue and yellow, to an immense landing where huge brass and china pots stood about filled with enormous thirsty plants, and books and laundry lay in amicable disorder together on the polished wooden floor.

"In here," Robert said. He flung open a door and showed Anna into a tall, dramatic room looking out at the back of the house. It contained a brass bed—a very big brass bed—several wardrobes and tables, two armchairs, a black-marble fireplace, a hatstand, a crowded bookcase and curtains of maroon plush.

"Make yourself comfortable," Robert said, "bathroom straight opposite. Hang on to the chain and count seven before letting go. I'll make some tea. Eleanor will be back in five minutes."

He closed the door. Anna looked about her. There was a copy of *The Times Literary Supplement* by her bed, and the nearest book she could see in the bookcase was called *The Ethics of Ecology*. Her bed had an orange cover on it and a pile of riotously embroidered cushions. The room smelled faintly of incense. Anna put her handbag down on an armchair, and felt suddenly very shy.

Eleanor, she discovered, had not so much changed as solidified. She was everything she had been as a young woman, but more intensely so—more articulate, more decided, more culturally avid, more impersonal. She was also fatter. Her averagely shaped body had swelled at the hips to fill her capacious jeans and large, jolly jerseys. She was not only now a very successful novelist, but also a voracious committee woman. She was, she told Anna, a campaigner, and as soon as Ptolemy was ten—the age that he had been assured would allow him to bicycle to school alone—she intended to throw herself into yet more activity. She told Anna that England had become shockingly philistine and repressive; she intended to promote the freedom of the pen.

Ptolemy was a quiet, snuffling child who gave the impression of having a profound inner life that he was protecting from his mother. His two elder brothers, both day-boys at a city school, had the lugubrious sartorial appearance of impoverished Victorian undertakers, and sloped sullenly about the house, slopping endless bowls of cornflakes and muttering for hours into the telephone. They were kept deliberately short of money by Eleanor—"The only practical answer, I'm afraid, to Oxford's drug problem"—and so were to be constantly caught unabashedly combing cupboards and drawers for the latest hiding-place of her purse. She seemed to think that this was perfectly normal behaviour and as much an inevitable part of the messiness of adolescence as spots (which they both had) and wet dreams. She informed Anna a great deal about her life, her children's lives and life in general, and after two days had not asked her a single question in return. Anna, who had read *No Joking Matter,* all the first night when she couldn't sleep, began to feel that she was in every way in uncharted country.

The pattern of the day was very decided, and fraught with argument since Eleanor and Robert believed in the right of every member of the family to discuss every topic from the threat to the environment down to whether Ptolemy or Gideon should be allowed the last helping out of a box of Ricicles. Breakfast happened about eight in an atmosphere of steady acrimony, and then Robert herded the older boys into the car for school—this provided a wonderful chance for prolonged defiance—before he went on to college, and Eleanor walked Ptolemy to his school. Anna offered to do this (Ptolemy's eyes gleamed dully at the prospect) but Eleanor said no, because she and Ptolemy had a weekly discussion programme worked out for each term which they got through in fifteen-minute bursts, as they walked. Anna asked what this week's topic was, and Eleanor said, "Racism," and Ptolemy said, "Boring."

When Eleanor returned from the walk to school, she shut herself in her study until lunchtime, and sometimes teatime, and someone called Mrs. Lemon, who bicycled in from Marston, let herself in through the front door and scattered dusters and tins of polish about to create a good impression while she went to make herself coffee in the kitchen and have a good read of the paper.

Anna felt she must be quiet. She explained to Eleanor about her translation and Eleanor said, "Splendid," without taking in what she was being told. Anna spread her papers and machinery manuals out on one of the tables in her bedroom, and could progress no further. She tried lying on her bed and reading—every modern novel of any significance was in the house, mostly inscribed by the authors to Eleanor—but unease and a sensation of pointlessness cut her concentration to ribbons. She tried being nice to Mrs. Lemon, but Mrs. Lemon came to work almost exclusively to get away from her mother's ceaseless talk, and said she was afraid she hadn't time to chat, not with a house this size (she was sitting down at the time, with her feet on a second chair, filling in a competition to win a holiday in Greece with the companion of her choice). So Anna went out, and walked. She walked all through Oxford, and the Parks, and the Botanical Gardens and Christchurch

Meadows. She went up the spire of St. Mary's, into all
the colleges that would admit her, and several times to
the Ashmolean Museum. She looked at things of great
beauty and great antiquity and great curiousness, and she
spoke politely to people who addressed her, and smiled
at porters in lodges, and at girls in coffee shops who
brought her coffee. And all the time, she felt with a
gathering strength that she had, to all intents and pur-
poses, simply ceased to be.

To cheer her up, the Ramsays gave a dinner party. Anna,
who only ever went to dinner parties as the Rural Dean's
wife, and that most infrequently, was mildly apprehen-
sive. Eleanor did not seem to notice this, but firmly said
that Anna would find the people coming most refresh-
ing—a poet, three academics, a flautist and a psychiatrist
specializing in paedophilia. Anna would have much preferred to spend the evening playing snakes and ladders
with Ptolemy, a game which was his furtive passion and
of which Eleanor disapproved.

There were no preparations for the dinner party until
about an hour before everyone was due to arrive.
Eleanor said how sweet of Anna to offer to help, but
really she did so prefer spontaneity, both for the atmosphere and the taste of the food. In practice, spontaneity
meant that the kitchen suddenly became an inferno of
chaos and screams, loudly scented with garlic and olive
oil and roasting peppers, and Eleanor grew scarlet in the
face and yelled that she didn't bloody well see why she
should have to work so hard to keep them all so fucking
comfortable and *still* be condemned to this sodding domestic slavery.

Robert gave Anna a glass of wine and indicated that
they should both leave Eleanor to it. With elaborate qui-

etness, he drew Anna across the kitchen—Eleanor's back was briefly turned while she shrieked and hurled chilli powder into a bubbling pot—and out into the hall, where he closed the door behind them. They sat on the stairs.

"It's always like this," he said. He sounded perfectly relaxed. "I don't think a creative temperament can successfully be otherwise. She becomes absolutely Wagnerian at Christmas. Wonderful woman."

"I wish she'd let me help, I feel such a drone—"

"Fatal, dear girl, fatal. It has to be her creation as much as her novels do. She needs, craves, the achievement as much as the applause."

"I see," said Anna. "So my role will be the washing-up."

"Exactly so," said Robert, beaming.

Anna went up to her bedroom and looked at her clothes. At least, with a mother like Laura, some of them had a raffish distinction not usually associated with the wardrobes of the Church of England. Ptolemy came in with his snakes and ladders board.

"You'll hate dinner," he said gloomily, "it'll be all red and pongy and your mouth will simply blaze."

Anna indicated the clothes on her bed. "What do you think I should wear?"

Ptolemy looked, without enthusiasm. After a while he said, "Oh that," in a bored voice, pointing to a voluminously skirted black dress, and then added, "No-one'll see, anyway. Will you play with me?"

They sat on Anna's bedroom floor and played three games. Ptolemy won them all. Then Anna said she must dress and Ptolemy said he might as well stay—he always saw Eleanor in the bath so there were no surprises for *him*. Anna put on the black dress and tied a golden

yellow Paisley scarf round the waist, and Ptolemy said
he was thankful he wasn't a girl. He picked up his
snakes and ladders board and went out of the room saying, "You can always come and play some more if it's
too ghastly," and trailed up to his bedroom on the top
floor.

Anna went out on to the landing and listened. It was
not only calm, but an aria from *Don Giovanni* was floating out of the sitting-room. As she stood there, Eleanor's
bedroom door opened, and Eleanor emerged in an evening pyjama suit of purple-patterned silk with barbaric
golden jewellery. She smelled of scent and garlic. She
was smiling.

"Anna. Perfect timing. As always at these moments,
I ask myself, why *does* one do it?"

It was an evening of extreme difficulty for Anna, because, when asked about herself, she could only say
truthfully that she was a parson's wife, it being clearly
out of the question to embark on a long description of
her relationship with Eleanor, and how that had once
been, and how it had changed. It was not, she found, in
this enlightened and intellectually fashionable company,
at all socially helpful to say that one was a parson's wife.
It froze conversation. Eleanor tried to get her to talk
about St. Andrews, but she said firmly that, as that was
ten years ago, it wasn't now relevant. Eleanor persisted,
demanding that she recount finding the half-brick
through the children's broken bedroom window.

Anna took a deep breath and said very clearly,
"Eleanor, I may be a clergyman's wife, but I am not a
party turn."

There was a silence. It was a very complete silence,
and it seemed to go on for an unnaturally long time.
Anna did not look at Eleanor because she did not wish

to see the expression of fury she knew she would be wearing.

Robert gave several little bleats that refused to develop into sentences and then the poet, who was sitting next to Anna, said, "You must make allowances for us. It is a long time since religion had any real relevance in Oxford."

Anna turned and stared at him. He stared back for a little while but he was shorter than she, and staring upwards (unless you are a cat) puts you at a disadvantage.

One of the academics—an appealing, ugly, elderly woman with a deep voice—leant across the table and said, "Do be careful, Fergus, or Mrs. Bouverie will think us so very ignorant," and then she winked at Anna and brandished her wineglass. "Now look at that. Empty again. Extraordinary," and there was relieved laughter.

After that, Eleanor took no chances. Anna had been graciously, *generously,* invited to shine and had been most churlish in her refusal: she would not—Eleanor intended to see to it—get a second opportunity. Conversation could now safely exclude her and follow the pattern they all preferred—a little mild intellectual showing-off to warm up with followed by the most excellent Oxford gossip.

Anna and Robert washed up. While they did this, Eleanor sat at the kitchen table analysing the evening, and smoking a Turkish cigarette: "My absolutely only self-indulgence."

When the last plate and fork and glass were dried— Eleanor had not moved—Robert said, "Come on, dear girl. Bedtime."

Unexpectedly, Eleanor said, "You go up. I want to talk to Anna."

Anna and Robert exchanged glances of surprise. He mouthed, "Better stay," at her. She looked at Eleanor.

"As a novelist," Eleanor said, lighting another cigarette, "I am, as it were, helplessly observant. I am programmed to it. I've noticed far more this week than you might think."

Robert went stealthily to the door. Anna was beginning to despise his kindness to her, which was, she saw, only part of his voluntary subservience to Eleanor. She said, "Good night," loudly, to his vanishing back.

Eleanor took no notice. She waited until Anna sat down and then she said, "Of course, my dear, the time has come for you to leave Peter."

Anna said nothing.

"Do I read your mind?"

Anna said warily, "I have a strange diffidence—"

"About what?"

"About abandoning a situation which I have been part of for so long. About being sure that changes in me are permanent changes. About how much confidence I have, real confidence, not just bursts of temper—"

"You weren't ever in love with Peter," Eleanor said, in a voice suddenly much more like her youthful voice, "were you?"

"Not *in* love, I don't think, but I believe I loved him—"

Eleanor leaned forward. "I believed I loved Robert. I was desperate to stay in Oxford and I thought he was clever and he was so admiring of my ideas and ambitions." She reached across the table for a half-empty bottle of wine and poured some into two glasses still warm from Anna's washing-up. "Of course, he isn't clever in the least, and I could in fact have stayed in Oxford anyway, and his slavishness drives me absolutely

177

insane.'' She took a gulp of wine. ''He's simply hopeless with the boys, no kind of notion of discipline, and
the moment there's any question of a decision to be
made, he vanishes to college muttering about his com-
mitments. As a lover, he's as much fun as an old sock,
and he's perfectly idiotic with money, going into a mad-
dening sort of goofy helpless routine when the bills
come in. But you see, Anna, the thing is, I've *pretended*.
I'm not just someone of significance in Oxford, I'm beginning to be so nationally—actually, there's talk, too,
of an American promotional tour—and I've said to
everyone, over and over again, that I am succeeding, that
I have life taped. I'd give my eyeteeth for a lover, but
who's going to ever think of tackling me with my loudly
trumpeted perfect life? Oh Anna,'' said Eleanor, reaching out for Anna's hand and bursting into tremendous
tears. ''Oh Anna, it's so wonderful to have you here with
all your wealth of knowledge of the human dilemma. I
never thought I'd say it, but thank heavens for your con-
nection with the Church. It's such a relief to have someone who understands to confide in, you can't imagine.''

When Anna climbed off her homebound train, she found
Patrick O'Sullivan waiting for her.

''I offered,'' he said, ''and I won. I offered and so
did Elaine Dodswell, but I won because I hadn't also
promised to take Mrs. Eddoes in to the arthritis clinic
this morning. Though if I live here much longer it may
come to that.''

Anna said, ''But where is Peter?''

''Busy. What does he usually do on Thursdays?''

''They vary,'' she said. She had promised herself, all
the journey home, that she would arrive in a mood of

generosity and optimism, that she would greet Peter with affection, that she would . . .

"Are you all right?"

She lifted her chin. "Fine, thank you. Rather a late night, last night, a grand finale—"

Eleanor had talked and cried until almost three in the morning. She talked herself through leaving Robert to staying with him after all to leaving him once again for a life founded upon honesty. When she finally allowed Anna to go to bed, she had embraced her warmly and said that she was absolutely thankful Anna had come and been able to make her see what, simply, had to be done, and that more self-respect was to be gained that way than via any kind of self-sacrifice. Anna, who had scarcely uttered, and was entirely uncertain which conclusion Eleanor had finally lurched to, returned her embrace, and then lay exhausted and wakeful until Ptolemy came in at seven-thirty and said Eleanor had relented, and Anna was allowed to walk him to school because it was her last morning, but that they were not going to converse because he was going to tell her jokes out of his *Hundred Worst Jokes Book*. Briefly, she considered relaying the one about a gooseberry in a lift to Patrick O'Sullivan, but decided to save it for Flora.

"I don't wish to be ungrateful," Anna said, getting into the car, "but I thought you were a very busy man. After all, this is a very domestic kind of errand."

Ella had in fact offered to come in Patrick's place, but he had declined. He said he was picking up some wine on the same journey. She had said, "Oh yes," in a voice loaded with sarcasm.

Patrick shut Anna into the car and came round to the driver's side.

"Don't sound so suspicious," he said, starting the engine. "I am merely learning to be a good villager. Doing my bit, as it were, for the Rector's support-group."

"The what?"

"It's in its first week. Can't remember whose idea it was. But we have all received an earnest circular about doing our bit for our overworked Rector and his lady, for which the accepted term seems to be lay involvement." He looked sideways at Anna. "I wouldn't mind," he said softly, "a little lay involvement myself."

Anna wasn't listening. "A group? Started last week?"

"Humming along. Beavering about going on all over the place. I expect you'll get home and find there isn't a thing left for you to do." He glanced at her. "Did you like my flowers?"

On the kitchen table sat a mauve-pink African violet with a little card propped against it. The card read, "Welcome home. Celia, Elaine and the parish group." There was also a note from Peter on the back of a brown envelope, saying that he would be back at twelve-thirty and that Celia had left something in the fridge. Anna opened the refrigerator door. Two perfect, technicolour salads lay on two matching plates (not Rectory plates) under plastic film. Anna banged the door shut. The kitchen smelled violently hygienic. The floor shone; the sink gleamed. "Be *thankful*," Anna instructed herself, fighting with rage.

She went upstairs; the staircarpet had been brushed. In her bedroom the air was fragrant with polish, and the dying lilies of the valley had been ostentatiously left in a bowl of clean water. Someone strange, Anna noticed with a spurt of fury, had made their bed, since the cover was arranged with hotel-like precision, tucked trimly in

under the pillows, smooth and neat. Peter's slippers lay
smugly together by the wardrobe, and the piles of books
on their bedside tables had been graded into pyramids.

She ran into the bathroom. All was shining and reg-
imented. The toothbrushes stood in a sparkling tumbler,
the towels hung in ordered oblongs. She sat down on
the edge of the bath, suddenly winded by the effrontery
of it, the intrusiveness, the heavily implied criticism of
everything she had previously done, from her behaviour
in the parish to the way she did (or didn't) polish the
taps.

She found she was shaking. Had these unseen hands
also been through her drawers, her medicine cupboard,
her linen shelves, looking for letters and tranquillizers
and compromising underclothes? She went back un-
steadily to her bedroom. Her translation table—oh, the
guilt about that, weeks and weeks behind and the silence
from the publishers so ominous—had been discreetly
but definitely tidied. Whoever had done it now knew
about it, just as whoever had ordered their books knew
what they were reading. A new thought came to her.
She sat heavily on the edge of the bed, too stunned even
to take pleasure in creasing its smoothly plump surface.
Peter must not only know about all this, but have sanc-
tioned it, given permission for his pyjamas to be folded,
his toothglass polished, his wife's sad little collection of
cosmetic jars marshalled, to—whom?

The doorbell rang. Anna got up off the bed and went
slowly downstairs. She opened the door to Elaine Dodswell, whose face, above one of her weekday tracksuits
in jade-green with a white stripe, wore an expression of
mixed welcome and apprehension.

"I just came—"

Anna held the door a little wider. "Come in."

"You're only just back, I know, I saw Patrick's car. I just wanted to say welcome home, you know. Did you have a nice rest?"

"No," Anna said.

She led the way into the sitting-room. The furniture looked as if it were standing to attention. The cushions were bosomy; there were no newspapers.

Elaine said, almost in a whisper, "Oh Anna, I'm so sorry—"

"I ought to be grateful," Anna said, softening at her evident distress. "I should be, but—"

"I wasn't at all certain we should do it, I mean, I said, look it's her *home,* but when Peter—" She stopped.

Anna sat down on the sofa. She patted the cushion beside her for Elaine to sit down too.

"Was it Celia?"

Elaine said, loyally, "It was the group, the new parish group."

"And what has the new parish group left for me to do?"

"Anna," Elaine said pleadingly, "we were *worried.* You must see that, what with your taking a job that's, well, that's beneath you and looking so tired, and having to put a brave face on your disappointment over Peter, we wanted to *help,* we wanted to show we *understand,* I mean, we're women too—"

Anna took her hand. "I know. I believe you. I think you are a kind woman, Elaine. But—and this will seem harsh and ungrateful to you—I need the sort of kindness that is tailored for me, not just the unimaginative sort that it suits other people to give. Do you understand me?"

"No," Elaine said. She took her hand away. "It took three of us all yesterday and two hours this morning. Celia and me and Trish Pardoe. We haven't moved anything." She got up and said in a voice now tinged with resentment because Anna had failed to soothe her anxiety with comforting, understanding gratitude, "Peter was ever so pleased. He said the house hadn't looked like this in years."

Anna stood up too. "And if Colin said that about your house, after someone else had cleaned it, and the cleaning of it was usually your responsibility, what would you feel?"

Elaine stared at her for a moment. Then she went bright-pink. "He'd never say it!" she almost shouted. "He'd never have cause to! I keep my home like a new pin!" And then she ran from the house.

Anna and Peter ate lunch almost in silence. Peter, Anna observed, looked much better for her absence, not so bony and with even a little colour. He ate Celia's brilliant salad with relish, wiping his mouth at the end with the little scallop-edged paper napkin she had so daintily provided. Anna blew her nose on hers.

By the time Peter had come home, Anna had had a private tantrum in the garden, and had washed her face and prepared herself to be calm but not particularly friendly. Peter clearly felt the same. She did not mention the spotless Rectory, so neither did he. Nor did she broach the subject of the parish group, a sleeping tiger he was clearly not going to poke awake. Instead he told her of uncontroversial parish matters and she told him of Eleanor's troubles and neither commented upon the other's information. When lunch was over, Peter gave

Anna a brief kiss, said it was good to have her back and
that he must go, to take prayers for the Thursday Club
at Snead. As he went out of the back door, he was humming. He sounded almost jaunty.

11

❖ ❖ ❖

WHEN HE HAD gone, Anna washed up, brushed her
hair, found the quilted Indian jacket that Charlotte had
discarded as being reminiscent of a sixties earth mother,
and locked the house. There were no afternoon buses
from Loxford into Woodborough, so she walked the
mile and a half to the main road, and caught a bus there.
She had brought shopping bags because she told herself
that she was going to buy supper before she collected
Flora, but she had also brought the paperback copy of
Ariel, which she had not read, because she knew she
was really going straight round to the Vicarage. She did
not, as she sat on the bus and stared out of the window
at the prosperous fields of wheat and barley, and the
blazing fields of rape, allow herself to articulate why she
would go to the Vicarage. Instead, she permitted herself
half an hour of mindless luxury of having a purpose that
would also be a pleasure.

The door of the Vicarage was opened by Miss Lambe.
She stood, as she always did, holding it only six inches
open and peering up at Anna in an anxious and mouse-

like way. Anna stooped a little and asked in a very kind voice for Mr. Jonathan Byrne. Miss Lambe whispered that he was working and wasn't to be disturbed until teatime.

"In that case," Anna said sadly, "would you give him this? Say that I'm returning it. With many thanks."

Miss Lambe nodded and shot out a paw for the book. Behind her, in the cavernous hall, a door opened and Daniel Byrne ushered someone out of his study. He was saying, "I do agree with you, but I don't want to do it so delicately that it ends up looking apologetic," and then he saw Anna and said, "Mrs. Bouverie! How extremely nice. Come in, come in."

"I was just returning a book—"

"Can't you just come in, too? Mrs. Bouverie, this is our new Methodist minister, here in Woodborough. We were having an ecumenical discussion about a joint confirmation service."

The Methodist minister looked as if he thought the subject of their discussion ought to be strictly private. He nodded stiffly to Anna.

"Miss Lambe," Daniel said, "could you rustle up yet more coffee?" He shook the minister warmly by the hand. "It's been such a useful discussion. Thank you so very much for coming."

When the front door had closed, he said, "A good man but he swallowed a poker." He took Anna by the arm. "How very nice it is to see you. Come in, come in."

She allowed herself to be led into his study and installed in a wing chair upholstered in faded tobacco-coloured corduroy. Daniel seemed entirely at ease, pottering round her, moving books off a stool for her coffee cup, stuffing papers into a cardboard folder, talking comfortably. He talked about Methodism for a little, and then about a Christian therapy group he had been asked to lead—"They all complained of the sensation of being lost, of not knowing where they were going but I said what about starting with the notion that you can only be lost if you have no destinations, and if you are Christians, as you say you are, then surely you *do* have destinations?"—and then about Miss Lambe—"A rare little bird, indeed, but her innocence is such a responsibility"—and then he settled himself in a chair opposite Anna's and said, "Now. Let's get down to business and talk about you."

She said, "I might behave just like your therapy group."

"You have a sense of humour—"

She looked down. "And a sense of shame."

"My dear girl—" He leaned forward. He waited.

She said reluctantly, "I'm very much afraid of sounding self-pitying. Self-pity is so absolutely disgusting."

"I think you should simply *speak.*"

She looked up. He was watching her, his head on one side. She would very much have liked to cross the room and sit on his knee, and her eyes widened involuntarily in horror at herself.

"Anna," Daniel Byrne said, "concentrate."

She blinked. She said, in a sudden rush, "I've been away for a week in Oxford, staying with a friend. It should have been a release but somehow it wasn't, it was simply quite foreign. And I came home this morning glowing with good intentions, and found that a newly formed parish support-group, with Peter's blessing, had scoured my house from top to bottom. All very well meant and yet absolutely outrageous. I am so offended, I hardly know how to express it, and yet I know any outsider would think me an ungrateful *cow.*'' She paused, took a breath, and hurried on. ''The thing is that the validity I am assured, almost commanded, that I have as a Christian, seems not to be carried out in my human life. I seem to have less significance not only than my husband but than most of the parish. I'm not a person, I'm simply a sort of function, and a pretty lonely sort of function at that. And when I think about love,'' Anna said, warming up, leaning forward, ''which I know to be absolutely vital, I can only think, except for what I feel for my children, of something rather monochrome and tired and dutiful. It isn't that I don't try, I try like mad, and then of course the lack of result seems even harder to bear. Sometimes, I've been known to yell at the sky just trying to get an answer.'' She stopped, wondering if she had overstepped the mark. She shot him a little glance. He looked exactly the same.

''Go on,'' he said.

She took a breath. ''Have you ever felt like this?''

''Of course. The dark night of the soul.''

''I suppose, though, if you were a monk—''

''If you mean sex,'' Daniel Byrne said comfortably, ''it stopped mattering quite simply when—and because—other things of much greater importance came to fill its place. But it was a shocking trouble before that.'' He put his hands behind his head. ''I wonder if you are confused about love? You are so determined to strive and struggle, to bash away. But divine love— don't look away—is about receiving, not giving. That's why it's so different, so instinctive, also why it's the easiest.''

The door opened, Jonathan put his head in. His face lit up.

''Anna!''

Daniel said, "That was a tactless bit of Porlocking. Haven't you the discretion to knock?"

Jonathan came right in. He was wearing jeans and an enormous dark-blue jersey and his hair was tousled. He said, "In case you have a choirboy in here?"

Daniel ignored him. He said to Anna, "I find you very brave. It's so wrong to think that spectacular courage is the best bravery. The noblest bravery is battling against these dreadful daily assaults, often very minor, on one's spirit."

Jonathan came to sit next to Anna. "Can I join in?"

Anna looked up at him. Her eyes were shining. Sitting here in this shabby, untidy, human room with the Byrne brothers suddenly seemed perfection, a happiness she could hardly bear to abandon. She said sadly, "I have to get Flora."

Jonathan said, "Then I'll drive you back to Loxford."

"The bus—"

"No," Jonathan said with vehemence, "no. Don't always object to everything. Don't be so bloody difficult."

"She's not difficult," Daniel said.

"I know that. I know that really. She's lovely."

"Stop it!" Anna said, "stop it!" She was laughing.

Daniel got up. "You just hold out your cup," he said to her, "just hold it out and let it be filled."

"Like letting me drive you home—"

"Only if that's what she *wants.*"

"Do you?" Jonathan said, turning. She nodded. "Good," he said, smiling at her. "I'll go and find the keys."

When he had gone, she said to Daniel, "I thought it was a requirement of maturity, and of grace, to be very hard on yourself, as hard as you were generous to everyone else."

He put his hand briefly on her shoulder. "It's all a deal, a two-way business, if it's man to man. That's what makes us undivine. But you try a little taking from God. Just relax into it. And in a while, we'll talk some more." He moved away, back to his desk. "We aren't all the same, you know. We all need something different, we all hear different messages." He paused and then he said softly, "So many people just lack the capacity to live richly, at any level. You aren't one of them. It's too easy to defend a castle that's never been attacked. Don't be afraid. And now here is your chauffeur."

It was a strange drive home. Flora had begun to write a play in her English lesson, and was so absorbed in her second scene (an encounter between her orphan heroine and a mysterious cloaked stranger) that she actually elected to sit in the back of the car and scribble furiously in her notebook. Jonathan had pleased her by saying seriously, "Ah, the second scene. Of course, it's the second act that is always notoriously so difficult," to which she had gravely nodded. From the back seat, she watched the back of his head and wondered if he would serve as a model for her stranger, when he removed his cloak and shed his mystery.

Jonathan talked most of the time. He drove better than Daniel, with an instinctive ease that freed him for talking. He talked with energy and fluency, mostly about the education of the feelings, and how important it was, and how feelings make or break men and women and give them their best capacity to understand other people. He told Anna that Stendhal had declared that you had to look into your own heart to discover who you were. He said that one of the messages of literature is that everything is different in the grip of strong feelings, and that is why passion is dangerous as well as wonderful.

Anna listened. She simply lay back in her seat and watched the sky swoop past through the windscreen, and listened. There was no need to say anything.

Jonathan said, "We all overlay our feelings with too much thinking. We are afraid of our feelings because they are arbitrary and volatile, and we often need literature to make our feelings intelligible to us, to make us see that our reaction to what we can't choose and what we can is what shapes our lives."

The journey was over too soon for Anna; she saw the village green slide by with apprehension. She said, "It's so nice of you. Just drop us by the church."

The car stopped. Jonathan said, "You see, it is so terribly important to stay *alive,*" and then, without warning, he picked Anna's hand from her lap, and kissed it.

Later, Flora said, "Why did he do that?"

"Because it's awkward to shake hands sitting side by side in a car." (Well done. Quick thinking.)

"You couldn't," Flora said clearly, "do that to a *man—*"

"But I'm not a man."

Flora regarded her. At the end of scene two, the mysterious stranger might take the heroine's small cold hand in his great gloved one and kiss it. "Telling me," Flora said.

In Woodborough Vicarage, Jonathan looked without enthusiasm at the slab of pork pie lying palely on his plate and said, "Can I ask what Anna came to see you about this afternoon?"

"Not really."

"Was it to tell you that she didn't love her husband

anymore and to ask you what to do about it?''

"If you knew what she came for," Daniel said, putting down his knife and fork, "why do you ask me?"

The evening passed with rigorous politeness. Luke had much enjoyed his week living in Woodborough and listened enviously to Anna's account of Eleanor's sons' lives in the wild paradise of Oxford. Flora explained about her play—"It's a tragedy so of course the end will be awful"—and Peter and Anna avoided looking at one another. After supper, Peter said he would wash up, but the telephone rang and a young woman from Church End said her father had died that afternoon and she couldn't do a thing with her mother, so he had put down the washing-up brush, and put on his jacket, and gone. Luke and Anna washed up instead, and Luke sensed that Anna didn't want to be back at home any more than he did, but he didn't wish this to be the case, so said nothing. Instead, Anna told him about coming home to find her gleaming, burnished house, and Luke said, "Interfering old cows. At least my room defeated them," and they laughed. Then he said, "I've got two hundred and eighty pounds towards India," and she said, "Wonderful. Well done," and he nodded, and the doorbell rang.

It was Elaine Dodswell. She was holding a pile of parish magazines for May. Luke looked at them. Elaine said breathlessly, "Would you give these to your mum? We thought perhaps—I mean, we know she likes to do them herself, so after all we thought—" She stopped.

"OK," said Luke, after a while, "if you want." He took the magazines.

Elaine stepped back a little. "Tell her—" Luke

waited. "Say I called," Elaine said. "No hard feelings." She turned and hurried down the path.

Luke shut the door and went back to the kitchen.

"What are those?"

"Guess."

"Who brought them?"

"Elaine Whatsit. From that house with those gross frogs. She said no hard feelings."

Anna sat down. "Do you know, I think they believe that by handing back the magazine round they are somehow restoring my *raison d'être*."

"Don't do it, then."

"I have to," Anna said. Luke was suddenly afraid she was going to cry. "I have to. I've painted myself into a corner."

Three days later, in the early evening, as Anna pushed a folded magazine into the gleaming brass letter box of the Old Rectory, the door was opened from the inside.

"Come in," Patrick said.

Anna shook her head. "Thank you, but I can't—"

"Just for a moment. I want to talk about Luke."

"Luke? Why, has he—"

"Don't look worried. He's wonderful, a real asset. No, it's a scheme I have."

Cautiously, Anna followed him into the hall.

"Come and sit down." He opened the door to the room where he had taken her before, and given her brandy. The fat chairs beckoned like pillows. She longed to sit in one.

"Drink?"

"No, thank you."

"Just innocent tonic water, then. Why do you treat me like Bluebeard?"

Anna did not want to encourage him by saying that all conversations with him immediately seemed to flicker with danger, so she simply said primly, "I treat you like any other parishioner."

He grunted. He poured tonic water into one of his extravagantly cut tumblers and added ice and lemon. "About Luke." He handed her the glass.

"Yes?"

"I want to help him."

"I believe you already are—"

"No. More than that. I want to get a bit involved in this fearsome trip they're all planning, see they have a roadworthy vehicle and so forth, and then, if you'll agree, help him with the next stage of his life, the right art school, that sort of thing."

Anna said with distaste, "A patron."

"If you like. Why should that matter? I'm rich and childless and I like Luke. There wouldn't be any sinister strings."

Anna shook her hair back. "I'm terribly sorry. I was disagreeable and rude. It's exceedingly kind of you to want to help and heaven knows, Luke could do with a guardian angel like you. May I mention it to Peter? And then—and then, perhaps talk some more?"

"Anna," Patrick said, "I do genuinely want to help Luke. But I must confess, I'd do anything on earth to get you to talk to me some more."

She stared at him. He took a swallow of the drink he had poured himself and then put the tumbler down on the tray where all the bottles stood. Then he crossed the few feet of carpet between them, removed her glass from her hand, set it down, put his arms firmly about her and kissed her. He kissed her hard and competently. Anna, who had been kissed by no man but Peter for over

twenty years and had come to assume that she was surrounded by some *cordon sanitaire,* was so entirely startled that at first she did nothing. She simply stood in his
embrace. Then panic set in; not the indignant panic of
outrage at being kissed but the hysterical panic of realizing that she did not dislike it. She brought her arms
up sharply and shoved hard against his chest.

He said, "And now you can say, 'How dare you!' "

She stepped away from him crying, "But I don't want
to be seduced!"

He said, "Do you know, for a second I could have
sworn you did?"

She ran for the door. He ran after her, and seized her
wrist. "Don't go!"

"What I hate," Anna said, swinging on him, eyes
blazing, "is this assumption that I'm easy game, that
I'm some sort of imprisoned innocent who will be grateful to you for releasing me. You are a stupid, arrogant,
insensitive man." She wrenched her wrist free. It hurt.
She cradled it with the other hand. "Just because I'm
inexperienced," she said furiously, "doesn't mean that
I lack perception or native wit. I'm not a *fool,*" and then
she flung the door open and vanished across the hall and
through the outer door, letting it crash shudderingly behind her.

Slowly, Patrick moved to the hall in her wake. Ella
came out of the kitchen, holding an oven glove. She
looked at Patrick. Without uttering a word, she com-
municated to him that she was pleased to see he had at
last met his Waterloo. He said, without returning her
look, "I haven't finished yet."

12

✦ ✦ ✦

IN THE SIXTH-FORM college's boys' lavatory, companionably peeing side by side, Luke said to Barnaby that home was really weird just now. Barnaby, who had always hankered after more weirdness than his mother's strong sense of order could stand, said how come? Shaking himself and then zipping up his jeans, Luke said kind of furtive.

"Furtive?" Barnaby said. "Like hassle?"

No, Luke said, not like hassle, in fact no-one was hassling him at all. It was more a sort of atmosphere, people not saying things when they were dying to, Mum and Dad kind of pretending the other wasn't there.

Barnaby considered this very briefly and abruptly lost interest in the whole topic. "Want a smoke?"

Later, on the last bus to Loxford, Luke's mind returned reluctantly to the subject. He wasn't much surprised, since his mind, just at present, lurched between the disagreeableness of home, and sex. Sex usually won. Luke was horrified and fascinated to find how much he thought about it and longed for it and was afraid of it. He couldn't see, usually, how he was actually going to *do* it for the first time but he feared that if that first time wasn't soon he'd probably explode. This state of affairs had come upon him quite suddenly and he was entirely at its mercy. He got erections all the time, without warning, and had fantasies of a slightly brutal kind about a girl in his art-history set, a girl called Alison with long, rough red hair and sneering eyes, like a cat. She was reputed to have slept around since she was fifteen. Luke's imagination returned constantly to what, if this were true, she might know that he did not. The power that she would have in possessing such knowledge made him almost sick with excitement. It also made this daily departure from Woodborough, where Alison lived and where she lounged about in the evening with Barnaby and a group of others, almost unbearable. Add to that the atmosphere in the Rectory, and Luke sometimes thought he couldn't take any more.

And yet . . . There was some little haunting thing about his mother that sang in Luke's mind. Ever since she'd come back from Oxford, she'd seemed secret, shut away, but the secret clearly wasn't a thrill like the secret of Alison, it was something sad, as if something had got broken. Luke didn't want to talk about it because he didn't really think he could cope with being confided in, but the look of her made him uneasy and sorry. His conscience drove him home, and then his feelings of being helpless and disconcerted drove him out again, to the Old Rectory, to cut the edges of Patrick's lawn, and polish Patrick's car and rake Patrick's gravel and to feel, as he did so, the healing balm of Patrick's prosperity and assurance.

When the bus got to Loxford, Luke found that he

simply could not face the Rectory yet. He got off at the far side of the green, and was immediately ambushed by old Mr. Biddle from behind his garden wall.

'' 'Ere,'' Mr. Biddle said. He beckoned Luke over. He wore a cap, winter and summer, and a sagging tweed jacket, and he had filthy fingernails and bright, sharp old countryman's eyes. "What about 'im?'' said Mr. Biddle in a conspiratorial, screaming whisper.

"Who?'' Luke said.

Mr. Biddle seized Luke's sleeve. He gestured at the Old Rectory. '' 'Im. O'Sullivan. Does he 'ave wimmin there?''

"All the time.''

Mr. Biddle licked his lips. "Wimmin from *London*?''

Luke nodded. "Belly dancers.''

"Cor,'' Mr. Biddle said. He let Luke go. He sketched huge breasts on the front of his jacket and grinned. "In the war—'' began Mr. Biddle.

"I'm late,'' Luke said. "I'm supposed to be working for him. Got to get the spuds in.''

"Spuds?'' Mr. Biddle said. He gave a little cackle.

Luke did not, despite lurking thoughts of Alison, want to know what spuds reminded Mr. Biddle of. "Gotta go,'' he said.

Mr. Biddle nodded. He took a step back, his glance suddenly clouded. Belly dancers! In Cairo, in 1942, he'd been offered a little girl, she couldn't have been more than ten. He hadn't remembered that for twenty years; he wished he hadn't remembered it now. He squinted at Luke. "You take care.'' His voice wavered a little. "You take care around that O'Sullivan. Money ain't to be trusted.''

Luke walked briskly away across the green, hoping that his air of purpose would prevent anyone else from accosting him. Patrick had not in fact asked him to come in this evening, but, as there were always things to do, Luke assumed it wouldn't matter. He went round, as usual, to the kitchen door and knocked. No-one came. He opened the door cautiously. The kitchen was empty and tidy and faintly fragrant with baking. A row of Ella's loaves—she was now highly proficient at bread-making and, to her scornful pleasure, in demand for demonstrations to local women's groups—stood on racks on the table under blue-and-white cloths. Luke's mouth watered.

He crossed the kitchen and knocked on her sitting-room door. No reply. He opened the door. Like the kitchen, the room was empty and orderly. Luke went back through the kitchen and out into the hall and listened. It was very quiet, but clearly someone was at home because the back door had been unlocked. He knocked softly on the door to Patrick's study.

There was a pause, and then Patrick called, rather absently, "Come!"

Luke put his head in. Patrick was sitting at his enormous desk, writing. This was most peculiar. Patrick never wrote, he only signed things. But now, he was writing what looked like a letter, in a very neat black hand on the stiff white paper he had had specially printed for the Old Rectory. He looked startled to see Luke, as if Luke had woken him up.

"Luke!"

"Sorry," Luke said, "I just wondered, I mean, d'you want anything done?"

"It's Wednesday."

"I know. I just wondered—"

"No," Patrick said, "no. Nothing. Tomorrow, as usual." He looked down at the half-filled sheet of writing paper, and then at the hand holding his pen, which seemed to hover with eagerness to get back to writing.

"Sorry," Luke muttered. He withdrew his head and shut the door. Patrick hadn't even smiled. There was nothing for it but to go home.

Only his father was at home. Flora had gone to tea with the Maxwells, which she liked to do because she was conscious of adding glamour and colour to their tidy lives, and Anna, said Peter, had gone to Brownies.

"But she doesn't do Brownies."

"Trish Pardoe is ill. Mum said she would step in."

A sudden childish misery settled on Luke. He wanted Anna to be there, as he had wanted Patrick to welcome him. "I'm hungry," he said, "starving—"

Peter looked at him. He said, "You know where the bread is." Luke's face was sullen. Peter felt, as he often now did, that he was too tired for his children, that he was so worn out by inner emptiness and the need to show outer confidence that he had nothing left over. He had never quite known what to say to Luke, had come to regard communication with Luke as Anna's business; now, he was bored by Luke, bored by his age, his unfinishedness, his mixture of obstinacy and apathy. Flora, luckily, was both more outgoing, and still a child. Peter said, "Make yourself a sandwich." He tried to sound helpful.

Luke sighed. He let his bag fall with a thud. He would have liked, with a sudden mindlessness, to have lashed out, to have slammed his fist into something—the wall, the closed sitting-room door, his father's face. Muttering, he turned away, and slouched into the kitchen, where he made himself a heavy crude sandwich, not bothering to put away the bread, and leaving the knife stuck in the butter. Then he went upstairs and shut himself into his bedroom, and turned his music on so loudly that downstairs in the study objects danced on Peter's desk and the furniture shuddered. Peter, writing a piece on "The Church in the Nineties" for the diocesan magazine, put his hands over his face, and despaired.

Two days later, Anna found a stiff white envelope in one of her Wellington boots. It was long and smooth, and it had "Anna" written on it in black ink. She took it down the garden with her, on her way to unpeg the washing, and opened it the far side of a screen of several sheets, two towels and a surplice.

It said, "Anna, I have to write because you will never allow me to speak. You are determined that I am unscrupulous, that I am amusing myself, that I am playing a seduction game. You are so wrong. I am in earnest." The "earnest" was underlined.

Anna's mouth was dry. What she held in her hand was a love letter. A *love* letter! Extraordinary. Being kissed had been strange enough—though not, she had told herself with rigorous insistence on the truth, unexpected—but a letter was even more unmanageable, because it prolonged what might have been just a mad moment into a mad situation.

"You accuse me," Patrick wrote, "of wanting to release you. Of course I do. Of course, because of admiring you as well as being in love with you (in love with me, Anna thought, in love with me. Dear heaven! What is *happening?*), I wish to rescue you from a life where you are neither valued nor fulfilled. If you were less determined to write me off as a bastard, you'd see that my intentions are gallant, not patronizing. I want to give you clothes and books and travel. I want to give you comfort, even luxury. I want to give you money. I want to take you among people who will appreciate you—not as my possession, but because I absolutely cannot stand to see you wasted here. You aren't just wasted as a person, you are wasted as a *woman*."

The letter was signed simply "Patrick." Anna folded it and put it back in its envelope and put that in her pocket. A few heralding drops of rain were beginning to fall. Anna turned to the washing line and began to tear the laundry down rapidly, thankful for any action that might calm her incipient hysteria. A man I hardly know, she thought, holding pegs between her teeth while she folded a sheet, a man I hardly know has asked me to leave Peter and come away with him so that he can shower me with glittering things and company. It's daft. It's not just daft, it's silly and ludicrous and not what happens in life. It's a stupid fairy story. It might even be a particularly disagreeable joke. She touched her pocket. She thought of Patrick's armchairs, his carpets and decanters, his hair, his clothes, his voice saying, in her own kitchen, "Now, what is a woman like you doing in a place like this?" If this was temptation, Anna thought, holding Peter's surplice against her unheedingly, then it had all the subtlety of a charging bull. Yet it also, undeniably, sang a soft and siren song. To exchange what she had for what she might have! She blushed for herself. "You must never," she told herself sternly, picking up the laundry basket, "make the mistake of underestimating what you don't have. Thinking that way shrivels the soul. But, oh—"

Back in the kitchen, Luke was sitting on a tilted-back chair talking to Barnaby on the telephone. When Anna came in, he dropped his voice to a mutter. He waited for her to say don't be long—the parish paid only half the telephone bill, as he was sick and tired of being told—but she didn't. She didn't really seem to take him in at all, just put the clothes basket down on the table in a dreamy kind of way, and then went over to unplug the kettle before filling it. Luke watched her. She was wearing an Indian skirt Laura had given her, of rough russet cotton with big pockets, and round the hem darker russet embroidery encircling tiny moons of mirror. Something stuck out of the top of one of the pockets, something white and oblong. Anna turned from the sink. Luke could see it was an envelope. For no reason he could think of, Luke felt abruptly horrible; sick and sweaty. "Yeah," he said to Barnaby, gripping the receiver tightly. "Yeah."

Ella had several broken nights. Being a person who prided herself on competence, this was annoying enough in itself (when you are flat in bed, my girl, you are there to *sleep*) but was made worse by anxiety. Patrick had accustomed her over the years to what she termed his scrapes, but this present business was another matter altogether. Ella was a fast learner. She might not have cared for the look of village life at first glance, but as it appeared to be her future she had decided to accept it. It had not taken her long to realize that what could pass invisibly in Fulham or Notting Hill Gate was laid bare for all to see in such a place as Loxford. In Ella's view, it was only a matter of days, rather than weeks, before all five villages knew that Patrick O'Sullivan was laying siege to the Rector's wife.

Ella had made friends. She had found in Celia Hooper and Sheila Vinson and Elaine Dodswell just that practicality that she rejoiced in in herself. They shared with her, too, a small but steady resentment of the upper classes as represented by the Mayhews, the Richardsons and Miss Dunstable—Patrick was exempt from this social disapproval because he was a bachelor, and approachable, and had clearly made his money himself, quite recently. Conversations between the four women fell only just on the right side of bitching. They were very confidential with one another, but Ella felt instinctively that Patrick's current adventure had to be kept to herself. This was hard, with her new-found companionship.

What troubled Ella was not only that Patrick was about to create a scandal, but that Anna Bouverie might help him. Ella quite sympathized with her new friends' view that Anna didn't pull her weight and that she was guilty of wearing an expression of separateness—almost of superiority. Country parishes, they were all agreed, were very different from urban ones, and most priests' wives would think it a privilege to live somewhere as friendly as Loxford. Anna's job at Pricewell's was, Ella considered, pure exhibitionism. It was this element in Anna that Ella feared might make her revel in the limelight of an affair with Patrick. It was all of a piece with that terrible purple cloak.

Then there was Luke. Ella, who did not like boys, liked Luke. Whatever Anna's failings in other directions, she had done a good job on Luke. He had nice manners, worked hard, and was clearly very fond of his mother. Ella showed her approval by treating him as she did Patrick, and by feeding him. He ate relentlessly. It was almost a luxury, Ella thought, to watch her excellent loaves and fruit cakes and scones disappear into Luke like coal into a furnace. She found that she felt very troubled indeed about Luke when she thought of Patrick and Anna Bouverie.

There was nothing to be gained by speaking to Patrick. He knew without question that she thought his behaviour both stupid and wrong. He believed himself to be thoroughly in love this time and was, as he had become accustomed, determined to have his own way. Ella had nothing to threaten him with. If she told him she was leaving, he would simply ring up an agency for a temporary housekeeper. Putting a kipper down in front of Patrick one breakfast, she said, "Well, if you haven't the sense to think of yourself, at least think of that poor boy," and Patrick had replied, in his genial way that contained just a hint of menace, "Mind your own business, my dear."

There was nothing Ella could do except get on with her job. Practicality, she discovered, was no match for power.

Luke burned with an inarticulate rage. He was haunted by suspicion and could not bring himself to hunt through Anna's drawers to find that envelope and have his suspicions confirmed. Instead, he was surly and oafish. He came home on the last possible bus, avoided going round to the Old Rectory and then announced that he was spending a few nights in Woodborough with Barnaby. Neither of his parents seemed to mind at all. Flora said, "Oh, *good.*" During one of those Woodborough evenings, he got drunk and aggressive, and then tearful, and Alison took him home with her. She lived with her divorced father, who was a salesman and often away. She made it very plain that she would allow Luke to fuck her, but only after he had done to her all the things she required for her own pleasure. This had never struck him as constituting part of the sex deal. He didn't like it very much. Parts of her tasted soapy and other parts salty or fishy. He came several times, helplessly, during the course of this, and, when he was finally allowed inside her, it was over almost before it had begun. He had slept afterwards as if poleaxed and woken feeling absolutely terrible. Over mugs of instant coffee before school, Alison said that now he'd had what he wanted, perhaps he'd kindly leave her alone; he was too young for her anyway.

The day passed in a furious, nauseous daze. Barnaby, who of course knew where Luke had spent the night, behaved with rare tact and simply left him alone. After the lunch break Luke, impelled by instinct rather than conscious thought, cut an English literature class (*Hamlet*—a discussion of the relative significance of action and inaction in the play) and caught the early afternoon bus to Loxford. Sometimes, after a morning shift at Pricewell's, Anna caught that bus too. Luke looked furtively round. She wasn't there; no-one he knew was there.

He sat slumped across the seat, staring out at the landscape. He knew every tree and hedge, every house and barn. All the things that usually pleased him—a gaunt dead tree alone in a shallow valley, a spire rising above a beech hanger, a secret lane that suddenly plunged downhill off the main road like a rabbit hole—looked as interesting as grey cardboard today. After a while his eyes grew gritty and strained with staring so he shut them. It made him feel slightly sick, but at least that was a diversion. He kept them shut until the bus stopped on Loxford green.

He went slowly, steadily, across it to the Old Rectory. This time, Ella was in the kitchen, doing household accounts at the table with the bills spread round her in little piles.

"Luke!"

He shut the door and leaned against it.

"You should be at school—"

"I've come to see Patrick."

Ella rose. "We thought you'd given us up. Revision, I said to Patrick, with A levels only a month away—"

"Sorry," Luke said. He dropped his bag.

Ella came nearer. "You look dreadful."

"Feel it."

"Luke," Ella said, "where have you been? What have you been up to?"

Luke made drinking movements with one arm. "I stayed in Woodborough last night."

"So you've come here for me to make you respectable to go home to your mother." Ella sounded pleased.

Luke looked at her. "I've come to see Patrick."

Ella's expression changed. "I don't think that's wise. Really I don't. I'll make you a sandwich and we'll chat—"

"No," Luke said loudly. "I've got to see him. Please."

"But what will it achieve? Just think a moment—"

"It'll stop it," Luke said, "that's what."

They stared at each other. Then Ella said uncertainly, "He's in his study. As usual."

Patrick laughed. He came round his desk and tried to put his arm round Luke's shoulders. Luke flinched away. "Come on," Patrick said easily, "no melodramatics."

Luke was trembling. He said, "Don't lie, don't lie, I *know*—"

Patrick laughed again. "My dear old fellow, you know nothing. How could you? You're only seventeen." He put his hands in his pockets. "I like it. Really I do. I like your loyalty, your protectiveness towards your mother. You're a good lad. I don't blame you for coming, it does you credit. But you have to believe me when I tell you that you don't actually understand what you've come for.''

Luke yelled, ''You're making a fool of my mother!''

Patrick stopped laughing. He looked grave and sad. ''Oh no,'' he said, ''that is the last thing I would do to someone who means as much to me as your mother does.''

Luke lunged forward. Patrick caught him easily and pinned him against a bookcase.

''Don't be such a bloody fool.''

''You're a shit,'' Luke tried to say, ''a shit, a shit,'' but tears were flooding down his face and he could not speak for rising sobs. Patrick propelled him out of the door. Ella was waiting in the hall. She took Luke from him and led him into the kitchen.

Isobel Thompson had had a trying afternoon. Her car had broken down on the way to her weekly session with the girls at a remand home some ten miles outside Woodborough, so that she was over an hour late and the girls, difficult and truculent at the best of times, were impossible. She felt out of touch and useless, with no spirit even to ignore the repulsive language they were deliberately using for her benefit, let alone rise above it. There was no question of love that afternoon, only of endurance. Isobel endured until four-thirty, and then nursed her complaining car slowly back to Woodborough. The garage had told her they would probably find her a reconditioned engine for five hundred or so, which would give the car another few years of life. Five hundred! And on something so dull. For three years, Isobel had been promising herself a trip to India, a walking trip in the foothills of the Himalayas before she was too old to take it on. She had £700 saved towards it. Isobel set her jaw and drove tensely on.

At home, the telephone-answering machine was loaded with querulous messages. Unmarried women deacons were, Isobel thought, assumed to have no life of their own worth having, and were therefore bound to be terribly grateful for all the unpleasant bits of other people's. She wrote down the messages in her notebook, and went out to the kitchen. If she had a pound for every time she put a kettle on each day, either in her own house or anyone else's, she'd have enough money in six months to go to India *and* buy the car a new engine.

She made herself tea. She longed for a biscuit, but she was steadily putting on that kind of solid, middle-aged weight there is no shifting, and was trying to resist all the sweet and comforting things, that, if taste was anything to go by, were her natural foods. Her mother, who despised sugar, had always been contemptuous of Isobel's preference for sweet rather than dry sherry, milk chocolate to plain, a bun instead of a cheese sandwich. In Africa, Isobel had never thought about sugar; in England, if she was honest, she thought about little else.

She took her shoes off and sat down with her cup and saucer. She looked at her stockinged feet. Serviceable things, no more. When she was a girl, she had been rather proud of her high arches, but these had dropped long since, padding about sandalled in Africa. Oh, she thought, closing her eyes, how much I left in Africa!

The doorbell rang. Isobel found she would rather have liked to say several of the things those girls on remand had said this afternoon. She put down her cup, found her shoes, and went stiffly and wearily into her little front hall. There was a telescopic spy hole in her front door. She put her eye to it and gave a little gasp. She flung the door open, and there stood Luke Bouverie, looking on the point of collapse.

When she had put him to bed—"I'm not discussing anything more, dear, until you've had some sleep"—Isobel rang Anna.

"He's quite safe. He's had a bath and he's asleep. I'm afraid he went drinking with Barnaby last night, and then cut classes this afternoon. He'll be fine in the morning."

"Oh Isobel," Anna said, "I'm so grateful. But I'm sorry too, it shouldn't have to be you—"

"I'd rather Luke than most of the people who end up in my spare room."

"He's having a bit of a phase, poor fellow. I don't think the atmosphere here is good for him at the moment." She stopped, just before she said, Any more than it is for any of us.

"I'm always here," Isobel said. "You know that."

"I do. Bless you. And bless you for having Luke. Did he confess to you?"

"About the drinking," Isobel said firmly.

She put the telephone down, and went upstairs. Luke slept on his side, his dark head deep in the pillow. Isobel stooped and picked up his clothes, which he had simply dropped on the floor. When she had put them into her twin-tub washing machine, she thought she would telephone the Archdeacon.

"I think it's just a bit of nonsense," Isobel said to Daniel. "Instead of a woman parishioner getting a crush on the priest, it's a male one on the priest's wife. But it's upset the boy a lot and he says he can't talk to his parents."

Daniel was scribbling with his free hand. The other was occupied with the telephone receiver. "Do you know the man?"

"Only by sight. He hasn't been there long. He came from London. And, of course, Anna's so attractive."

"Hasn't she put a stop to it? It isn't difficult, for a clever woman."

Isobel hesitated.

"Oh dear," Daniel said.

Isobel said hurriedly, "Things have been so difficult at Loxford recently—" She wanted to say, Since you got the job Peter wanted, but contented herself with, "It's often the way after ten years in a parish. And the children are growing up—"

"I understand you perfectly," Daniel said. "I've spoken to Anna recently and I know something of her situation. If I speak to her again," he said musingly, "I'm taking her into a confidence her husband isn't sharing, and I think he is even more isolated than she, just now. Do you agree?"

Isobel said, "He's a very difficult man. He knows he is, which makes it worse."

Daniel made a resolution. "I will go and speak to them together. This is, after all, a difficulty for them both."

"I never listen to rumours," Peter said, "I never have. You can't afford to in the country."

"But, if your son is distressed—"

"Luke is taking A levels and is not at an age where anything is easy. He gets overwrought."

"All the same," Daniel said patiently, "I should like to come out to Loxford and talk to you and to Anna."

"No, thank you," Peter said. He sounded as if he

were holding the telephone receiver well away from his mouth. "I appreciate your concern but there's nothing the matter. Temporary tittle-tattle. I'm afraid Luke got led astray by friends and overreacted. Isobel Thompson has known him since we came here, so it was natural he should go to her. Perhaps she—she gave more weight to things Luke said than she ought."

"Peter, may I not suggest even that you and I might meet, just briefly—"

There was a pause. Then Peter said, "Perhaps, when I'm not so committed. In a few months. Thank you for ringing. Goodbye."

Daniel replaced the receiver and sighed. He looked out of his study window at the white clouds sailing briskly across a cool May sky.

"Over to You," Daniel said, out loud.

13

❖   ❖   ❖

LAURA MARCHANT'S TELEVISION commercial had proved rather a success. Although it hadn't reached the screens of the nation yet, it was much talked of in the offices of the company that had made it. There was a strong sense that Laura was something of a find. She was put on a retaining fee not to accept work from any rival until the effect of the original commercial could be assessed.

This made her more comfortable, but it was boring. She was like an old hound scenting the chase—the relief and pleasure of acting again had given her a renewed taste for it. While she waited to see whether she and the Irish stout proved to be something—or nothing—of a triumph, she auditioned down at Chiswick for a small part in a new play, and got it. The part was a seaside-hotel landlady and, although she hadn't many lines, she was on stage a good deal and she intended to make the most of that. Given her dimensions and the exuberance of her personality, she thought her mere presence on stage might be one of those things the audience found they could not ignore.

She adored rehearsals. She loved the purposeful travelling to them, the gossip and coffee breaks, the reborn contact with the theatre and its people. She became the auntie of the company, the source of consolation and liquorice allsorts. All thoughts of selling St. Agatha vanished from her mind since not only could she now squirrel away weekly sums to help Luke and Flora, but St. Agatha was clearly the cause of her new-found success. All those years of confiding in the saint, of treating her as a true companion, had reaped their reward. On St. Agatha's painted plaster face, despite the scars and chips of her arduous life, Laura was now sure she could detect a faint but unmistakable animation.

The play in Chiswick was not admired by the critics or by the public; the only person to get even reasonable notices was Laura. After its allotted three weeks it closed, with no mention of a West End transfer, and Laura went back to St. Agatha, determined to audition for something else as soon as possible. Mutely and powerfully, St. Agatha indicated that, perhaps, before she started to badger her agent once more, Laura should pay a little attention to matters closer to home. The word "Loxford" emanated from St. Agatha as powerfully as if she had spoken it.

"My dear girl," Laura said, "you are perfectly right."

St. Agatha made it very plain that that was what saints were for.

Laura telephoned Loxford. Peter answered. He sounded polite and a little formal. He said that Anna was out—in such a way as to make it plain that Anna was always out—and that Flora and Luke were at school. Laura proposed herself for the weekend. Peter said he was sure that would be fine and that he would get Anna to confirm the arrangement that evening.

"Darling boy," Laura said, "I don't like the sound of you. What is the matter?"

Peter said he had rather a cold, thanked her for telephoning and rang off. Laura dialled Kitty, in Windsor. Kitty's employer had started a tea shop for the summer months and Kitty's duties now included making scones and showing people to their tables, as well as selling souvenirs in the shop, and taking the Pekinese out to spend constant, minute, senile pennies. She'd had a payrise too, and had booked herself a holiday in Jersey, a week in October, her first holiday in years. She was going with her employer, who knew a lovely hotel where they did all their own baking . . .

"And have you heard from the family, Kittykins?"

"The—"

"Do concentrate, darling. Life isn't all lardy cakes. Have you heard from Loxford?"

"I ring every week, dear. Just for a little word. Flora loves her school—"

"Kitty," Laura said, "I spoke to Peter just now and he sounded perfectly morbid."

"He never could rise above knocks, not even as a little boy. I remember—"

"No," Laura said, "no reminiscences. Have you spoken to Anna?"

Kitty rather thought Anna was overtired. Of course, shopwork was terribly tiring, she ought to know, and Anna's standards were so high, always had been, whereas hers had got lower and lower until she realized, before her job came along, that she was simply never cleaning the bath, because no-one saw it but her, and she didn't care . . .

"I am worried," Laura said emphatically.

"Are you, dear?"

"I don't like the atmosphere. I shall go down this weekend."

"You're so decisive," Kitty said. "I do admire it. I've found that if you dust the tops of scones with flour before you put them in the oven they come out as light as air."

Laura put the receiver down sadly. As light as air. As light as Kitty's heart and head. Scones! Laura dialled the number of a national long-distance bus company and, in an exaggerated German accent for her own amusement, asked the times of the service to Woodborough, on Friday afternoons.

In the garden of Woodborough Vicarage, Anna and Jonathan Byrne sat on a bench in the sun. It was a wooden bench, on whose back had been carved "Our God Himself is Moon and Sun." Jonathan said it was a quotation from Tennyson. Above the bench hung a few branches of white lilac, and in front of it a lawn stretched in a neat oblong to a solid border of hostas beneath the boundary wall. Anna thought it a dull garden, but she was very contented to be sitting in it, in the late May sunshine, with Jonathan Byrne.

He had come into Pricewell's at the end of her shift, and dissuaded her from the errands she was then intending to do. She had said, automatically, "Why?" and he had said, "Because I need to see you." In Anna's present bemused state of mind, this had seemed as good a reason as any for obliging him. Daniel had gone to London for the day, Miss Lambe was having her weekly afternoon off at the Wednesday Club (an outing, this week, to nearby water gardens followed by tea in St. Paul's Parish Room) and the Vicarage was empty and quiet. Anna followed Jonathan docilely out into the garden, as she had followed him from Pricewell's. He sat her on the bench, and then he went back into the house and returned with a tray bearing a loaf, a piece of cheese, two apples and a jug of cider. Anna took off her shoes and sank her grateful bare feet into the grass.

While they ate, Jonathan told Anna about his and Daniel's childhood. They had been brought up in York. Their mother had been a Baptist, simple and stern, and their father a most unlikely mate for her, a ranting and eloquent Scot who ran a timber yard. Daniel was born ten years before Jonathan and had, from his birth, treated his younger brother with peculiar tenderness.

"So how old is Daniel now?"

"Fifty."

"So you are younger than I am."

Jonathan looked at her. "Not by much. And not to judge by appearances."

Anna surveyed her feet. She said calmly, "I love Daniel."

"Yes," he said, "I know." He waited for her to say something more, but she didn't, only sat and stared at her feet in the grass. So he said, "Could you love me?"

Very slowly, she turned to look at him. After what seemed like a very long time, she said, "I think so."

"Only think?"

She said seriously, "I have to be honest. I love Daniel and that's one kind of love. I believe I love Peter, and that's another. I'm being besieged by a parishioner with yet another brand. But when I'm with you I feel that, in a way I can relax best, I've come home.''

He didn't touch her. He bent down to the tray and refilled their glasses. He held Anna's out to her. She said, ''I'll go straight to sleep.''

''Not straight—''

The hand she had stretched out for the glass shook a little. She withdrew it. He said, ''I'm in love with you. I had thought I wouldn't say it because the words are so weary, so overused. But I want to be quite plain with you, I want you to be quite sure of what I'm saying.'' He leaned towards her and kissed her mouth lightly. Her eyes were full of tears.

''Oh Anna. What is it?''

She gave herself a little shake. ''Relief,'' she said.

Jonathan stood up. Then he bent and took Anna's hand and led her after him back to the house. She felt heavy and peaceful. They crossed the cavernous hall— the Victorian tiles, patterned with crude imitations of medieval designs, were cold and smooth under Anna's bare feet—and climbed the gaunt staircase to the first-floor landing, where narrow strips of brown carpet led off down various dark passages, like arrows. Jonathan led Anna along one of these to his study, to which he had now become so attached that he had moved a divan in, and started sleeping there. He opened the door. Anna burst out laughing.

''What a funny room!''

''Is it?''

''Yes,'' she said, ''yes.'' She was enchanted by it. ''So mad and so exuberant and so grim—''

He seized her. ''Too grim to be seduced in?''

She stopped laughing. "Oh no," she said, "and anyway it isn't a seduction."

"What?"

"It would only be a seduction," Anna said, leaning into his embrace, "if I wasn't as willing as you are. Which isn't, as it happens, the case."

When Anna got home, there were, as usual, several telephone messages (Peter had said that the parish group was going to raise money to give them an answering machine and Anna had said, "Are you sure Celia wouldn't rather just sit here and take the messages herself?"). There was one from Sir Francis Mayhew about the honey rot he had spotted in two beech trees in the churchyard, one for Luke from Barnaby, and one from Laura. At the bottom of the list, Peter had written, "Out until 6.30. P."

Flora said, "Sarah Simpson at school says Barnaby takes drugs."

Anna put her arms round Flora. She wanted to hold her, to feel the great warmth she was full of spreading into Flora. Flora squirmed.

"Do you mean he smokes pot?"

Flora wriggled free. *"Much* worse."

"Barnaby's mother is a pillar of rectitude. And his father likewise. What do you know about drugs, anyway, Flora Bouverie?"

"Heaps," Flora said.

Anna wrapped her happy arms about herself instead. "I think you just like gossip."

"I do not like Barnaby Weston."

"I see," said Anna.

Flora went pink. "I don't!"

221

"No, darling. Are you hungry?"

"Starving—"

Anna unwrapped herself, and delved into a carrier bag. "There."

Flora's eyes bulged. "Chocolate hazelnut spread! We *never* have that!"

"We do now."

Flora looked at her. She appeared to Flora to be sort of—*shining.* Flora said fervently, "Thank you."

Anna smiled, "Not at all. Don't eat too much at once. It's for sandwiches, not spooning. I'm going to telephone Ga."

"Is she coming?"

"For the weekend," Anna said, turning to the telephone. Behind her back, with infinite stealth, Flora extracted a teaspoon from a drawer and unscrewed the lid of the chocolate jar. What, after all, was the point of a treat in half-measures?

Laura decided at once that she didn't like the look of any of them. Peter looked withdrawn and offended, Luke looked ill and Flora was thoroughly out of hand. As for Anna . . . What was the matter with Anna? She looked fine really, better than Laura had expected, but it wasn't somehow a reassuring fineness. Her eyes were full of energy, a quick, restless energy. It was, Laura decided, as if some bright inner life were both firing and alienating her. Was her behaviour, Laura wondered, just a little mad?

She tried to corner Anna. Saturday was hopeless. "You know Saturdays here," Anna said, "almost worse than Sundays. Definitely Rabbit's Busy Day."

In the afternoon there was a sad, amateur, little fête

at Snead Hall, where the headmistress prided herself on insisting that the girls use their own initiative. As they were aged between eleven and sixteen, and were spending these precious years of their adolescence being irrationally disciplined and indifferently taught, most of the pupils at Snead Hall either had no initiative or were damned if they were going to use any. Under a lowering sky, a scattering of stalls had been set out on the ruined lawn of what had once been a beautiful garden. The five villages, drawn to the fête by the same instinct that drew them to jumble sales and carboot fairs, poked about among the secondhand paperbacks and lopsided offerings from the cookery room, and obligingly guessed the name of a giant, pink, plush teddy bear, donated by the husband of the school secretary, who was a traveller in soft toys. Laura said, "Satan." The child detailed to write down the suggestions (10p a time) wrote the name down without a glimmer of comprehension.

It was obligatory for Anna and Peter to visit every stall. Laura, discouraged by her anxiety out of almost all her natural ebullience, trailed after them. She bought a gloomy little bag of melted-together fudge, a paperback of a historical novel about Joan of Arc and a pair of curiously lumpy oven gloves from a craft stall, whose holder explained breathlessly that she'd had to use old tights in them as their needlework teacher had run out of wadding. Flora brought a stout pink child with spaniel's ears of brown curls to meet her, a child called Emma something, but they didn't stay, being too much occupied with showing off to the poor prisoners of Snead Hall. Clutching her purchases, and feeling the fudge soften unattractively under her fingers, Laura resolved that, before night fell, she would tackle Anna.

However, Luke got to her first. He came into Charlotte's bedroom which she was as usual occupying, while she was repinning up her luxuriant dark-grey hair before supper. First he said it was great of her to have given him the money for India but he didn't know if they'd be going now, it was all a bit difficult and Barnaby's mum was anti the whole thing, he'd have to see. Laura said did he have to go with Barnaby and Luke looked shocked and said there wouldn't be any point otherwise. Then Laura said, "Is that why you look so awful, darling? Or is it looming exams?" and Luke ducked his head and muttered that it was Mum.

"Mum?"

Luke said, "Well, not Mum, really, her and Dad. And this bloke—"

"What bloke?"

"The one I worked for, the one with the Daimler."

Laura put down her combs and pins. She came over to the bed where Luke had slumped and sat down beside him. He smelled sad and unwashed.

"Darling, tell me all you know."

"I don't *know* anything—"

"Then—"

Luke turned on her. "That's just it, I don't know anything, nobody says anything, but the atmosphere's awful, I hate it, they're hardly speaking—"

"I noticed."

"Ga," Luke said, "Dad makes it hard, you know, hard for all of us. And Mum . . . This bloke fancies her."

"The Daimler bloke?"

"Yeah. He wrote to her. This letter—"

"You never saw it—"

"Not the words."

224

"And Mum. What does Mum think of Signor Daimler?"

"Dunno."

"Then what does it matter?"

"I don't like it!" Luke shouted suddenly.

"Why?"

He glared at her. Couldn't she see? Couldn't she see that he was full of love and loyalty and confusion, none of which could possibly be explained? Could she not also see that, by doing something wrong, or clumsy, he might unwittingly break some magic rule and lose the thing he loved?

"Sorry," Laura said, "sorry, darling. I shouldn't have asked. I'll talk to her, I'll talk to Mum."

"No! No!"

"Why not?"

"I don't want to squeal on her," Luke said, "not on her."

"No. Of course not. Though I don't see how I can help if I stay silent."

Luke looked at her. "That's the problem," he said in exasperation.

On Sunday, Laura accompanied Anna to church. It was a sung eucharist. The church looked very bright and clean and there were horrible stiff triangular flower arrangements on the altar and by the chancel steps. "Freda Partington," Anna hissed. "Fields full of cow parsley just now and she buys, actually buys, chrysanthemums." There were not many communicants. Sir Francis Mayhew limped round with the collection bag, having first put in his own five-pound note, in full view of the congregation. Laura watched her son-in-law and reflected that, however difficult and unapproachable he was in real life, he still took services with grace and dignity. Beside her, Anna thought much the same thing.

Anna also thought about Jonathan. What astonished her was not so much that she had been to bed with him—and was now an adulteress—but that it should have been so natural to do so, and even more, so natural in its doing. Her every dealing with the Byrne brothers had been characterized by sheer ease, from that first drive to Loxford with Daniel, to Jonathan saying into her shivering skin, "And do you like this? And this? But not that?" She had slipped along in her relationship with them like a fish in a stream, seeing at last, because of them, her passage clear to the sea. She was perfectly certain that she would continue to go to bed with Jonathan and that her love for him would grow until—she looked at Peter's surpliced back before the altar—until she saw unquestionably what she should do next. For the moment, she would just gratefully draw strength from this astonishing new source. A thought shot into her mind like a bolt from the blue. Had Jonathan actually been *offered* to her?

Going out of church, she and Laura were accosted by Patrick. He shook hands fervently.

"I'd adore you," he said to Laura, "to see my garden."

"Dear boy, I'm hopeless at gardens."

He said, "Hopeless?"

"Can't see the point of them. But mountains! Ah now, *mountains*—"

Patrick, sensing he might be being made fun of, stepped back a little. "Can't offer you those, I'm afraid."

Anna hadn't looked at him. Nor had she replied to his letter. Both omissions gave him heart. He said, rallying, "Perhaps I can manage a mountain for your next visit—"

Laura smiled at him. He was very attractive. "Do try."

At the lich-gate, Miss Dunstable paused to say, "Terrible flowers," to Anna.

"I quite agree. But you'll have to complain to the parish group about them. They've taken over the rota."

"Let them try taking over my altar frontal!"

Later, in the Rectory kitchen, making coffee, Anna said with no self-consciousness, "I'm being besieged by Patrick."

Laura affected outrageous surprise. "Darling!"

"I expect Luke told you."

Laura deflated. "Actually—"

"Poor Luke. There's nothing for him to worry about. I feel nothing for Patrick except temper."

"Sure?"

Tiny pause.

"Sure."

"You must make that plain to Luke."

"Does he think—"

"He's afraid to think. Anna, I had one golden rule for affairs. No teasing."

"I'm not having an affair," said Anna with her back to her mother.

"But Patrick thinks you soon will. He's blazing with that caveman certainty of incipient conquest, simply blazing. You must tell him once and for all. It's perfectly easy to make yourself quite plain."

There was a silence.

"For Luke," Laura said.

"Of course."

"One last meeting. Face to face. Finish."

"There's nothing to finish."

"Oh yes, there is," Laura said. "In Patrick's mind, at least." She looked at Anna, leaning against the sink, her dark head bent. Poor darling, Laura thought, poor wasted darling. What a life! And Peter. What had withered Peter? "Anna," Laura said, holding a hand out to her daughter, "Oh darling," and felt as if her heart would burst.

That night, Anna attempted to comfort Luke. She explained that Patrick had developed an infatuation which she didn't in the least return, and that she was angry and sorry that such adult foolishness had spoiled his own relationship with Patrick. She said she was going to put a stop to everything. It was, she said, very easy for a woman to make sure a man never tried anything again. (Remembering Alison, Luke could at least believe that part.) She said he was not to worry any more and that she felt most remorseful that he should have worried in the past over something so silly and fantastic. He allowed her to kiss him. He wanted her to stay a bit, but not to talk any more, but he didn't say so, so she went. When she had gone, he lay on his bed and felt worse than he had done before she came in.

Two days later, she caught the early afternoon bus back to Quindale. Jonathan had put her on it, having walked with her from Pricewell's to the bus station. He said he was in such a frame of mind and heart at the moment that he was inclined to walk into walls. When he had found her a seat on the bus, he put an envelope in her lap and said, "I'm afraid there'll be a lot of this. Letters and poems. I'm bursting with the need to communicate with you."

She read the letter in the bus. It described Jonathan's sense of joyful recognition at meeting her. She read it several times. Then she put it away in her skirt pocket and leaned her head against the shaking glass of the bus window, and uttered a mute and fervent prayer of thankfulness.

It took a quarter of an hour to walk from Quindale to Loxford. The lane between the two villages was travelled only by local people, and ran between peaceful fields used for grazing cattle and sheep. They were, at the moment, full of lambs, as raucous as a primary-school playground. Anna walked along the verge—the lane twisted a good deal and the hedges made visibility difficult—and looked at the lambs and the new, soft, bright growth on the trees and thought of her letter and her good fortune. One field, brilliant with buttercups, seemed to her to be almost a symbol. She stopped in the gateway to gaze.

When, half a minute later, Patrick drew his car into the gateway behind her, she felt a mixture of irritation and relief. It was exasperating to have her reverie broken, and yet this was clearly an excellent chance to say what she had to say, a chance that avoided all kinds of disagreeable contrivings. All the same, as he got out of the car and came round it towards her, she felt suddenly nervous.

"Anna."

"Hello."

"What a chance. I was going to pick up some new greenhouse glass." He leaned on the gate beside her. "Why haven't you replied to my letter?"

"There is no reply," Anna said.

"Oh yes," he said, "there is. And you know it."

She was silent, resolving exactly what she would say.

"I asked you to come away with me. I'm asking you again now. I'll ask you until you come because I know it is what you want."

A car was coming along the lane. Immediately, Anna moved away from the gate to put a prudent distance between herself and Patrick, but he leaned forward and seized her wrist.

"I love you," Patrick said.

The car passed. Anna dared not look at it. She said, as contemptuously as she could, "Let go."

He dropped her wrist. "Please," he said.

"This is the last time we shall have anything to say to one another."

"Why, what do you mean—"

"I despise you," Anna said. "I despise your arrogance and your insensitivity. I was a fool to believe you wanted to help Luke." She turned and began to walk hurriedly along the lane towards Loxford. After her, Patrick called, "But I did! I do." She didn't hear him. She began to run, dreading to hear the Daimler's sleek purr behind her, catching her up. But it didn't come, nobody came, except Mr. Biddle, pedalling slowly on his creaking bicycle, never looking at her but simply shouting at her as he went by.

"Want to get yourself a bike, Mrs. B!" Mr. Biddle bellowed. "Want to get yourself modernized, you do!"

"It's true," Trish Pardoe said. She stood in the Old Rectory kitchen, confronting Ella. She had driven straight to Ella even though it would make her late for picking up her mother at the Woodborough Pop-In Club.

Ella, who knew all too well it was true, simply nodded.

"They were holding hands," Trish said. Her voice

shook. "In a gateway. Broad daylight. I nearly crashed the car."

Ella said, "It's been going on some time. He got a bee in his bonnet about her the minute he got here. I thought it was just a fad. He's like that." Unaccountably, she found she wanted to defend him, to say that he was a romantic, that he saw himself rescuing a princess from a tower, that he wanted to give her all the things she had plainly never had. But Trish Pardoe's expression was not conducive to any defence of Patrick.

"It's disgusting. That poor vicar."

"I suppose she's a human being, like the rest of us—"

"Ella!"

Ella said sadly, "Perhaps it's a good thing it's come to a head. That you've seen them—"

"I saw them all right." Trish peered at Ella. "What'll we do?"

Ella sighed. "I suppose I have to go and talk to the Rector."

"I'll come—"

"No."

"Why not? I saw them—"

"Because it will be easier for Peter if he thinks only I know. If he doesn't think it's general village gossip."

"Soon will be—"

"It needn't be," Ella said with emphasis.

Trish hesitated. "Of course, I wouldn't say a word—"

"No."

"What's she got to complain of? Tell me that. How many vicars' wives get the help she gets, I'd like to know? Gives her all the time in the world to mess about with her fancy man—"

"Shut up," Ella said.

"I beg your pardon—"

"Go away," Ella said, "I've got to think. And keep your mouth shut. If I hear any rumours, I'll know where they started."

"Whose side are you on?"

Ella looked at her. "Peter's."

"Me too," Trish said.

Flora brought a note home with her from school. It was from Luke. He had delivered it to St. Saviour's at lunchtime. It said, "Dear Mum, I'm going to live at Barney's for a while. Till the exams are over. Mrs. Weston says it's fine. I can give her a bit out of my savings to help with food. Take care. Love, Luke."

14

❖ ❖ ❖

PETER SAT ALONE in Snead church. He had gone to
take the midmorning Thursday communion service, to
which almost nobody came, but which was clamorously
defended whenever he suggested dropping it. He liked
Snead church. It was the simplest of his five churches,
a Norman nave with a single shallow transept in which
the wheezing organ lived. There was no coloured glass
in the windows and the Parochial Church Council of
Snead preferred sisal matting in the aisle to the red car-
peting favoured by the other four churches. The restraint
appealed to him.

He sat in the north side of the choir stalls and looked
out at the waving plumes of a willow tree in the churchyard. He did not really see it, any more than he saw the
sky beyond it, or the greyish stone window that framed
it. He was conscious of very little except the quiet and
his unhappiness, which filled his whole being like cold,
still water. It was water he was afraid to disturb, to dive
into, because he couldn't bear even to begin to analyze
why he felt as he did. He shrank from his thoughts, just

as, these days, he shrank from Anna. If their limbs brushed each other in bed, he could feel his withdrawing, flinching. In the same way, his eyes turned away from meeting hers when they spoke. He was terribly afraid that he was going mad. Long ago, as a theology student, he had had a crisis about prayer, a period of alarming doubt. His tutor, a man of enormous experience in ministerial matters, had simply counselled him not to struggle. Throw out the idea of God, he had said, just forget it. Think instead about something about which there can't be personal anguish, something more abstract, like a desire to be good or kind, or the wish to love, and voice that wish in your mind, over and over. After a while, try saying it to Christ, but only when you feel you want to. This had been sound advice. When things were difficult, he had thought about the qualities necessary to ease those difficulties; but of late, he had only thought of how to endure. All softness in him seemed imperceptibly, involuntarily, to have hardened. He didn't feel in the least interested in love or goodness or kindness; the only thing that stirred him was a determination not to give in.

He sighed, and slipped automatically to his knees. Footsteps sounded in the porch, and the heavy iron latch on the door was lifted. A slice of sunlight fell in and a woman said, "Oh, I'm ever so sorry, Mr. Bouverie, I'd no idea—"

He looked up. It was Emma Maxwell's mother, clutching a dustsheet.

"I just came to clear away last week's flowers. But I can easily come later—"

He got stiffly to his feet. "No, no, please come in. I was just going."

"You sure?"

"Quite," Peter said. He smiled at her. She was plump and pink and her hair curled cheerfully, exactly like her daughter's.

"We're so pleased Emma and Flora are such friends," Mrs. Maxwell said, encouraged. She advanced up the aisle. "St. Saviour's is a lovely school. So kind."

"Flora seems very happy."

"She makes us laugh. What an imagination!"

"Too vivid, sometimes."

"Oh, I don't know. Most children never use theirs, because of television, so it's lovely to see a child like Flora. The nuns are dears."

"I only—"

"So tactful," Mrs. Maxwell said, rushing on, pressing her dustsheet to her bosom in her enthusiasm. "I mean, if you don't mind my mentioning it, they make no distinction between the fee-paying children and the free-place ones. I shouldn't think the other children even know. Emma certainly doesn't know about Flora."

Peter came out of the choir stalls. "I beg your pardon?"

Mrs. Maxwell blushed. How clumsy and stupid to bring it up! Probably little Flora didn't even know herself.

"I'm so sorry. I've no tact. Please forget I ever said such a thing."

A small light was dawning in Peter's comprehension. He said quietly to Mrs. Maxwell, "Please don't worry. Don't think of it."

She nodded. She said quickly, wishing to make amends, "I hope you know that Flora is welcome any time, at our house. Very welcome."

"Thank you," Peter said, "thank you." He smiled again. "And now I'll leave you to your flowers."

He drove home in a very different mood. The paralysis of unhappiness had abruptly given way to the energy of anger. He left the car in the drive and hurried into the house. The telephone number for St. Saviour's was written up, in red, on the emergency list that Anna had stuck to the wall. Peter dialled it. He stood up straight by the telephone, almost to attention, looking out of the window. The school secretary answered.

"This is Peter Bouverie speaking, the Reverend Peter Bouverie, Flora's father. I wonder if I might speak to Sister Ignatia?"

At lunchtime, Peter made himself a sandwich and a cup of coffee. After he had eaten, he washed his cup and plate, and then he had a good look in all the cupboards. There was nothing in any of them that wasn't familiar, nothing new, or exotic, only a virgin cheese-grater still in its plastic film and an untouched, sealed tin of shortbread.

He went upstairs, quietly, as if he were a burglar. He looked in the bathroom; same towels, same toothglass that the Quindale garage had given away at Christmas with every twenty gallons of petrol, same cracked and charming Victorian soap dish. He crossed the landing to his and Anna's bedroom. Methodically, one by one, he slid out drawers and opened cupboards. Anna's colourful and wayward clothes lay and hung there in absolute familiarity; her shoes were in the tumble on her wardrobe floor that had always so exasperated him and were all, in any case, unquestionably well worn. There were no new books beside her bed, no scent bottles on the chest of drawers, no evidence anywhere that Anna had spent a single penny of her earnings on herself or her house.

So where were those earnings? They wouldn't be

much, but there would be, Peter reckoned, at least £500.
Why had she concealed Flora's free place? Why was
she hoarding? In all their married life, anything she had
earned he had thought of as pin money, holiday money,
money for violin lessons for Charlotte (a failure) or a
school trip to Venice for Luke (a success). He believed
she had thought of it in the same way, that they were
well-suited in their approach to money, that she had
grown accustomed to frugality, adjusted to it. Of course,
being an archdeacon would have brought in substantially
more and of course it was only human to regret that; but
why deceive him? Why take this attitude of secrecy and
defiance?

He went downstairs again, and into his study. He was
not going to conduct this war Anna had started using
her own guerrilla tactics; he was going to act decisively
and openly. Sister Ignatia had, unsurprisingly, been
much startled to hear Peter's question, and, although she
had said nothing even faintly condemning of Anna, her
tone of voice had been unmistakable. Sister Ignatia was
the first step. The next two seemed to him perfectly
plain. When he had taken those, Anna could not but
confront the reality of her actions. What would happen
after that, Peter chose not to think.

Peter said to the supervisor on the checkout that he
would like to see the administration manager. The supervisor hesitated. Peter had no appointment, and there
were rules in Pricewell's about appointments, but he had
a dog collar and was therefore in an unusual category
of visitor. After a moment, she asked Peter to follow her
and led him up the aisle between pet foods and washing
powders to the staircase to the office.

Even though he knew Anna's shift was over, and that

she was on the bus back to Loxford, Peter kept his eyes on the supervisor's back. He followed her up the gaunt staircase and along a corridor to Mr. Mulgrove's office. Mr. Mulgrove was very startled. The sight of Peter gave him the same sensation as being visited by the police.

He offered Peter a chair in his tiny office. When he resumed his own seat, their knees almost touched, which horrified him as it seemed so disrespectful. He thought Peter had probably come to ask Pricewell's to make a donation to some local cause, and, as Pricewell's had a charities policy, he had his patter all ready for that. But Peter said nothing of the sort. He said that his name was Peter Bouverie, the Reverend Peter Bouverie, and that he believed that his wife worked part-time in the shop.

Mr. Mulgrove stared. "Anna!"

"Yes," Peter said, "my wife."

Mr. Mulgrove's eyes strayed to Peter's dog collar. A vicar's wife! Anna, a vicar's wife! He started to say that Anna was one of their best staff but of course she was really management calibre only he couldn't persuade her—but stopped himself. It didn't seem, somehow, an appropriate observation to make in the circumstances, with Peter turning out to be a vicar, sitting there almost in Mr. Mulgrove's lap.

"Were you unaware that she came from a rectory?"

"Why, yes, I mean, I knew her address, of course, but so many people now live in old rectories I didn't think. I knew she was, well, not exactly what we usually—" He stopped.

"No," Peter said. He wasn't smiling.

Mr. Mulgrove had a flash of loyalty for Anna. "She wanted the job to send her daughter to St. Saviour's. My sister went to St. Saviour's."

"My daughter has won a free place at St. Saviour's."

238

They looked at each other in silence.

"She's a good worker," Mr. Mulgrove said, and then, "This is a good company to work for."

"I don't doubt it. But there isn't any need for her to work here any more." Peter had a brief battle with the precise truth, and lost it. "Not now that St. Saviour's has given Flora a free place."

"I see."

"So from the end of this month, my wife won't be working for you any longer."

Mr. Mulgrove hesitated. When he had first begun at Pricewell's, as a school leaver of sixteen, it was quite common for the husbands of women with jobs in the store to organize their wives' working lives for them, accompanying them to interviews, complaining to the manager about poor working conditions or low pay. But things had changed now. Mr. Mulgrove doubted that any of his female workforce even consulted their husbands about where or when they should work. He supposed that vicars were a bit old-fashioned. He said, "She's said nothing to me."

"No. I think she preferred it that I should speak to you."

"I'll have to confirm it with her—"

"Of course." Peter got up with difficulty.

Mr. Mulgrove stood too. He was taller than Peter, and younger, and it struck him that Peter was not just old-fashioned but stuffy. He couldn't somehow see Anna as Peter's wife. Looking down at Peter before he performed the necessary contortion to open the door, he said, "We'll be sorry to lose her. She's very popular." He paused and then he said, with just the faintest hint of aggression, "We're proud to work here, you know. We're proud of this company."

Anna was not on the bus to Loxford. Anna was lying on the headland of a sweet-scented bean field in flower, five miles out of Woodborough, with Jonathan. They had started to make love but it had been terminated by Anna's sudden violent distress at recalling Luke's going off to live with the Westons. It had shaken her dreadfully. She had been to see Mrs. Weston, who had been kind and ordinary and talked sensibly about exam pressures. She said she'd fill Luke up with bread, and in any case she was glad to have him; his presence made Barnaby less truculent. Luke would clearly be safe and well provided for with the Westons, which was bearable, but the probability that he would also be happier was hardly bearable at all.

Jonathan was very comforting. Anna said sternly to him that he mustn't feel he had to comfort her because her family troubles were hers and she certainly wasn't about to offload them on to him. He held her in his arms and told her she was a perfect fool; didn't she realize that he loved the whole package of her, not just the bits and pieces that related directly to him? He said he would go and visit Luke, that he would like to.

"To my amazement, I like adolescents. You'd think, after fifteen years of teaching them, that I'd have developed a violent antipathy. But I really like them. They interest me. I don't at all mind that they haven't got their acts together. I like all that passion and confusion."

"Luke has all that," Anna said, sniffing, "and he's so loving." Her voice shook.

Jonathan began to kiss her face. "So am I."

"Jonathan—have you told Daniel?"

"About us? No."

"Will you?"

"In time. Have you told Peter?"

"No."

They looked at each other. Jonathan traced the outline of her mouth with his finger.

"All that'll come soon enough, you know."

She caught his finger in her teeth. "I quite want it to. I want action—"

He burst out laughing. Then he swooped down on her. "Then you shall have some!"

Flora lay in bed. It was late, but it wasn't dark. She hadn't pulled her curtains because there was, tonight, a romantic view of a new, pale moon which would do very well as the subject of a poem for her newspaper. (This was not going well. Emma was becoming restive at the lowliness of her role, but anyone with half an eye could see that Emma had no *vision*.) "Oh moon of May," Flora began. She didn't seem to feel like poetry. She wished Luke were there, through the wall, with his thudding music. She'd thought she'd love to be at home without him, but she found that she didn't at all. She felt lonely, and it was dull.

She got out of bed and peered out of her window. The garden was all shadowy and mysterious in the gleaming, dark-blue light. She could see the line of sticks Anna had put up for the sweet peas, and the neat clumps of the new-potato leaves. It was very quiet. She tiptoed across the room and out on to the landing. She thought she would just go into Luke's room and smell his smell for a bit. He might even have left a Twix bar somewhere.

The landing, however, was not quiet. From downstairs came the sound of voices, cross voices, behind a closed door. Flora went to the banisters and peered over. The hall was dark, but there was a line of light under Peter's study door. Behind it, her parents were quarrelling.

"You can have it," Anna said, "take it. I don't want it."

"I don't *want* it," Peter said. He sat at his desk, staring down at his green blotter, furiously rolling two pencils.

"I was going to tell you about Flora's place. When—when you seemed a little more approachable. But I knew if I did you would insist on my leaving Pricewell's, which I didn't want to do because I like it. I like the people, I like the ordinariness, I like being out of Loxford. The money isn't for myself, anyway. I've bought a few things, a few wickedly, sensationally extravagant things like a jar of chocolate spread for Flora—"

"There's no need to be sarcastic."

"But you are implying that I'm hoarding for myself. The money was for the children, for you if you wanted it. It's sitting tamely in a building-society account. Take it. I said so."

"And give you the evidence you want that I don't provide adequately for you?"

"Peter!"

"Well, what else is all this about?"

Anna took a controlling breath. "It's about my not telling you that Flora had a free place at St. Saviour's."

"About your *concealing* from me—"

"God!" Anna said. "You'd try the patience of a *saint*! Well, you know now, so that's all over. I'm going to make some tea."

"One more thing—"

"What?"

"I am not remotely interested in how much money

242

you have or what you've done with it or do with it. But there won't be any more from Pricewell's.''

Anna leaned towards him. ''Oh my dear, don't always kick me when I'm down. If it upsets you so much I will try and get a more prestigious job, but not yet. Just let it ride a bit, just let me get Luke a little launched . . .''

He did not look at her. ''I went to see the administration manager today. There will be no more work for you from the end of this month.''

Anna stood up and leaned against the end of his desk. She closed her eyes for a moment but the swirling angry darkness behind them made her feel dizzy, so she opened them again and looked at Peter. He seemed to her all at once as familiar as herself and an absolute stranger.

''You went into Pricewell's and you cancelled my job.''

''Yes.''

''After you had spoken to Sister Ignatia.''

''Yes.''

''But you didn't think of speaking to me.''

''You would have refused.''

''I do refuse,'' Anna said. She held the rim of the desk in both hands. She was so angry she was afraid.

Peter said, ''So you will make our—difference—plain to Mr. Mulgrove?''

There was a pause while Anna struggled with herself. Peter didn't look at her. She said at last, ''Peter, I've asked you this before but I'll have to try once more. What is it that you want of me?''

He thought. Even six months ago he would have said he wanted her to be a loving wife, a helpmeet, an ally. Now all he wanted was to have her out of his study. He said in a voice that shook with the impact of this realization, "If you can't see that, I can't possibly explain it to you."

"Mummy."

Anna looked up. Flora's nightied figure was dark against the dim landing.

"Flora! You should be in bed."

"I hate it when you cry—"

Anna came up the stairs. "I'm not crying, darling."

"All that shouting," Flora said, "I hate it. Why are you quarrelling?"

"Money," Anna said.

Flora's chest contracted. "About St. Saviour's?"

"No, no. St. Saviour's is quite safe. It was a very dull adult quarrel. Nothing to worry about." She reached the landing and put her arms around Flora. "Isn't it quiet without Luke?"

"Horrid," Flora said.

"He'll be back soon."

Flora said into Anna's shoulder, "I don't want to be Emma's friend anymore. I want to be Verity's."

"Can't you be both?"

" 'Course not," Flora said scornfully.

"No unkindness to Emma, Flora."

Flora tensed a little. "No unkindness to Daddy then." She withdrew from Anna's embrace. "I'm going to sleep in Luke's room."

"All right."

Flora marched across the landing. She put her hand on Luke's door and pushed it open. Anna didn't move. Suddenly, Flora didn't like her little victory. She turned and scuttled back to Anna, dissolved in tears, and Anna, soothing her, thought that all these years of her own self-sufficiency seemed to have conditioned her for nothing, since all she now longed to do was to telephone Jonathan. Which, of course, she couldn't.

Patrick told Ella he was going away. In the past, this would have meant nothing, Patrick was always going away, but since coming to Loxford he had hardly stirred. His business, those mysterious companies in which he played an unspecified but clearly significant part, had taken him to Germany a good deal, to Frankfurt, and Munich, and also to America. He always brought Ella something if he was away for more than a week. She couldn't help noticing that, after the past months of rural life, she was running low on duty-free scent. She had always liked the fact that Patrick bought her scent.

When he announced he was going away, Ella felt a huge relief. She had put off going to see Peter because she found she could hardly face it. It wasn't just the errand itself, but having to confront, because of it, the fact that Patrick was wildly attracted to Anna. His long-term mistress had been someone Ella could assimilate, an idle, witty, impractical creature with none of the qualities Ella thought important, because she possessed them herself. But Anna was different. Anna was original and attractive, with a suppressed wildness about her, like something caged. Ella herself had no wildness; as a quality it alarmed her and so she disapproved of it.

Her sister, Rachel, had prophesied that Ella would fall for Patrick if she went to work for him, but Ella had snorted and produced her good sense, her age and her pragmatism as evidence that she was proof against a thousand Patricks. So it had been, and a relationship had developed that had never overstepped the mark into either formality or informality, its tone dictated, Ella was sure, by her own cool head. Patrick could be such a boy

... But he was a man, too, and the man in him had clearly now got the upper hand and was bearing him away to Germany to collect his wits.

"He's going to Germany," she told Trish Pardoe in the Loxford shop. "For three weeks." The shop was full, it being a Friday, but she lowered her voice all the same. "I think he's come to his senses."

"She looks terrible," Trish said. "I saw her getting on the early bus. White as a sheet."

"Perhaps he said something."

Trish rooted in a box of crisp packets for the cheese-and-onion-flavoured ones. "Will you go and see Peter, all the same?"

"I don't know. Not if—"

"Leave well alone, I think."

"But you thought—"

"I was upset," Trish said, "wasn't I? It was a shock, seeing them. But I've got enough to worry about, what with Mum and the Brownies being threatened with amalgamation with Quindale. I ask you! Poor little mites. Might as well send them into Woodborough and have done with it. There now. I always put these on top, because they're the most popular."

"Then why," said Ella, nettled, "don't you put them at the bottom?"

She packed for Patrick with exaggerated care, feeling that this trip was of great significance. He seemed, she had to admit, very cheerful, almost jaunty, and not in the least like a sober adult taking a blow bravely. But then, Patrick was resilient. When his mistress had left, Ella had heard him whistling while he shaved less than a week later.

He surveyed his suitcase. "You're a pearl."

"Nonsense," she said, "I'm paid for it."

He grinned. He said, "I may not be a whole three weeks, of course. Why don't you go away, go to your sister? You don't want to be stuck here—"

"To my great chagrin, I like it here."

"Me too."

She set her mouth. "Time you got away, though."

"And what is that supposed to mean?"

"You know perfectly well."

He laughed. He picked up his case and started across the hall.

"I read your mind like an open book, Ella. Keep an eye on the Rectory for me, while I'm gone."

She said grimly, "There'll be nothing to see."

He stopped at the front door and turned to her. "Oh, I hope there will. That's the chief reason I'm going. Absence, as they say, makes the heart grow fonder." And then he let himself out into the sunshine.

Anna read the letter several times. It was quite a courteous letter, but it was firm as well. It was from the publishers of her translations, a firm in Bristol. They were sorry, they said, to have received no work from her for some months now, despite frequent reminders (oh, help, those envelopes pushed into the kitchen-dresser drawer in the hope of their just vanishing) and assumed that she was no longer in a position to work regularly for them. As they themselves were now under increasing pressure from European manufacturers extending into the British Isles, and vice versa, they had to be certain of the reliability of their translators. They therefore thanked her for past work, requested the return of anything unfinished and begged her to regard this letter as the termination of any arrangement between them.

It should be a relief, Anna thought, and it's the reverse. She felt a sudden, irrational affection for that mad Oriental table upstairs at which she had sat for so many resentful, disciplined hours, coupled with a sharp nostalgia for those past times when things had seemed under her control. She might not want to translate another word, but she might not want to see it go from her either. This was not in the least logical, she knew, but sometimes the least logical things were the ones that twisted a slow knife in you until you cried out.

She went upstairs and looked at her books and papers. The last manual—of which she had only done twenty pages—was the German specifications for a machine that laminated plastic. She closed it sadly, and made a little pile of it, and her few typed pages of translation, and another manual, in French, that she hadn't even opened. Then she typed a letter to the publishers, saying that she was sorry, and took everything downstairs to make a parcel.

Later, she showed the letter to Peter. He read it without comment, and handed it back to her.

"Aren't you pleased?"

"I assumed this would happen."

The parcel, ready for posting, lay on the kitchen table between them. She longed to pick it up and hurl it at him.

"Aren't you triumphant? Isn't this what you wanted? I've got no job now, nothing. You can disband the parish group, if you want. Here I am, Peter, here I am. Just the Rector's wife."

He looked at her. After a pause he said, not unkindly,

"I'm afraid, Anna, that simply saying it doesn't make it so."

The telephone rang. Peter made no move to answer it. Anna picked up the receiver.

"Anna? This is Celia. How are you? Good, good. Now, I hardly like to trouble you, knowing how busy you are, but what I'm going to ask won't take much time—"

"Celia," Anna said, interrupting, "just ask away. I've got all the time in the world."

15

❖ ❖ ❖

ON ANNA'S LAST day at Pricewell's, she was presented with a double begonia in a china pot and Mr.
Mulgrove said to all the staff who were assembled for
their lunch break that it had been a pleasure to have
Anna working for them, and that they would miss her.
Anna, clutching the curious and un-English flower, felt
slightly tearful and said she would miss them too. Only
Tim, her erstwhile supervisor, who clearly felt a personal
betrayal at her departure, asked her why she was going,
just when she'd got used to it. Anna, shackled for new
reasons by old habits of loyalty, said, "Because I ought
to be at home more."

Tim looked unconvinced. In his world, the women
were always out, took all kinds of jobs, seemed to feel
no obligation to do anything they weren't inclined to do.
His own mother had weekly rows with his father over
both her job at a launderette and her regular expeditions
with girlfriends to watch the male stripper down at The
Royal George. Tim was used to seeing his father's ap-
oplectic flailings at his mother's independence; he

thought it was something that probably afflicted you as you got older. Perhaps it had hit Anna's old man, perhaps he'd said she'd got to stay at home and visit the sick or whatever vicars' wives did. But then Anna didn't seem to Tim like the kind of wife who took orders, even from a vicar.

He said, truthfully, "I'll miss you. I don't know anyone like you."

Mr. Mulgrove said, "I'm really sorry about this. We hoped you'd have a future with us."

Heather from flours and dried fruits said, "Don't blame you. Who wants to spend their life stacking bleeding sultanas?"

Anna took her last pay envelope, drank her last cup of subsidised canteen coffee, hung up her blue overall and went out into the market-place. In her bag, she carried the plastic badge she had worn, the badge which said, "I'm Anna. Can I help you?" Glancing up at the sky, behind whose high summer clouds dwelt that inscrutable power whose presence she could not quite get out of her mind, she thought of her badge and its slogan, and said to herself: It wouldn't hurt *You* to wear one . . .

It was market day, and Woodborough was full. The country buses brought people in after breakfast and took them away before lunch, their carrier bags bulging with fish from the woman who travelled up from Devon, jeans and T-shirts from the Pakistanis who travelled down from Birmingham, and cheese from the man who made his own from herds kept in pastures not five miles from Woodborough. Threading her way among the stalls, Anna bought some vacuum-cleaner bags, a bargain box of soap powder and a punnet of strawberries for Flora, who had crept into her bed at dawn that morning and said uncharacteristically, "I'm worried about you."

"Don't be. I'm fine."

"Mothers always say that. Verity says when her mother says it, it means she's got a migraine."

Flora couldn't cuddle, never had been able to. She lay awkwardly against Anna for a few minutes, then bumped a clumsy kiss on her, climbed out of bed again and padded back to her room. Peter didn't stir. Missing Flora, Anna took revenge upon his stillness by wishing the bed was just hers.

Now she looked at the strawberries. Should she buy another punnet for Peter? Would he notice? Was he remotely concerned as to whether she gave him strawberries or a banana? Or a black eye? She glanced at her watch. Half an hour before she collected Flora, half an hour in which to dawdle about Woodborough while her mind scurried round and round its new trap, like a mouse on a wheel.

She left the market-place and turned down Sheep Street, a narrow street forbidden to traffic which Woodborough Council had dotted with tree-shaded benches usually occupied by clumps of dismal teenagers waiting, without much hope, for action. Ahead of Anna, a tall young woman was pushing a pram. She stopped the pram outside a newsagent, stooped to pick up the baby (it was new, Anna could see, from its size and the swaddled oblivion of its tiny head), and then, as if recollecting something, abruptly put the baby back, tucked it in decisively and pushed the pram onwards. Anna, who had not thought of it for years, suddenly remembered her twenty-three-year-old self outside a newsagent in a Bristol suburb, making the abrupt decision not to buy chocolate. She had half lifted Charlotte from the pram,

even, just as that young woman had done. She could see
Charlotte clearly, a neat, small baby with a dark, downy
head, and her own hands holding her, hands emerging
from the sleeves of a scarlet duffel coat Laura had given
her, a stiff, thick coat with a hood and black-lacquered
toggles. That was twenty years ago, that October afternoon, twenty years, nearly half my life . . .

Anna crept to one of the benches and sat down. There
was a gloomy girl at the far end, her feet thrust into
huge, black shoes, smoking ferociously. She didn't look
at Anna. Anna sat cradling her parcels, inhaling the peculiar, synthetic, red smell of the strawberries, grappling
with herself. Where had she come, in the last twenty
years, but round in a huge, slow circle? Even the children, even now Jonathan, were they enough, was he?
Should she now just break cover and run for dear life,
literally for her dear life? But it wouldn't do to run to
Jonathan, she could only do that if she was running a
hundred per cent away from something else. All the
same, thank heavens for Jonathan. She thought she could
hear him, she was sure she could hear his voice. She
looked round, enchanted, and there he was, coming lei-
surely up Sheep Street, accompanied by Luke. Luke
looked just as usual, in jeans and a T-shirt, his denim
jacket slung over one shoulder. He was listening intently
to Jonathan, slightly turning his head towards him. Jonathan was deep in explanation, gesturing for emphasis.
They walked slowly past Anna, quite absorbed, not seeing her. As for her, after a first, quick, involuntary gesture of greeting, she didn't move, simply sat there and
watched them drift obliviously by.

The girl on the bench had watched them too, particularly Luke, with resentful interest. Anna said, on impulse, to her, "That's my son."

The girl stared. Then she shrugged. "Yeah," she said, "and I'm the Queen of England," and slouched away.

Flora ate her strawberries on the bus, throwing the hulls out of the window. Anna told her about seeing Luke, and Flora said Luke had been to St. Saviour's and seen her, too, and he'd said living in Woodborough was great and she thought she'd like to stay with Verity for a few nights and live in Woodborough as well.

"Suppose," Anna said, "just suppose I wanted to live in Woodborough?"

"You couldn't. You have to stay in Loxford."

"Do I?"

Flora ate the last strawberry. "You know you do. That's what happens."

The village green was already showing signs of summer wear. The mothers, waiting for the bus, had trampled their habitual spot in a depressed, yellowing circle, and there were bare patches in front of the two benches and the litter bin. Anna and Flora climbed down the steps of the bus and the mothers said, "Warm enough for you, Mrs. B?" and, "Like your hat," to Flora, who scowled and put her convent Panama behind her back. They trailed together across the green, Flora bumping her school bag behind her like a recalcitrant dog, and Anna holding her begonia tightly, as if it were a talisman.

From the landing windows of the Old Rectory, Ella watched them. She hardly knew Flora, who seemed to her a precocious and unattractive child with none of Luke's undoubted warmth of heart. She glanced at Flora, in her striped St. Saviour's summer dress, red and white, and thought, for a brief and disquieting moment, of motherhood, a state she could hardly even visualize. Anna was a mother, and Anna interested Ella far more. Walking beside Flora in a long, full-skirted, dark-blue dress sashed in buttercup yellow—why, Ella thought crossly, why were Anna's clothes so irritating?—she looked as if she belonged to Flora, and was, at the same time, separate. She looked, too, thoroughly despondent. Ella studied her. Her shoulders drooped a little, her head was slightly bent, both noticeable in a woman who usually carried herself with assurance. She seemed to be bent over some lurid, pink-flowered plant she was carrying, as if she were protecting it. Ella took a breath. It couldn't be a plant Patrick had sent. Could it? It didn't look Patrick's style; he would send lilies or an orchid, something exotic and showy. She thought of Patrick. "Absence makes the heart grow fonder," he'd said as he left. Looking at Anna, Ella now thought, with a sinking heart, that perhaps he might have been right.

Anna put the begonia on the kitchen table.

"It's an awful colour," Flora said.

"I know. But I feel very fond of it."

Flora began to rummage for biscuits. "What job'll you do now?"

"Celia has given me a piece to write for the parish magazine. To try and encourage people to help clean the church. I think you should have bread before a biscuit."

"That won't take long," Flora said, finding two digestives and ignoring the bread bin, "that's not a job."

"No. I'll find something else. Don't worry."

"You keep saying that. You said that to Luke."

"I mean it."

"You can't just switch off worry," Flora said. "You can't just take an aspirin."

Anna ran water into the kettle. "What exactly worries you?"

Flora spread her arms, showering crumbs. "The feeling here."

Anna said nothing. She put the lid on the kettle and plugged it in.

"When I grow up," Flora said to her mother's back, "I'm never, ever going to marry a vicar."

Daniel and Jonathan Byrne sat in Daniel's study. They had not put any lamps on, because the light was fading so beautifully outside the window that it seemed a pity to outshine it. Miss Lambe had given them coleslaw for supper, and Daniel was revolving in his mind how to tell her tactfully that he found coleslaw disgusting. He thought he might say that it gave him indigestion (it didn't; nothing did) because that would let them both out so easily. Caring for the tenderness of Miss Lambe's feelings—as small and vulnerable as seedlings—was becoming an exhausting and full-time job.

Jonathan was not thinking about coleslaw. He was less chivalrous towards Miss Lambe—perversely, she adored his mild carelessness towards her—and simply hadn't eaten his, pushing the pale, glistening heap to the side of his plate, and leaving it there. He was thinking about Anna, and about Luke, whom he was getting to know and getting to like. Luke's conscience was deeply troubled at leaving home, at abandoning his mother, but as he could see no way to improve anything and was being driven demented by the atmosphere, getting out had seemed the only course. He had said this quite directly to Jonathan, on their second meeting, and Jonathan had said there was only point and merit to sacrifice as long as it achieved something. The next natural step would have been to talk about Anna, but both avoided it. Jonathan had talked to no-one about Anna; he simply thought about her.

He said to Daniel now, "I want to tell you something."

Daniel's mind, which had abandoned coleslaw for tomorrow's meeting with the Bishop, came swiftly back. "Of course."

"I'm in love with Anna Bouverie."

There was a fractional pause and then Daniel said, "Yes, I know."

"How do you know?"

"Little things. Remarks. The look of you."

"And?"

"What do you mean?"

"Does a sermon follow? Will you try and stop me?"

"Have I ever," Daniel said, "tried to stop you doing anything?"

"But what about Peter Bouverie? He's a priest of yours—"

"Are you asking me to make up your mind?"

"Oh no," Jonathan said, "I've done that. I want to marry her."

"She is married."

"Daniel—"

"I can't encourage you. I may understand why you feel as you do, but I can't encourage you to act on it. Marriage is difficult enough, these days; for one thing it tends to go on for so long, but it mustn't be attacked, undermined, by people who have the power to withhold themselves, even if they haven't the inclination."

"And Anna?"

Jonathan couldn't see Daniel's face in the dark, but he could hear that his voice had softened.

"Ah. Anna."

"Throw Anna to the wolves in the name of ortho-
doxy? Is that what you think?"

"I think individuality of choice and personal convenience are inadequate as moral principles."

"Choice and convenience! Is that what you think has
brought about Anna's situation?"

Daniel swung round in his chair. "Don't cheapen
what I say. For wisdom and balance, humanity must give
its unequivocal support to the defence of human life and
to Christian institutions such as marriage."

Jonathan got up. He crossed the room to stand over
Daniel.

"There speaks the natural celibate. Sacrifice of the
spirit, however futile and destructive to the individual,
is to be encouraged as long as appearances are main-
tained for the comfort of your *Christian* society."

"Not comfort. For morality."

"Morality! And is it moral for Peter Bouverie to
starve his wife and parish of everything but pure form?"

"He's a sick man," Daniel said.

Jonathan shouted, "Well, do something about him!
And leave his wife to me!"

Daniel bent his head. "Has she said she would like
this?"

"Not in so many words."

"Then your love isn't returned?"

"Oh yes. But she's encumbered. She can't rush forward freely as I can. There's her husband and children.
And there's your damned Church. Where's its tolerance
and intellectual subtlety? Where, for God's sake, is its
vision?"

Daniel rose too. He said sadly, "You know what I
think. You know I think the modern Church lacks ho-

liness because we've played about with the truth. I hate its narrowness of spirit.''

"Yes. So you say. But may Anna not be allowed to hate it too and to try to escape from it?''

Daniel turned and put his hands on his brother's shoulders. "Give me a day or two. Let me talk to the Bishop.''

"What good will that do? What bishop can ever decide anything? And what has the Bishop got to do with it, anyway?''

"I must,'' Daniel said, "for Christian and Church reasons. For you and Anna. And for poor Peter Bouverie.''

It was the first time for weeks that Anna had been at home at lunchtime. She made Peter a salad and called him to the kitchen. He said that he was terribly busy and would like to have it on a tray in his study. Anna carried it in, in silence.

"You are very kind,'' said Peter, as if speaking to someone he hardly knew.

"Not at all.''

"Have you had a good morning?''

"No.''

"I'm sorry to hear it.''

"I spent the morning being congratulated by the village. Celia Hooper even stopped her car to say with a merry laugh that I'd now put them all out of a job. She sounded quite resentful.''

Peter turned his head away. Would she never stop? Would she never admit defeat, but make a grievance, a point of discord, out of everything? He had never thought, until recently, that Anna was a greedy woman. He didn't look at her; he didn't want to. He looked instead at his salad, at the slices of cold chicken, at the lettuce leaves sprinkled with herbs. He said, "Thank you for this."

Anna paused by the door. "I'm going into Woodborough. To collect Flora."

"I thought she came on the bus."

"She does. I want to go with her. I need the occupation. I suppose I mayn't have the car?"

"I'm afraid not."

"And I suppose we couldn't have a walk together. Instead?"

He sighed. He said, "I have parishioners coming." Patrick O'Sullivan's housekeeper had asked to come, he couldn't imagine why.

"Please," Anna said.

Peter didn't reply. After a second or two, she went out and closed the door gently behind her.

In the kitchen, her own salad lay on the table. She felt tremendously unhungry and put it in the fridge, thinking: Never mind, Luke can make it into a sandwich later. But Luke wouldn't be here later. No-one would be, except herself and Peter and poor Flora, who didn't like the feeling in the house. Who could blame her? Who *could* like the feeling? Standing by the refrigerator and gazing out of the window at those orderly, green rows of vegetables she had planted, Anna felt that, almost without realizing it, she had turned some kind of corner. There was nothing to be gained anymore from steeling herself and ploughing on—and there was plenty to lose. I've given him every chance, she told herself, every chance to come close to me, and every olive branch I offer he breaks across his knee.

She glanced at the clock. It said five past one. Over three hours until Flora returned, three hours in which she had more than half intended that she would go and see Jonathan. But on reflection, she decided she would not do that. She would instead walk down her garden past her beans and peas, past her washing blowing on the line and through the neglected gate at the bottom. Then she would make her way to the hills beyond the river, just going straight across country like a wild animal, and climb the slopes to that mysterious copse. When she got there, she knew she would have decided, she knew she would be sure what she would do.

She opened the back door, her spirits suddenly lifting, and closed it firmly behind her. The few clouds were high in a clear sky and the air smelled clean, full of the scents of grass and earth. Then she paused, checked by an impulse to go back into the house to say goodbye to Peter. Why? He thought she was going to Woodborough; he expected her to be out. She shook her head at the thought of him. Does one ever know, she asked herself, the difference between love and habit? Above her, a blackbird sang, and then another answered it from yards away, quite sharply, as if in reprimand. Thrusting her hands into her pockets, Anna stepped out along her garden path towards the distant hills.

When Ella got up to go, Peter rose and showed her courteously out of the house. He seemed perfectly calm. He had been perfectly calm all the way through their interview, so that it was impossible for Ella to tell whether he knew the whole story already. At least his apparent tranquillity had made it much easier for Ella, who had been able to relate what she knew unemotionally, as if she were reciting facts to a police sergeant. Peter had nodded once or twice, and glanced at her occasionally, but mostly he had looked past her, at a picture hanging just behind her which she saw, when she got up, was a seascape, a watercolour of waves and foam and sky and, in the foreground, a little wooden dinghy beached on shingle.

On the Rectory doorstep, she said, "Goodbye. And thank you for seeing me."

Peter said, "Goodbye." Ella waited for him to thank her for coming, but he didn't, so she turned, a little clumsily, and went down the drive beside the churchyard wall. She felt tremendously depressed and not at all relieved. It was certainly the right thing to have done, and it was equally certainly a most unpleasant thing to have done. Her sister Rachel would have said she should have done it weeks ago, nipped the whole nasty business in the bud.

She reached the lane and squared her shoulders. Across the village green, Elaine Dodswell was planting petunias in two urns that guarded her little bridge in summer, in addition to the frogs. A pang of envy seized Ella. What wouldn't she give, at that moment, for a cottage of her own, with her own untroublesome petunias, instead of this ill-defined life, half prefect, half parasite, on the coattails of Patrick O'Sullivan's wishes and whims? She quickened her steps and Elaine, seeing her, brandished a trowel at her and called out the offer of a cup of tea. Thankful for the distraction, Ella nodded, and hurried towards her.

After Ella had gone, Peter went into the sitting-room and sat carefully on the sofa. He sat there for a long time, slipping his thoughts through his mind like the beads on a rosary. One thing was very plain and that was that he wasn't at all surprised; indeed, he felt almost relieved to know the key to Anna's extraordinary behaviour recently. What was more, knowing the key, being in power by possessing his new knowledge, made him feel, for the first time in months, curiously elated. He looked around the room, reduced once more to its habitual untidiness, and found he even wanted to smile. It was such a relief, such a violent, savage, unspeakable relief to know that he hadn't imagined things after all, that his revulsion from Anna had been instinctive—rightly instinctive—and that he wasn't, oh, joy of joys, going off his head. His unconscious mind had known what his conscious mind had refused to know. In a curious way, he felt himself to be free, as if shackles had fallen from him. He found that he was trembling.

He got up and began to pace the room, rhythmically banging one closed fist into the other open hand. His father used to do that, and it always, Peter remembered, made Kitty nervous because she never knew how to react to her husband's perturbations of spirit, being incapable of either dealing with them or leaving them alone. Peter thought of Kitty with great affection. There was a loyal woman! A selfless, devoted, faithful woman! He forgot that most of his life she had almost driven him mad with her indecisiveness, her fluttering mind, and that it was Anna who had kept up communication with her. Now, pacing his sitting-room, Peter thought of his mother as someone almost noble. Even so, he did not contemplate telephoning her. He simply pictured her in his mind as a symbol of good womanhood and as a contrast to Anna with her perversity, her rebelliousness, her seething dissatisfaction.

He paused by the window and looked at the church, across the drive and the churchyard wall. He felt no urge at all to go and sit in it, no flicker of desire to pray. He felt he could never forgive Anna for having perceived in him this growing hollowness, and the fear that accompanied it. Oh, her behaviour had been so calculated, almost cynical, a carefully orchestrated campaign against him, culminating in this offensive revelation of a liaison with Patrick O'Sullivan! Well, at least this was a culmination. It had made up his mind for him. Either Anna repented and made amends for what she had done, or he would divorce her. Simple.

He left the sitting-room and went upstairs to wash. He combed his hair, looked at himself without affection in the bathroom mirror, and exchanged his cardigan for a jacket. Distasteful though it was, his first obligation, as a clergyman, was to confide the details of his troubles to his superior, the Archdeacon of Woodborough. He thought he would simply call, on the off-chance, so that by the time he faced Anna with her choice of futures the facts would already lie safely in official hands and she could not distort them. If Daniel Byrne wasn't in, Peter thought, he would just wait.

He left Anna a note on the kitchen table. It said, "Back later, P," and he wrote the time, "3.10," underneath, and the date. Then he locked the back door and put the key under the brick, which was, he had been telling Anna for ten years, the most blindingly obvious place to put it, and went out to the garage.

He drove slowly through Loxford, raising his hand in response to the few people who waved to him. He was conscious of his hand going up and down steadily, regally. How calm I am, he thought, how released, how free. Lady Mayhew was crossing the green with her dogs and she began to gesture towards him, as if she wanted to speak to him, but he felt that he had no obligation to anyone that afternoon because he was, serenely and composedly, bound upon something that was almost a mission. As he turned away from the green towards the main Woodborough road, he could see, in his driving mirror, Lady Mayhew's obvious exasperation. He almost smiled because it mattered to him so little.

He drove on between the still green wheatfields. He observed that the barn on the right which had been so damaged in the winter gales was having a new roof put on, and beyond it, a field of linseed was in full, blue flower. He saw scraps of litter in the verge and wild, purplish cranesbill in the hedge, and ahead of him, swerving blackly across the tarmac, the tyre marks of a skidding car. He felt acutely observant, as if the world had come into a sharp, clear new focus now that he possessed the key to what had been the matter. It wasn't just relief either; it was something more akin to triumph.

The lane turned sharply just before the main road. Peter braked, as he always did, changed gear, and drove smoothly round. The main road was quiet ahead of him. He pushed his foot forward to step on the brake, and as he did so a bright, detailed, unwanted, unbearable picture came into his mind of Anna, naked, in the arms of Patrick O'Sullivan. Peter gave a little cry, which turned into a much greater cry, and the car sprang forward of its own accord and as if in response to his sudden agony. Blinded by tears, Peter simply let it go.

At the inquest, the bus driver said he had had no chance. He'd been coming along, all slowed down and ready to turn down the Loxford lane, when the Reverend's car had shot out, without any warning, and headed for him, straight for him. It was all over in seconds. He'd braked, of course, braked as hard as he could, but there was no avoiding it. He said that if it was all right, he'd like to express his real sympathy for the Reverend's family and tell them he'd be haunted by those ten seconds the rest of his life. Then he broke down and had to be comforted by a constable.

16

❖ ❖ ❖

LOXFORD CHURCH *WAS* packed for Peter's funeral.
Anna had said she would like it to be full of flowers,
and it was, most touchingly, with all the fragile, impractical flowers that she loved, like delphiniums, already shedding petals, and cow parsley, distributing its
peppery dust. The Bishop came, with his wife, and he
and Daniel officiated together, and Peter lay before them
in his coffin, below the chancel steps.

Anna sat in her usual pew, with the children and the
grandmothers beside her. Charlotte had come down from
Edinburgh on an overnight bus and, despite having hardly slept, was composed and controlled. At one point, she
even briefly took Anna's hand. On the other side, Luke
and Flora wept and wept, Flora out of fear and Luke out
of anguish.

"I didn't love him," Luke had hissed to Charlotte in
the few moments they had had alone together. "Don't
you see? I'm a bastard. I feel so guilty."

"You did love him," Charlotte said, who had had all
night in a bus to think about this. "You did. You just

267

didn't like him much recently. He didn't like himself.''

They neither of them said anything of this to Anna. She was most affectionate to them, but nothing she said invited a confidential conversation.

"She's working it out herself," Charlotte said. She felt extremely old suddenly, tired and experienced. "None of it's straightforward for her."

"It's shock," everyone else was saying. How could it be otherwise? What would you feel, they said to each other, if you came back from a country walk and found a policeman in your garden with such news as that? Of course, Peter and Anna hadn't seen eye to eye just recently, but what marriage is ever all plain sailing? You had to admire her dignity. Really, her dignity was perfect. So brave; too brave, of course, there'd be a reaction soon, a breakdown. Most of the congregation, craning round each other to look at the occupants of the Rectory pew, speculated with an uneasy excitement about Anna's precarious future.

So, without excitement, did Laura. She stood beside Charlotte in a hat waving with funereal plumes, and felt anxiety almost obliterate her grief. She thought intermittently of Peter, of young, student Peter painstakingly scrubbing a corner of her kitchen table to make it fit to eat off, but she thought predominantly of Anna. Her heart sank when she thought of Anna, because it seemed to her that Anna was about to embark, and not out of choice, upon exactly the shapeless, unstructured, struggling life that she had had herself, and that she knew to be such a weary battle for the spirit. She had believed Anna wasted in her marriage to Peter; now that he was dead, the uncertainty of the future seemed more destructive than the waste of the past. Laura heaved a gargantuan sigh and a shred of feather detached itself from her hat and floated down on to Kitty's prayer book.

Kitty couldn't see her prayer book for tears. She couldn't believe that she was not simply a widow now, but childless too. What have I been for? she asked herself over and over again. When the fragment of feather alighted on her book, she thought it was a spider for a moment and gave a little shriek. Behind her, the congregation murmured in sympathy. Poor little woman, and Peter her only child! She mopped and blew, and around her feet crumpled paper handkerchiefs gathered like fallen petals. Must pull myself together, she told herself, stand up like Laura. It won't help Anna if I give way, or the children, it won't help anybody. She heard her father's voice of half a century before saying, "Tears, Katherine, should only be shed for others." But I can't, Kitty thought desperately. I can't, I can't; I only know how to cry for myself. Silently, majestically, Laura passed her an enormous handkerchief of plum-coloured silk.

As the priest who had known Peter the longest, John Jacobs climbed into the pulpit to give the address. He said how sad he was to be in Peter's pulpit on such an occasion. He said how his heart went out to Peter's family. He described Peter's great spirituality and his devotion to duty and his kindness and his work for the diocese. He spoke of a man of God who had understood the needs of the rural church. He spoke of a priest who had never, for all his faith, compromised his family. He spoke for a long time and illustrated his address with anecdotes about Peter that seemed appropriate to almost any clergyman in the diocese except Peter. He concluded by saying that, if ever a priest had been a square peg in a square hole, that priest was Peter in Loxford. The congregation listened politely. The Bishop looked out of the south chancel window. Anna looked mostly at the floor.

Then they all filed out into the churchyard for the burial. It was a proper burial, in an old-fashioned grave, as Peter had wished, his father having had a full burial before him. Luke led Flora away from the graveside and sat on a tombstone, holding her on his knee. Charlotte took Anna's arm. Kitty took Laura's hand. When the coffin had been lowered in, they all threw flowers down after it.

"You OK?" Charlotte hissed. Her arm clamped Anna's to her side.

Anna nodded.

"What," Charlotte demanded, "what, what?"

Anna turned and kissed her.

"I'm so relieved," she said, "so relieved. For him almost more than for me."

There was tea afterwards at the Rectory. The parish group had made it, plates and plates of sandwiches and scones and ginger biscuits and slices of fruit cake. They had set up the Mothers' Union tea urn in the kitchen, and borrowed the Loxford village-hall teacups, all six dozen of them, and it looked as if they would all be used. Anna, feeling tea was somehow not sufficiently encouraging, had bought some bottles of sherry from Pricewell's, and Luke was detailed to be butler. He came upon Anna, with his tray of glasses, and said to her, "I'm sorry, Mum, I'm sorry, I'm sorry."

She looked at him. She wanted, violently, to embrace him, tray and all. She said, "You drink one of those. Straight down. We'll talk later."

The atmosphere in the sitting-room was heady with relief. It was full of people holding plates and the plates were full of food. The Bishop was slowly eating sandwiches, one after another, almost absently. He said to Anna, "You are all so much in our prayers."

"Yes, indeed," his wife said. She looked keenly at Anna. Anna was very interesting to her.

"I want to talk to you," Anna said.

The Bishop looked mildly alarmed.

"Not about the past," Anna said, "about the future."

The Bishop thought of housing, of the three Bouverie children. His brow cleared. "Of course."

"No," Anna said, reading his mind. "About my future, what I should do."

He peered at her. His wife watched.

"I'm not putting this well," Anna said, "and I don't suppose now is the time. But I have a plan, you see, a plan that will involve the diocese. At least, it ought to involve the diocese."

The Bishop said, "Come and see me. In a week or so. Just ring my secretary and come and see me."

"Thank you." She smiled up at him. Celia Hooper appeared with a plate of sandwiches, flagged "cucumber," smiling too, but in a hostessy way.

"I say," said the Bishop, taking two.

"His favourite," said his wife. She looked after Anna, who had moved away. "Wonderful, really. So composed."

"One always hopes there won't be a reaction," Celia said.

The Bishop's wife looked at her. "There's usually a reaction," she said crisply, "if there's guilt. Guilt is much harder to live with than grief." She thought of Peter Bouverie coming out of her husband's study when he knew he would not be Archdeacon. "I wish," she said with some vehemence, "I wish I had taken the trouble to get to know Anna Bouverie months, years, ago. I wish—'' She stopped. Celia and the Bishop looked at her.

"Have some of Mrs. Pardoe's fruit cake," Celia said.

"I say," said the Bishop.

Daniel found Anna in the kitchen. She was refilling the urn with kettles of boiling water, her hand muffled in a tea towel.

"My dear."

She put the kettle down. Daniel took her in his arms. She said, "I've only said this to Charlotte, but I'm so relieved—"

"I know."

"The service was terrible, so false, except for the lovely bit by the grave."

Daniel let her go, and she picked up the kettle again. "The burial service," Daniel said, "is the most triumphant, the most exhilarating of all the services. I know no music as resoundingly confident as the English of the burial service. Perhaps that very confidence is what people shrink from now."

"I don't," Anna said, pouring. "I'm thankful for it. I'm desperately sad that Peter got so empty and that we grew so far apart, but there wasn't a remedy. It was all too deep in him and in us, and too complicated."

"Did he know about Jonathan?"

Anna looked straight at him. "No."

"Oh Anna—"

"Why?" Anna said. "Why, 'Oh Anna'?" Her gaze was candid. "Why should I feel guilty? I'm not guilty. While he was alive, I was always racked with guilt, but now he's dead it's stopped. I know I was a good wife to him. I was a good wife until he didn't want me anymore."

She turned away to fill the kettle again and plug it in.

"You had an affair with Jonathan."

"And is that morally worse than having an affair with duty? The withdrawing of the essence of yourself, of your emotional and imaginative generosity, is what kills relationships. I never withdrew mine. Look," Anna said turning back, "I've come to love you dearly, and to admire you, but there are things about men and women that I now know better than you."

Daniel bowed his head. Anna watched him and thought of the previous evening when poor distraught Ella Pringle had come round and had told Anna that she had been the cause of Peter's car crash. Anna, who had never liked Ella much, had found herself being genuinely tremendously sorry for her. She had taken her into the sitting-room, and had sat beside her on the sofa, soothing and patting. Ella's story seemed to her a sad and scruffy little business, and not significant.

"It was pure coincidence," Anna said, over and over again. "You are not to blame. He was in a very sad state, very wound up."

"I'm leaving Patrick," Ella said. "I can't stand his attitude anymore. I believed him. I believed he had a relationship with you."

"No," Anna said, "he was playing a game." She looked at Ella. "Are you in love with him?"

"No," Ella said. "Yes."

"It's harder to leave than to stay," Anna said. "If it's any comfort to you, I had decided to leave, the very afternoon Peter was killed. I came down from the copse to tell him that, and found the policeman. I've been given freedom, but I would have left. You must, too. Patrick is too arbitrary to live with, too tyrannical."

Joanna Trollope

And Ella, who disliked touching women, leaned across and kissed her.

"I've learned so much in a week," Anna said now to Daniel, "that I'm quite exhausted."

He smiled. "Life certainly never gets any easier. Or simpler."

The kitchen door opened. Elaine Dodswell came in, followed by Trish Pardoe. They were carrying piles of empty plates.

"I'm ever so sorry," Elaine said, looking from Daniel to Anna, "I'd no idea—"

"You weren't interrupting," Daniel said. "Nothing that can't be resumed."

Elaine said to Anna, "Oh, I do hope you've eaten, you must eat, you know, it doesn't help not to eat. Oh Anna, I'm so sorry, I'm so terribly sorry. What are you going to do?"

"Do?"

"Yes," Elaine said. She put the plates down and gestured at the kitchen, at the table and the cream-painted units and the blue-checked curtains overprinted with vegetables that had been a present from Kitty. "What are you going to do, poor Anna, now that you aren't the Rector's wife anymore?"

Anna stood by the front door so that they could all say goodbye. Most people, particularly those she hardly knew, kissed her with fervour. The sherry had clearly been a good idea. Flora came and leaned tiredly against her, and so got kissed as well. Her eyes, behind her glasses, were swollen and tender from crying.

Isobel Thompson kissed Anna warmly. "Come and stay. Don't be alone. Don't hesitate to ask for anything."

"I won't," Anna said.

"Sometimes it's so much easier to talk to a woman—"

"I'll talk to you because you're Isobel. Not because you're a woman or a priest."

"Oh Anna," Isobel said. "You don't change—"

"Oh, but I have. I've stopped pretending."

"Yes," Isobel said uncertainly, moving back a little. "Yes."

Colonel Richardson embraced Anna with relief. "My dear," he said. He knew what to do with her now; she had stepped back into a category he could manage, the plucky little widow putting on a wonderful front. Damned good-looking, too, good carriage, great dignity, never a public tear. "Don't forget," he said, "Marjorie and I are always there. Anything you want. Only have to ask. Anything. Frightful business." He wrung her hand.

Marjorie Richardson brushed her face with a powdered cheek. She looked at Anna oddly, as if about to speak, but said nothing.

"Mummy," Flora said.

Anna bent. "Yes, darling."

"Where," said Flora, her eyes widening in alarm, "where exactly did Daddy go?"

Several people were waiting. Anna looked round at them; Lady Mayhew, Miss Dunstable, that poor deaf man from Snead, even Mr. Biddle in a bursting decent dark suit. She said, quite clearly, to Flora, "To paradise."

Ella put Patrick's chicken casserole for supper into the Aga, and went upstairs to brush her hair. She also put on some scent, her new lipstick and her pearl earrings. She felt she must be armoured.

Patrick was in his small sitting-room, in the armchair

Anna had briefly occupied on the night he had heard her crying in the lane, with a tumbler of whisky and a financial newspaper. He had not been to the funeral; he had not commented, even, on Peter's death, beyond saying to Ella in a tone she didn't at all care for, "I wonder what triggered him off?"

She said now, "May I speak to you for a moment?"

"Of course," he said. He got up and indicated a chair. "Drink?"

"No, thank you."

"I see. So I'm in for some kind of wigging."

"No," Ella said. She sat down and crossed her legs. He surveyed her with approval.

"How was the funeral?"

"Sad," Ella said. She waited for him to ask her about Anna, but he didn't, he simply went on watching her.

"I've come down to say that I am leaving at the end of the month." She paused.

"And?"

"And?"

"And why are you going and what are you going to do?"

"I've applied to be matron at Snead Hall."

He laughed. He stared at her and he laughed. Then he sat down again.

"My dear Ella, they'll pay you half what I do and you'll moulder—"

"Anything," Ella said, "anything is better than staying with a man who plays games with other people's feelings."

"Who have you been talking to?"

"It doesn't matter."

"I can guess," Patrick said. "She doesn't matter either. Not now." He looked at Ella with a queer sideways glance. "I didn't play games with Anna Bouverie, you know. She played them with me. She used me. It's never happened to me before and I don't like it."

"I don't want to talk about it," Ella said.

"I've had everything generous I've done thrown back in my face. Luke, Anna, now you. Can you imagine how I feel?"

"Oh yes—"

Patrick leaned forward. "Please stay. All the usual inducements, of course, more money, more time off, but really because I need you to. I want you to."

Ella stood up. "So sorry, but no. I'll stay until the end of August. Then I shall go. You'd be better off with a couple to look after you, in any case. There are so many jobs for a man."

"I may not even stay here—"

"I didn't think it would last long."

Patrick looked up at her. "I believed in it all, you know."

"All I know," said Ella briskly in her usual voice, "is that now Anna Bouverie is free for the having, you don't want her anymore. And that you are furious with her for that." She marched to the door. "If I ever marry, Patrick O'Sullivan, I shall make sure that my mate for life is a decent woman, or even, maybe, a book." And then she went out quickly before he had time to collect his wits to reply.

Anna lay in the centre of her and Peter's bed and gazed up into the pale summer darkness. The doctor had left sleeping pills, but she thought she wouldn't take one until it was perfectly plain that she wouldn't sleep naturally. All around her in the Rectory's other bedrooms lay her relations, also probably, except for Flora, staring

into nothing. Anna had climbed into bed with Flora and
held her until she slept. On the floor beside her bed lay
the dictionary, where Flora had wanted to look up "paradise." The dictionary had said that it was an ancient
Persian pleasure ground and a place of bliss and the final
abode of the blessed dead. It went on to describe paradise fish and paradise birds, gorgeous in colouring and
plumage, and Flora's brow had cleared a little. She
looked very small, to Anna, small and childish. It was
a relief when her body relaxed and Anna could see she
was truly asleep.

Then there had been Kitty. Kitty was not to be comforted with descriptions of Persian pleasure grounds.
Kitty sat and nursed a tiny glass of sherry and said that
her human landscape had quite fallen away and that she
was not only desolate but absolutely no bloody use to
anyone. No-one had ever heard Kitty swear before.
They looked at her with new respect. She blushed and
tossed off her sherry and said loudly that she'd do her
best to die soon, too, so that Anna could have her
savings and her amethysts, and then she burst into
tears again.

Laura said why didn't they have a suicide pact? She
thought they might dress in black velvet and do it with
poison at midnight. She meant to make Kitty laugh, but
Kitty cried harder. Laura took Charlotte into the kitchen
and they fried bacon and eggs and discussed the future.
Laura said she was going to sell her flat and offer the
money to Anna, and Charlotte said she was going to
leave Edinburgh and get a job, any job. They took the
bacon and eggs into the sitting-room and distributed the
plates around to Anna and Kitty and Luke. Kitty said
she couldn't face it, so Anna fed her little bits, like a

baby, and after a while she stopped crying and ate by herself, until her plate was empty.

After supper, Laura took Kitty up to Charlotte's room, which they were sharing, and Charlotte said was it all right if she made a phone call.

"She's got a new bloke," Luke said, when she had left the room.

"Oh? What sort of bloke?"

"He's called Adam. He's reading engineering." He looked across at Anna. "Mum—"

"Yes," she said. She was so tired she felt as if she were floating, as if her mind were hovering some distance above her body like a little spotter plane.

"It wasn't Patrick, was it?"

"No."

"It was Jonathan."

"Yes."

Luke dug himself out of his armchair to come and collapse on the floor by the sofa where Anna lay.

"I'm not going to India."

"Oh Luke—"

"I don't want to."

"Don't decide anything," Anna said. "Not yet. It's too soon. One longs to decide everything, it's a kind of reaction, but we mustn't. We'll decide the wrong things."

"Are you going to decide about Jonathan?"

Anna turned her head to look at Luke. "I decided that before Daddy died."

"He's a great bloke."

"Yes."

"Are you going to marry him?"

Anna put out a hand and ruffled Luke's hair. "I'll tell

you that the minute I've told him. Promise.''

"And Dad?" Luke said.

"The funny thing is," Anna said, "that now he's dead I feel I can be fond of him in peace."

Luke rolled over so that his face was buried against Anna. "I want to love someone."

"You will."

He gripped her hand. "It's the waiting," he said. "That's what I can't stand, the waiting."

When Charlotte had come back into the room, she carried a little private glow with her. She sat down beside Luke and described Adam the engineer. He was six foot two and his parents lived in Cheadle Hume. He played the clarinet and she had known him three weeks, at least, three weeks seriously, although of course he'd been around all her time at Edinburgh. She said he'd offered to come down and sort of be around, if it would help.

"Of course," Anna said. It would clearly help Charlotte.

They sat there for a long time in the growing dark. The telephone rang several times and solicitous people asked if they were all right and did they need anything. To all of them, Anna said they were fine, thank you, and that all they needed was time. Then they took the telephone off the hook, and went upstairs together.

Charlotte went into Flora's room, where she was sleeping on a mattress on the floor. Luke paused before going into his room, just long enough to say, "Will you be lonely?"

Anna said carefully, "I don't think so."

Now, lying awake, she wondered about it. What exactly did lonely mean? What had she meant by it, in the past, when she had declared herself to be so lonely within inches of Peter's living, breathing self? She switched the light on again, and picked up the dictionary from the floor. "Alone," it said, "solitary, standing by oneself." Yes, Anna thought, yes, I am all those things. "Abandoned," the dictionary went on, "uncomfortably conscious of being alone." She closed the book emphatically. She was neither of those last two things. She reached out and switched off the light. Those two things had been the loneliness of the past.

Miss Lambe was polishing the brass in Woodborough Vicarage. It was a huge task, involving over thirty pairs of door knobs, not to mention the front-door knocker and the letter box and the Archdeacon's study fender. Miss Lambe had chosen it deliberately, because it took her mind off things. The thing she wanted her mind particularly taken off was Jonathan's leaving the Vicarage. At the end of the week, he'd said to her in the kitchen that morning, at the end of the week he'd be going back to his university and then to Greece. Miss Lambe had little enough idea of the whereabouts of his university, and none at all about Greece, but they both sounded a long way off. He said he'd be back, of course, but Miss Lambe knew that that would not be the same as knowing, on a daily basis, that she'd find his blue shirts in the linen basket to be washed, along with the Archdeacon's grey ones.

She knew that he and the Archdeacon had had a long talk the night of Mr. Bouverie's funeral. She hadn't been able to sleep, and had pattered downstairs, anxious not to be seen in the intimacy of her all-enveloping pink woolly dressing gown, and had noticed a line of light under the Archdeacon's study door, and heard their voices, just as the clock struck midnight. It did not occur

to her to listen, but, as she scurried by, she could feel
through the closed door that the atmosphere of the conversation was grave. It was, in consequence, no surprise
to her to hear that Jonathan was going, but it made her
feel most peculiar all the same, shaken and unsteady,
and prone to snuffle. Polishing was a good antidote to
snuffling.

She was painstakingly rubbing polish into the front-
door knocker with a toothbrush when Anna appeared.
Miss Lambe did not like Anna, who seemed to her not
a good churchwoman, not properly modest and unas-
suming. Anna smiled at Miss Lambe. Miss Lambe
clutched her toothbrush.

"I wonder if Mr. Byrne is in," Anna said.

Miss Lambe gave a tiny toss of her head.

"Mr. Byrne is working."

"Do you think I might interrupt him very briefly?"

"No," said Miss Lambe.

"I think," Anna said, putting her hand on the door,
"I think I just will, all the same." She gave the door a
little push.

"Stop!" said Miss Lambe.

"No," said Anna. She pushed the door again and it
swung open. The tiles of the hall were still damp from
Miss Lambe's morning mopping. She stepped forward.
Miss Lambe sped after her.

"He's private!" Miss Lambe cried, prodding Anna
with her polishing toothbrush.

"Oh Miss Lambe," Anna said turning. She was
laughing.

Miss Lambe was full of sudden hatred. "Stop that!"
shrieked Miss Lambe.

A door opened on the landing and Jonathan appeared.
They looked up at him.

"She wouldn't stop!" Miss Lambe cried to him. "She wouldn't, she wouldn't!"

He began to descend the stairs. Anna could see he was fighting laughter. She said, "Miss Lambe was very properly defending your working privacy. But I'll only be a moment."

"I hope not," Jonathan said. He put his hand under Anna's elbow. "Thank you," he said to Miss Lambe, leading Anna away. Miss Lambe watched them go up the stairs together, his hand still under her elbow. She would not, she decided, make them any coffee.

"Now," Jonathan said, holding Anna hard against him. "Now, my darling. At last, at last. Are you all right?"

"I think so."

"I love you." He led her to the divan and sat down on it, drawing her down close to him. "Daniel has dismissed me. Very kindly and nicely and inevitably. To do me justice, I think I should probably have dismissed myself, to make things easier for you. For us."

Anna leaned against him.

"I came to dismiss you too."

"Did you?" His voice was indulgent. "How comfortable, that we should all be in unison. I shall go back next week and set things in motion."

"Things—"

"For you to join me. For you, after a decent interval, to become a don's wife and thus exchange one set of stereotypes for another." He was laughing again.

"Not that," Anna said softly.

"Not quite that, of course, but I fear not so different—"

"Jonathan," Anna said, "I love you and you saved

my sanity and I want to be in bed with you. But I'm not marrying you."

"I'm sorry," he said, "I'm so clumsy. Peter's only been dead a fortnight."

Anna picked up his hand and separated the fingers. "You aren't clumsy at all. And it isn't Peter. It's two other things. One is that I don't want another relationship just now, I don't want the involvement again yet. The other is that I have things to do."

"What things? I'd never stop you—"

"Things," Anna said, "that I haven't done for too long, for twenty years. Things I can do for their own sake, not in relation to other people. I have to learn, you see, to live with myself, I have to learn what I can do. It's so trite to talk about being oneself, but it's what I feel, what I truly feel."

"Why should marriage stop that? I'm the least possessive of men."

Anna turned to look at him. "To be perfectly honest with you, I'm desperate for a rest from marriage."

"But—"

"I know marriage to you would be unrecognizably different from marriage to Peter, but I still don't want it just now."

"Darling Anna," Jonathan said, putting his arms around her and pulling her down to lie beside him. "You are very difficult to follow. Could you please tell me exactly it is that you do want?"

"Yes," Anna said. She looked straight at him. "I want a lover."

17

❖ ❖ ❖

THE BISHOP'S STUDY was a modest room. It was painted pale green and it looked out on to a long lawn lined with herbaceous borders that ended with a fine view of the Cathedral's Chapter House. It contained comfortable, ugly furniture, a great many dark, grave books and several photographs of the Bishop's grandchildren, all of whom appeared to have spent many, many years without any front teeth. There was a vase of yellow roses on his desk, and a very old mongrel asleep on the hearthrug.

When Anna arrived, the Bishop said he was so sorry, his wife was out, so they would have to make coffee for themselves. Anna said she would be delighted, and they spent a long time in the kitchen while the Bishop opened cupboards full of saucepans, and bags of flour, looking for cups. Once he said, "Ah, biscuits," in a pleased voice, and put a tin on the table. Then, in the midst of these explorations, his secretary came in, and looked crossly at Anna, and shooed them both into his study. Ten minutes later, she appeared with coffee on a tray laid with a tray cloth, and biscuits arranged in a fan on a flowered plate. The Bishop, who was deep in thought over what Anna had just said to him, failed to acknowledge her arrival, or her indignant departure.

Anna took a cup of coffee and the sugar bowl over to the Bishop. He said, spooning sugar, "So what you are suggesting is a series of local support-groups for clergy wives?"

"Not exactly," Anna said. "That could turn into precisely the sort of bossy, ill-defined, do-gooding group that makes parish life so difficult. I think it ought to be a diocesan project. Like the ministerial review, or whatever you call your care-of-priests scheme. What's wrong is that the top administrative end of the Church doesn't know what it's like to live out in a rural parish. And I have to say that it often feels as if they don't much care, either."

"You'd be quite wrong about *that*," the Bishop said with some energy.

Anna said nothing. The Bishop stirred his coffee. He cleared his throat. "Would you wish to be part of this scheme? In this diocese?"

"Oh yes," Anna said, "of course. After all, I know the other side. Trying to live with someone with a strong sense of service is taxing enough, so what must it be like being married to a vocation?"

The Bishop looked at her. "What about a wife's sense of service?"

Anna looked back. "A sense of service to God is one thing. It's independent, you chose it, you chose how you fulfil it. A sense of service to a husband who has chosen God is quite another. Handmaidens of the Lord have a much better time of it than handmaidens of husbands."

THE RECTOR'S WIFE

The Bishop began to feel relieved that his wife was out. He had felt a little uneasy at seeing Anna and had wished for his wife's presence, but now that he knew her errand, it seemed to him that his wife might not altogether have taken his part. He could not fault his wife's loyalty, but he had felt, in the last few weeks, a certain steel in her that he had not observed before.

"A clergy marriage," Anna said, "isn't immune to anything a lay marriage is vulnerable to."

The Bishop leaned forward. "I shall talk to my council."

"Will you?"

"Can you think of any specific examples—"

"Yes," Anna said. She got up. She was suddenly weary.

"I doubt we could pay for your help. I imagine such advice as you might give would have to be voluntary."

"I never imagined otherwise."

"My dear Mrs. Bouverie," the Bishop said abruptly, getting up too, "how are you managing? What is your future?"

"We have to leave the Rectory, of course. But I have plans—"

He peered at her. "Do you? Are you getting help? From the Archdeacon?"

"I am inundated with help," Anna said, "which I don't at all seem to want to accept."

"Don't you?"

She regarded him. "Would you? In my position? Or, for that matter, at any time in your life? Would you like to be beholden?"

The Bishop smiled. He put out his hand and grasped hers. "I should absolutely loathe it," he said.

Everybody had made offers. Laura and Kitty had offered to sell their flats; Sir Francis Mayhew had suggested the old coachman's rooms over his stables; Eleanor had telephoned from Oxford saying that she had finally decided to leave Robert and—this was added rather perfunctorily—she was so very sorry to hear about Peter, so why didn't they join forces and set up house together in Oxford? No sooner had she declined all these than Daniel came out to Loxford to suggest, rather diffidently, that they might all move into the Vicarage, which needed people, as he did, and to be quite honest, Miss Lambe . . .

"No," Anna said gently. "No. But thank you very much."

"Because of Jonathan?"

"Because of independence."

"But I would regard you as being wholly independent—"

"Daniel," Anna said, putting her hands on his shoulders, "I think I believe in God now more than I ever have, but at the moment, I simply can't stand the Church."

Soon after Daniel had gone, the telephone had rung. Luke had answered it and came to find Anna, who was pulling early carrots, saying that it was the Diocesan Secretary. Anna looked amazed.

"Who's he?"

"I dunno. Said his name was Warbash. Brilliant."

"Mr. Warbash?" Anna said into the telephone.

"Commander Warbash, actually. Mrs. Bouverie, could you run into Church House this week for a moment?"

"Is it about my idea?"

"No," said Commander Warbash, who regarded clergy wives as a pretty low priority in his scheme of things. "No. It's about something much more to your advantage. Something practical."

"Can't you tell me on the telephone?"

"No," said Commander Warbash.

Three days later, across his well-marshalled desk, he offered Anna a house. It was a cottage on glebe land the far side of the diocese. It had three bedrooms and an orchard and it was on a bus route. Anna might have it rent-free for five years.

Anna explained that Flora was at school in Woodborough and that Luke was probably going to do a foundation art course at the polytechnic. Commander Warbash said that both those facts might be regarded as details.

"I don't think so," Anna said.

Commander Warbash said that the suggestion of a house had been made by a well-wisher of Anna's on the Diocesan Board of Finance, and that he, Commander Warbash, had assumed that, in her position, she would leap at the offer.

"I think," Anna said boldly, "that the test of true kindness is whether it benefits the recipient more than the donor."

"So you decline Glebe Cottage?"

"I'm afraid so. I'm very grateful for the offer, but I can't disrupt all our lives by moving twenty-five miles away. Also—"

"Yes?" said Commander Warbash.

"Let's just say that the Church doesn't owe me anything any more. I'm—" She paused. She wanted to say "free" but thought it would sound aggressive, so she said instead, "separate now."

"So how will you live?"

"I don't quite know yet."

"You have your children to consider."

She wanted nothing so much as to lean across the desk and slap him. She looked at his healthy, cleanly shaven, decent, insensitive, English face and imagined how it would feel under her hand. To restrain herself, she put her hands in her pockets.

"I imagine," Commander Warbash said, "that we have nothing more to say to one another."

"Nothing."

He rose and held out a hand. "Then I will bid you good morning."

Anna smiled. "Good morning. And thank you for your time. I do hope," she said with great warmth, "that you will find a nice, amenable, *grateful* tenant for Glebe Cottage."

"So do I," he said. But when she had gone, and he reflected upon Glebe Cottage's dismal downstairs bathroom and four windows only a few feet from a main road, he rather doubted it. He began to hum. Confrontations always stimulated him a little, particularly with pretty women.

Anna said, "I'll have to go and thank Colonel Richardson. It was his idea, clearly, and at least he really meant to be kind."

Flora was drawing at the kitchen table. She wanted to live in a house like her new friend Verity's, with a conservatory and a double garage. She hadn't chosen to grasp the fact that there was even less money than before, only the fact that she was no longer committed to living in a Rectory. She said, "It would be kind to me to live in a real house."

"It would be quite kind to me, too," Anna said.

Flora drew a blobby tree and began to add apples. "If you died now, I'd be an orphan."

"Would you like that?"

"No!" Flora said in terror.

"Then why say such things?"

Flora drew a rabbit under the tree. "To scare you. To *make* you stay alive."

Anna bent and kissed her. "I'm going to see Colonel Richardson. Luke's upstairs if you want him."

"Yes," Flora said. She drew a second, smaller rabbit. "Drive carefully."

It was curious and exciting to drive so much, to feel that the car was hers to drive. She reversed slowly and drove down to the lane. She passed the Old Rectory without looking at it; the thought of Patrick O'Sullivan filled her with a dull rage mixed with shame. She drove across the green, waving to Mrs. Eddoes, who was tying up her sweet peas with raffia, and to Sheila Vinson, who was washing her front-door paintwork, and turned down the lane to Quindale. She decided, as she drove, that she would not attempt to rehearse her explanation for turning down Glebe Cottage. She would simply, when confronted with Harry Richardson, tell the spontaneous truth.

But Harry Richardson was not at home. It was Marjorie, in a blue-and-white-patterned summer dress of immaculate cut, who opened the impressive front door of Quindale House. Anna was rather thrown.

"Marjorie. I'm so sorry to disturb you, but I wondered if I might have a word with Harry, he's been so kind—"

"I'm afraid he's out," Marjorie Richardson said. "Regimental reunion in London." The hand that was not holding the front door crept to her double row of pearls. "Come in," she said unexpectedly.

Anna came. She followed Marjorie across the beautiful old rugs on the hall floor to a pretty back sitting-room with a door open to the garden. Out on the lawn beyond, the Richardson Labradors lay stoutly in the sun.

"Coffee?" Marjorie said. "Or gin?"

Anna said, startled, "I suppose it'd better be coffee—"

"Why? Wouldn't you rather have gin?"

"I've almost never drunk it—"

"I've drunk it all my life," Marjorie said. "All my generation have. We're nothing like so fond of wine, but we all grew up on gin. I'll make you a weak one."

Anna sat down, slightly dazed, on a fat, chintz-covered chair. Marjorie went over to a lacquered tray full of bottles and began some competent mixing. She came back to Anna with a small stemmed glass full of ice and lemon.

"That's a dry Martini. There's no pick-me-up like it."

"Heavens," Anna said. She took the glass gingerly.

Marjorie Richardson sat down opposite with her own much fuller glass. She waved it. "Cheers," she said.

Anna took a tiny, electrifying sip. She said, after a moment, "Harry did something very kind. He got the diocese to offer me a cottage for five years. I'm terribly touched, but I'm afraid I've turned it down. It was such a kind idea."

"It was mine," Marjorie said.

Anna stared.

"Yours?"

"Yes, I thought it would be easier to accept from them than from any of us."

Anna put her glass down. "Then I'm even sorrier I turned it down—"

"Don't be," Marjorie said. She crossed her handsome legs. "I'm not surprised. I'd have turned it down too."

"What—"

"You've had enough, haven't you? You've had an absolute basinful of being towed along behind some male institution, haven't you? I think you want out." She paused and took a swallow. "I think this because I think it too. Church or Army, what does it matter, they're all the same. Fill a man with notions of duty and obligation and then expect his wife to feel privileged to fall in with him. Makes me sick."

Anna leaned forward. She wondered briefly if Marjorie had begun on the gin some time before her arrival.

"But you've always disapproved of me being a maverick! You were furious over Pricewell's—"

"Fury born of envy and admiration. I never had your guts, you see, I never had the guts to rebel. I went along with Harry and the Army for forty-three years, while everyone told me what a brick I was and ideal for an Army wife. Even Harry began to believe it. I don't think it's crossed his mind to wonder if I can look back on my life with even a fraction of the satisfaction he can look back on his. These male institutions—" She paused, took another swallow and went on. "I'll tell you something. Our elder daughter, Julia, was married to a sailor. He's a bit older than her, and he was a captain during the Falklands War. While he was away, Julia became responsible for all the wives and mothers and girl-friends of the men on his ship. They rang at all hours, all the time. She travelled all over England seeing these women, in her own time, at her own expense. When the

Task Force returned, her husband was promoted, went off with a WRNS officer and the Navy never even said thank you. Not a postcard. Nothing. As a service wife she was expected to do all that and feel honoured to do it. You should hear Julia on the subject. You'd like Julia.''

"Marjorie," Anna said, "you've absolutely taken my breath away.''

"I owe you an apology, really," Marjorie said. "I've been pretty hard on you. I suppose suggesting the cottage was part of a wish to make amends. I'm glad you've turned it down. Now you're free, stay free. Would you let me lend you some money?''

"No," Anna said gently, "I wouldn't.''

"Damn. Though I don't see why you should take it just to make me feel better. You aren't drinking your drink.''

Anna picked up her glass. "I'm rather startled by it. The combination of it and you has made me feel as if I'd already drunk several—''

"Where are you going to live?''

"Woodborough," Anna said.

"Good. So I can come and see you? You'll accept veg and stuff—''

"Oh yes. I'd love to see you.''

"I'll bring Julia.''

"I'd love to meet Julia. Marjorie," Anna said, "will you tell Harry about the cottage? Will you explain that I'm so grateful but that I must be independent now? I'm afraid—I'm afraid that the cottage I was offered sounded rather—''

"Grim? I bet it did. Of course I'll tell Harry." She looked at Anna and then tossed off her drink. "Funny old fellow. Terribly protective, without one clue as to how we tick. Not one. I hope you'll keep in touch, let me know where you are, what's going on. I'm stuck now, of course, but I don't half get a kick out of watching you throw over the traces.'' She brandished her glass. "Want the other half?''

Anna hadn't been in Sister Ignatia's study since the day of Flora's interview. Sister Ignatia seemed quite unsurprised to see her, but then, she reflected, nuns did not seem to go in for visible surprise about anything. Anna sat down and let Sister Ignatia tell her all that St. Saviour's was doing to comfort Flora over the loss of her father. Anna felt that the expression in Sister Ignatia's sharp eyes did not quite match the gentle platitudes of her speech. She said how grateful she was, what a difference the school's sympathy made to Flora. Then she waited. Sister Ignatia waited too, for a few seconds, to allow her a decent transition of mood, and then she said, in quite a different tone, "And how can we help you?''

"I need a job,'' Anna said.

Sister Ignatia nodded.

"I'm qualified to teach French and German in language schools, but not in the state system. I have also taught English as a foreign language.''

"And why have you come to me?''

"Because you don't have the same requirements as a state school, and because I know you a little and because I saw your advertisement in the *Woodborough Echo* for a languages teacher.''

"It might not benefit Flora.''

"It would do her no harm to learn to accept it.''

They looked at one another. Sister Ignatia remembered that Mrs. Bouverie had concealed Flora's free place from her husband. She also remembered that, after her initial surprise, she had remarked to herself that Mrs. Bouverie doubtless had her reasons.

"You are my first attempt at getting a job," Anna said. "I won't be surprised if you turn me down. But I'd like to teach here, I think."

Sister Ignatia folded her hands under her scapular.

"I thought you might come to me."

"And did you think what you might say to me when I did?"

"I thought I might agree. At least to a term's trial."

"I'd be very grateful." Anna leaned forward. "How did you know I'd come?"

"You've a very ecumenical archdeacon here in Woodborough."

"No!" Anna said. "Not Daniel! This isn't a plot, is it, between you and Daniel Byrne? Will I never be free of the Church?"

Sister Ignatia gave a tiny, ironic smile.

"Oh Mrs. Bouverie," she said, "it's not the Church you'll never be free of—"

When she left St. Saviour's, Anna made her way to the market-place. It was market day, and busy, and the busyness added to Anna's sense of elation. Sister Ignatia had offered her a term's trial of full-time French and German teaching, a position to be reviewed at Christmas. It was, Anna could not help realizing, exactly the kind of job that would have earned Peter's approbation. It was also, she could not avoid admitting, exactly the kind of job she would not take while he was alive. Flora would, of course, be most indignant. Anna's presence at St. Saviour's would unquestionably cramp her style.

"A most imaginative child," Sister Ignatia had said.

"Do you mean not strictly truthful?"

Sister Ignatia hadn't smiled. "I simply mean what I said."

Anna's goal in the market-place was the clutch of estate agents' offices, which huddled together for safety, rather as building societies and antique shops tend to do. Her errand was, she thought, quite simple; she wanted a house to rent with a minimum of three bedrooms. A garden would be nice. A garage didn't much matter. The first two agents she visited said they had nothing to rent whatsoever and the third offered her a sad-looking bungalow behind the fire station. All three said she would find rented property very scarce; very scarce indeed. They shook their heads. They tried to interest Anna in small houses they had for sale, dull little houses on residential estates. Anna said she had no capital and could thus make no down payment. They looked at her pityingly, but made it plain that it was not their business to do any more for her.

The fourth agency produced two houses. One was a sturdy villa in a suburb of Woodborough, the property of a businessman currently living in the Far East, the second a narrow slice in a Victorian terrace. Anna said she would like to look at it. The agent urged the villa.

"But I'd rather be in the middle. And it's cheaper—"

"Nothing like so pleasant, though. And only three bedrooms."

"May I see it? May I?"

The agent sighed. He knew it would be a waste of time. The house had been on his books a year. He called a girl from a back office where she was photocopying particulars.

"Debbie. Take Mrs. Bouverie to 67 Nelson Street, would you?"

"You won't like it," Debbie said to Anna, on the pavement.

"Won't I? Why won't I?"

"It's ever so dark. Creepy."

"Is this a very good way to do business, do you think, putting clients off before they even get there?"

"Only trying to help," Debbie said. It might be a stupid errand, but anything was better than the photocopier. "You're the ninth person I've taken. That's all."

Nelson Street was five minutes from the market-place. It was too narrow, and it lacked front gardens, but the far end of it opened into the old abbey grounds, an eighteenth-century park designed picturesquely round the ruins of Woodborough's medieval abbey. Number 67 was exactly like its neighbours; flat-fronted, built of brick, with a window beside the front door, two above it, and one in the top-floor gable, under cuckoo-clock eaves of painted wood.

"Terrible, isn't it?" Debbie said.

Anna did not think so. She took the key firmly from Debbie and opened the front door. A smell of old, damp newspapers greeted her. The hall was narrow and dark, with a sharply rearing staircase, but beyond it Anna could see sunlight through a back window and something green further off. She turned to Debbie.

"Why don't you go off for ten minutes, and I'll explore on my own?"

"I'm not allowed to do that. I'm not allowed to leave the client."

"Even if the client refuses to look at the property with you standing scowling at her?"

Debbie gaped.

"Go away," Anna said. "Go away and come back in a quarter of an hour."

"Mr. Rickston—"

"I'll deal with Mr. Rickston."

"Barmy," Debbie said. But she backed away through the front door. Anna shut it behind her.

"Now," she said to 67 Nelson Street.

It waited. It allowed her to open doors and windows and climb the staircase and investigate cupboards and trap doors. It let her look into the bathroom (very bad) and the kitchen (worse) and observe the discouraging boarding-house decor. Not until she had looked out through the back windows and seen the wholly neglected little garden surrounded by old brick walls, in which an apple tree was growing (an apple tree laden with infant fruit), did it begin, tentatively, to defend itself. Coming away from the window—the garden was full of sunlight—Anna saw that, although the walls were covered in embossed and terrible papers, and the paintwork was ochre and lime-green, the fireplaces and mantelpieces were still original, there were proper cornices and deep skirting boards, and, above all, an unmistakable atmosphere of profound benevolence.

"I don't think you're dark or creepy," Anna said out loud. "Nobody could hope to look their best under salmon-pink gloss paint."

The doorbell rang hoarsely. Anna went down the stairs and opened the door saying, "That wasn't quarter of an hour—"

"What wasn't?" Jonathan said.

"Jonathan!"

"I followed you. I saw you in the market-place. Are you going to live here?"

She drew him in. "I might. I think I like it."

He looked round. "I have no eye at all. Never know

299

what I like in houses.'' He looked at her. ''Only in people.''

She took his hand. ''Come and see. There's room for all the children and a garden.''

''Is there a room for a lover?''

''Not as well as the children.''

He kissed her.

''Worth a try—''

She led him into the kitchen and pointed out through the window. ''Look. An apple tree. And lovely walls. I'm going to teach at St. Saviour's.''

He put his face into the back of her neck. ''Try not to be too self-sufficient. Try to need me a little. There are my feelings to consider after all.''

She said, ''It was you who said seize the moment.''

''That was before I was as deep in as I am now.''

She turned and put her arms round him. ''I'm in love too, you know. It's just taken me in rather a different way. Just as Peter's death has taken me in a way I never dreamed of.''

He regarded her for some time. Then he smiled and said, ''I understand, you know. And you thrill me, the way you're behaving, you really do. Now, show me your house.''

18

THE NEW RECTOR of Loxford had not been ordained until he was forty-five. He'd been an insurance agent before that. He was called Philip Farmer and he had a wife called Dorothy and two grown-up sons in the computer industry. He was a big, solid man with a genial expression and spectacles, and he told the Parochial Church Councils of the five parishes that it had been his and Dorothy's dream for ten years to come to a rural living, and that they felt very privileged to have been accepted.

Dorothy Farmer was evidently capable. Within weeks of her arrival, new curtains of her own making blew out of the constantly, healthily open Rectory windows and the WI Friday market had benefited from jars of her excellent chutney. The parish group found themselves somewhat disconcerted. Celia Hooper, Trish Pardoe and Elaine Dodswell had all paid an eager early visit to the Rectory, to explain their willingness. Dorothy Farmer had shown them into the newly painted, trimly furnished, almost unrecognizable sitting-room, with a single picture (a quiet landscape) hanging dead centre over the fireplace, and a row of African violets in copper pots on the gleaming windowsill.

"Now then," said Dorothy Farmer, bringing in a tray of coffee and home-made biscuits, "tell me about yourselves."

They tried. They told her about the Brownies and the old people and the Sunday school Christmas play and the difficulty of finding volunteers for the church-cleaning rotas. They attempted to explain delicately about their efforts to help Anna. They pointed out what a lot of work five parishes gave a priest, and how they knew that clergymen and their wives were under a lot of stress these days and that it was their fervent wish to help alleviate this.

Dorothy Farmer listened. She made notes in a note-book. She smiled a good deal, and nodded, and looked at them through her well-polished spectacles. When they had finished, she let a little pause fall, and then she picked up the coffee pot, and went round their cups with it saying, "I can see you've had a very difficult time. I'm so pleased Philip and I are here. I shall of course, being a trained physiotherapist, do a bit of work at the hospital to keep my hand in, but the rest of the time I shall be here, in the parish." She paused and smiled again. "Very much so, in fact."

They watched her. She sat down again in her neat oatmeal chair.

"Between you and me," Dorothy said confidingly, "I think there's a lot of nonsense talked about clergy stress. It's a question of attitude, to my mind. If you ask me, most clergy wives these days are a lot of moaning minnies."

• • •

Anna was invited to Philip Farmer's induction service. Laura was staying with her at the time, and so she came too, in the gilded velvet coat she had worn for Anna's wedding. As she had just signed a contract for a new series of Irish stout advertisements—the first batch having become a cult success—she bought a new hat. It was a straw cartwheel with the crown swathed in golden satin. Laura added artificial flowers and ears of corn and a huge glistening brooch shaped like a dragonfly. Her final appearance made Anna feel very affectionate.

Apart from regular visits to Peter's grave (it had no headstone yet because there were arguments over the lettering), Anna had not lingered recently in Loxford. She had not, for one thing, had time, and for another, it seemed only fair to stay out of Dorothy Farmer's way. She had paid a single, brief courtesy visit to the Rectory and come away astounded. "You wouldn't believe," she said to Luke, "that it was the same house." Luke, who had contentedly painted his attic room in Nelson Street black all over, merely grinned. Life in Loxford seemed to him, at times, already as remote as the moon.

Loxford church was not as full as it had been for Peter's funeral. It looked tremendously clean—almost too clean, Anna thought—and there were the usual lovely flowers, which bore the mark of the skilled hands of Lady Mayhew and Miss Dunstable. In the Rectory pew sat Dorothy Farmer in a fawn-checked two-piece, and beside her, two large sons and one small daughter-in-law. They were, from head to foot, impeccably brushed and polished.

Anna and Laura sat at the back. Several people turned round and made welcoming faces and grimaced at them to come further up the church. Anna shook her head. She wished Kitty was there, but Kitty had refused to come. She had sent Anna her amethysts, with a note saying that as she might as well be dead, why didn't Anna have them now? Anna had sent them back, saying that (a) nobody could enjoy a present sent in such a spirit and (b) she wanted, please, Kitty to stay alive as long as possible. Kitty had sulked after that, and refusing to come to the induction was part of the sulking. "Poor Kittykins," Laura said, "she thinks it makes her glamorous."

The Bishop conducted the service. Daniel was there too. Philip Farmer looked very pleased at the whole proceeding and beamed confidently at his new flock. He had plans for them, evangelical plans, plans that he had been shrewd enough not to reveal in front of the likes of Sir Francis Mayhew and Harry Richardson, before they had finally accepted him. He thought he would start with the music; a good modern song book, some young mothers with guitars, a few Taise choruses. Then he would turn to the services and replace Rite B with Rite A. It would be nice to encourage the congregation to participate in the services; some personal confessions, perhaps (surely even Loxford had a reformed alcoholic or two—even perhaps a drug addict?), and the warm exchanging of signs of peace. Loxford needed bringing to God, he could see that, plain as the nose on your face. It had got fossilized, poor old Loxford, fossilized by notions of "the Church." Well, Philip didn't call it "the Church," and nor did Dorothy. They called it "the Jesus Movement." Dorothy had played the recorder at services in their last parish and she would undoubtedly do it again here; it was a wonderful ice-breaker, a wonderful way to bear witness to the Lord. Philip Farmer's smile grew and grew. He looked upon his unsuspecting parishioners with love. He had so much to share with them.

In the churchyard afterwards, Celia Hooper came up to Anna. She said, "Oh, I'm ever so pleased to see you," and then to Anna's amazement, she kissed her. "Are you all right?" she said. "Are you settled?"

"Yes," Anna said, recovering. "Yes, I am. We all are. It's a funny little house but we like it."

"Oh Anna," Celia said. Her eyes were unnaturally bright. "We miss you—"

"I expect it's just the change—"

"No. No, it's more than that. You ask Elaine."

Anna looked across the churchyard. Dorothy Farmer was saying something to Daniel. Even from this distance, her demeanour looked arch.

"She seems terribly efficient—"

"Oh yes, she's efficient all right. I suppose I shouldn't say this, but I feel, we all feel, that there isn't the same humanity, somehow. We've lost the colour."

"It's very early days," Anna said, battling for the right platitudes.

Two precise tears spilled from Celia's eyes. "We miss Peter—"

"Of course."

"I shouldn't say this, to you of all people, but you felt you could get close to Peter, that he needed you in some way—"

"I'm so glad."

"Am I offending you? I'd do anything rather than offend you."

"Don't you think," Anna said, "that you and I have got quite beyond this kind of conversation? You did offend me, in the past, quite tremendously, but then, in a sense, I offended you by not being what you thought I should be. It's all over now, all of that.'' She glanced round the churchyard. ''This isn't my parish any more, this isn't my patch. I'm not part of the Church now, not the way I was.''

Celia looked at her. ''You seem so controlled—''

''I know.''

''Don't you feel sad, being back here? Don't you hate seeing her being what you were? And what about Peter—''

''What about him?''

Celia looked suddenly nervous. She said, ''I didn't mean to suggest—''

''Shall we leave it?'' Anna said. ''Shall we just leave it there?''

''Except—''

''Except what?''

''I'd love to do something to help. Really I would. Make curtains for you or something.''

Anna stared at her. Would she never understand? Then she touched her arm briefly. ''Thank you so much, but I'm making my own. Not very well, but I don't seem to mind that.''

And then Laura came up, and said that the Bishop had told her that her fleeting appearances on television were about the only reason he ever turned the thing on these days. She glanced roguishly at Celia. ''Rather a feather in one's pagan cap. Don't you think?''

Patrick O'Sullivan had seen Anna arrive in Loxford. He had told himself that he wasn't looking out for her, but that he would have been reading the paper in that particular chair by that particular window just then, in any case. It was chance that he should happen to look up and see her helping Laura out of the car, followed by a brief pantomime with the wind and Laura's hat. He had craned forward. Anna looked very well, he thought. She wore clothes he didn't recognize. She was a schoolmistress now, he told himself. He tried to smile.

He did not go across to the church. He wasn't particularly interested in this new Rector and even less so in his purposeful, bolster-shaped wife. Ella, who came to see him sometimes on her half-days off from Snead Hall, said that there was a lot of muttering in the parishes about Dorothy Farmer. As a leaving present, Patrick had given Ella the deposit on a bungalow at Church End, which she would use in the holidays, and when she retired. She seemed to like Snead Hall. She said it was a relief to work with other people.

In her place, Patrick had hired a Spanish couple. They had lasted three weeks, and then the wife had said that the country gave her allergies, and they had gone back to London. The agency Patrick used had replaced them with a quiet Scottish pair. Patrick had the feeling that the husband—courteous, unobjectionable, industrious—had once been in prison. It was something to do with his self-effacement and his wife's watchful protectiveness. The wife cooked better than Ella, but she had no sense of humour. Patrick missed Ella.

He looked out of the window again. Below him, in the shrubberies around the front drive, his silent Scots manservant was pulling out bindweed. Everyone was coming out of church, and the privileged few were straying off in the direction of the Rectory. Another tea party. Was the Church of England wholly sustained on tea and coffee and custard creams? He saw Anna from a distance. There was quite a crowd round her, an eager-

307

looking crowd; he could even see Miss Dunstable in it, and Lady Mayhew, of all unlikely people. The crowd moved slowly out of the churchyard and across the green to where the cars were parked. Anna stopped by hers, unlocking the passenger door for Laura. Then she turned and said something, laughing, to Sheila Vinson, who was standing quite close to her, and for a moment Patrick could see her face very clearly, and she looked suddenly very young, and very like Luke. Patrick gripped his newspaper. It wasn't just Ella he missed. He missed Luke. And Anna.

Sixty-seven Nelson Street was much improved. Charlotte had brought Adam, the engineer, to stay for a fortnight—this had caused great complication in sleeping arrangements, with Anna and Flora ending up quarrelsomely sharing Anna's bed—and he had steadily, good-humouredly, obliterated most of the fearful wallpapers under coats of bargain emulsion, bought from a stall in the market. Then he had taken Charlotte off to Italy, with backpacks, and Luke and his friend Barnaby had, to Anna's amazement, offered to clear the garden. They did it with enormous gusto and lack of finesse, lighting vast belching bonfires that brought Anna's new neighbours round at once in high states of indignation and leaving the garden looking like a lunar landscape. "There," Luke said with evident pride. "Now that'll give you a really clear start."

Luke, she observed, was very happy. He had acquired a girlfriend—a small, dull, sweet thing with huge brown eyes and a perfect rosebud mouth she hardly ever opened—and a holiday job collecting trolleys for Pricewell's. (It took some self-control for Anna not to tease him about Pricewell's.) Above his bed in his blackened eyrie, Luke had pinned reproductions of paintings he admired, a poster Barnaby had given him advertising a new political group at Leningrad University (in Russian, which he did not speak or read), and a photograph of Peter. It was an official photograph taken for the Woodborough paper when Peter became Rector of Loxford. He was in his cassock, and a surplice, and he stood gravely in front of the south porch of Loxford church. It was not the one Anna had on her dressing table. That one had been taken when Luke was born, and Peter was standing by a gate to a field holding the baby, and looking at the camera, and laughing. Flora didn't like that photograph. She didn't like the fact that the baby Peter was holding was Luke and not her.

People began to come, quite soon, to Nelson Street. Daniel came, and Isobel Thompson, and a fellow teacher from St. Saviour's. Flora brought friends home; so did Luke. Marjorie Richardson brought her magnificently outspoken daughter, Julia, who stayed to supper and then put herself to bed on the sofa. And then, quite unheralded, Patrick came. Anna opened the front door, expecting Isobel, and there he was, standing on the pavement, looking up at her. Her heart sank a little at the sight of him.

She said, quite truthfully, "You are the last person I expected."

He followed her into her sitting-room. He said, "This room could belong to nobody but you." He looked odd in it, so ordered and expensive amid Anna's possessions, which seemed to crowd round him in this little room with almost an air of eagerness. He held out a paper-wrapped bottle. "Something for you. To christen the house."

She knew it would be champagne even before she

opened it. She said, "How very kind," and put the bottle down carefully on a little table by the fireplace. Then she waited.

Patrick sat down on the Knole sofa, which now dominated Nelson Street like a dead mammoth.

"Are you happy here? Not cramped?"

"Oh yes, we're cramped. But it doesn't matter, it isn't important."

"I've wanted to come, for weeks," Patrick said, "but I've managed to restrain myself. I wish you'd sit down."

She sat, on a low chair across the room from him.

"Ella accused me of playing games with you. She nearly admitted that you had said so to her. And then she accused me of losing interest in you the moment Peter died, the moment you were free. I simply can't rest until I've told you that neither are true."

"I've got some deeply ordinary wine," Anna said. "Would you like some?"

"I'd rather you listened to me."

"I was only trying to lubricate the occasion—"

Patrick shouted, "Don't mock me!"

"I don't have to listen to you," Anna said. "I certainly don't have to if you shout."

He leaned forward, his elbows on his knees, staring at her. "I suppose this is some kind of revenge."

"Revenge?"

"Once I had the upper hand. Now you do. And you're enjoying it."

"Patrick," Anna said, "you don't have a clue, do you?"

"I have more than—"

"No," she said, interrupting, leaning forward herself, "no. You don't. You talk of revenge. Revenge has never crossed my mind. All that I'm interested in just now is independence.''

He smiled. ''That's just this modern woman thing.''

''It has nothing to do with gender. It's to do with humanity. Do you know what independence means?'' Anna said. ''It means not being subordinate. It means thinking and acting for yourself. It means not depending on anyone else for your sense of value. Wouldn't that describe you?''

''I'd like to think so—''

''Well, I'd like to think it described me, too, now.''

''But have you enough money?''

''Yes,'' she said, suddenly furious. ''Yes. Heaps. Billions. More than I know how to spend.''

He sighed. ''If I can't help you, and clearly I can't, is there any way we could have some kind of relationship?'' He looked at her. ''Would you come to bed with me?''

She said, ''I do have to admire your continuing nerve—''

''But you responded when I kissed you.''

''I did.''

''So you liked it.''

''I did.''

''So you would like some more.''

''No, I wouldn't.''

''There's another man,'' Patrick said.

''Correct.''

''Anna,'' Patrick said, holding his hands out to her, ''why not me?''

She stood up. She was weary of him. ''Because you're a bully,'' she said, ''and I'm tired of bullies.''

• • •

The Farmers were eating an early supper in Loxford Rectory. It was the evening of a Parochial Church Council meeting at Quindale. Celia had just resigned as secretary. Philip Farmer proposed to suggest that Dorothy should take her place. Dorothy had always been excellent at that sort of thing.

They ate their supper in the kitchen. It was newly painted in lemon-yellow and looked out on to the beginning of the patio with which the Farmers intended to replace Anna's vegetable garden. They would certainly go on growing vegetables, but at the far end of the garden where there was that terrible wilderness. It would be a good spot for Dorothy's rotary clothes-dryer too, out of sight of prying eyes.

Between them, on the table, by the salt and pepper mills, lay a letter from the Archdeacon. It was about a new diocesan project to help the wives of clergymen who got into difficulties. The help would cover a whole spectrum of domestic problems—lack of money, loneliness, marital misery. The Archdeacon asked all the priests in his area to think of anyone they knew who might be in trouble of this kind. The names of such people, and the source from which they came, would be treated, of course, with the utmost confidentiality.

Philip said cheerfully, reaching for the water jug, "Well, we needn't put you forward, dear."

Dorothy reread the letter. She said, "You know, I think it's shutting the stable door after the horse has bolted. I think they all got their fingers burned over Anna Bouverie and now they're trying to stop anything like that happening again. Though I must say, I'm amazed he's got the nerve to send out a letter about it himself."

"The Archdeacon? Why?"

Dorothy folded and rolled her seersucker napkin and pushed it through her napkin ring.

"You know how I am about gossip—"

"Yes," said Philip, who did. He went on eating, as if he didn't care.

"Of course, one must be terribly careful in villages."

"Certainly."

"I think I wouldn't have given this tale any credence if it hadn't tied up with so much evidence."

"Of course not."

Dorothy folded her hands on the table. "The rumour is," she said, "and mind you, I can hardly believe it—but the rumour is that Anna Bouverie formed a liaison with the Archdeacon of Woodborough."

"Polyester!" Miss Dunstable shouted.

Anna held the telephone a little away from her ear.

"Modern!" Miss Dunstable bellowed. "That's what she said to me! 'This is the modern Church,' she said to me! 'We need easycare altar linen.' Easycare!"

"Oh dear," Anna said, "I'm so sorry—"

"It's blasphemy!"

"Perhaps she really wants to save trouble—"

"Don't you start," Miss Dunstable said. "What's trouble beside standards, I'd like to know? She's a frightful woman."

"Are you sure," Anna said, leaning against the wall of her tiny hall and smiling, "that she isn't just different?"

"Vulgar," Miss Dunstable said. "Wants dried flowers in the Lady Chapel. It'll be plastic poinsettias at Christmas next."

"I'm so sorry. Really I am. But I don't think I can do anything."

"No. No, no. Of course you can't. I just had to let off steam. You know."

"Of course I do—"

"I've saved you some of my Californian poppy seed," Miss Dunstable said, in a different tone.

"How nice of you—"

"I'll give you some pinks when I divide them."

"That would be lovely."

There was a little pause and then Miss Dunstable snorted, "Easycare, indeed," and banged down the telephone.

Luke was in the kitchen, cooking pasta. This week, he thought he would probably be a sculptor. Last week he had toyed with photography. He called out, "Who was that?"

"Miss Dunstable."

"What did she want, for heaven's sake?"

"I think," Anna said, "that that was yet another apology."

Luke twirled long, pale lengths of tagliatelle out of the saucepan on a wooden spoon. "Weird," he said.

Seventy miles away, in his unremarkable university rooms, Jonathan was writing to Anna. He wrote to her a great deal, long, discursive, loving letters which were, he found, small but vital compensation for not seeing her as much as he would have liked to. His need to see her troubled him considerably, because it was a need that was new to him, and because it interfered with the self-sufficiency he had grown accustomed to, and dependent upon. He was also troubled by thinking that not only did Anna not seem to need him as reciprocally as he needed her but also that part of her remained elusive. Another part of her, which he also found difficult to come to terms with, seemed to be particularly attached to Daniel. It didn't, in Jonathan's mind, make all of a piece, it didn't seem to be consistent. When he looked back on his relationship with Anna, he saw an image of her, standing in a cage surrounded by people who were either longing to rescue her or determined that she should not escape. And then suddenly, it seemed to him, the cage was empty and Anna had eluded all those people and had run ahead of them, away from them. It was almost, now, as if she were in hiding, and they were all looking for her, guided only by bursts of slightly mocking laughter from her hiding-place. The tables were turned—but how had she done it?

For the first time in his life, Jonathan thought a good deal about the future. He thought about it because it had begun to matter. He found he wanted to plan. He had to stop himself from saying to Anna, In two years' time, will you—or even, Next Christmas, can I—because he wasn't inclined to tempt providence. Her life looked predictable enough, but its essence was so changed from her former life that it hardly seemed to belong to the same person. She had said to him once, seeing his anxiety, "I will need someone else one day. I think I will. When I've got used to myself." He had to be content with that.

Yet her growing degree of self-government disturbed him. You could see it reflected in her children, in her appearance, in her actions, which seemed to him sometimes arbitrary, because they weren't predictable. She excited him terribly, her personality quite as much as her body. He felt he was on some marvellous quest, at the best of times, and utterly lost in a hostile maze, at the worst. He was more deeply interested than he had ever been in his life before, more committed, more afraid.

He wrote, "I am afraid." He looked at it. He didn't like the look of it, so he crossed it out blackly and wrote, "Damn, damn. Mustn't whine. Won't whine," instead. He put his pen down. What was there, after all, to be afraid of? What was there to fear in placing his hopes and fears in Anna's hands? Of all the people Jonathan had ever known, besides his brother Daniel, Anna had a faithful heart, that commodity he had never thought to value before and which he now knew to be more precious than pearls. Smiling to himself, Jonathan seized his pen again and began to write rapidly.

19

❖   ❖   ❖

ANNA SAT ON Peter's grave. When it had been covered over, the turfs had been put back, like a roughly torn green rug, and they were at last slowly beginning to knit together once more. The mound of earth had subsided as well. It was starting to look, Anna thought, much more harmonious with the surrounding churchyard.

It was November, a soft, dove-grey day with no wind. Beside Anna lay a spade and an empty black plastic flowerpot which had contained the old shrub rose she had just planted at Peter's feet. At his head, there was nothing. There should have been a headstone, a simple upright slab of local stone from the quarry beyond New End, but Anna had only just won the battle over the lettering; her last battle, she sometimes thought, of the whole long business.

"Are you listening?" Anna said. She looked round. The churchyard was empty, and so was the lane beyond it. If anyone was watching from behind the shining Rectory windows, Anna thought, well, let them.

"Peter," Anna said, "I have to talk to you." It was easy to talk to him, sitting on his grave in the mild, still afternoon, with her arms wrapped round her knees. "We needn't pretend now, need we? We needn't avoid the fact any longer that we had come to the end of our happy times together. Do you get the feeling that we were, in some way, rescued? I wish you hadn't been the one to pay the price, I violently wish that, but I can't help wondering what would have become of us, with my growing appetite for life, and your increasing distaste for it."

A little, diffident gust of wind blew a few yellow leaves across the grass towards her. She picked them up. They came, she noticed, from the silver birch by the Rectory garage that she had so despised as suburban when she first came to Loxford, and had then grown to love for its grace and colouring.

"It's lovely now," Anna said, laying the leaves down Peter's mound like a row of buttons. "I can love you in peace, I can remember things without bitterness. I think you can understand that now, can't you? If you can't, if you still feel I ought to be doubled up in self-abasement, then you haven't been in paradise long enough. But I don't think you do. I don't feel you haunt me."

She looked at the space at the head of the grave.

"I want to talk to you about this headstone. You know what the parish wanted? They wanted 'Peter Bouverie' and then your dates, and then 'Rector of this parish from thing to thing,' and then 'Beloved husband, father and friend.' Well, I struck. I mean, you don't want that kind of meaningless, sentimental claptrap, do you? I struck and I've won. I'll tell you what you're getting and it's from me to you, Peter, from me to you."

She turned and put her hands on the grave, as if on his chest.

"In very simple letters, we will put your name and your dates. And then underneath, this will be carved. Listen: 'Pray for me, as I will for thee, that we may merrily meet in heaven.' And the emphasis, Peter, is on the 'merrily.'"

"Oy!" someone shouted.

Anna looked up. Mr. Biddle, unchanged in every degree, was leaning on the churchyard wall. He took off his hat and shook it at Anna.

"Waste of time!" he bawled. "Waste of time, Mrs. B! 'E can't 'ear you!"

He cackled with mirth. Anna got up off the grave and stood looking down at it, calmly, dusting her hands together. Then she waved at Mr. Biddle, smiling.

"Oh yes, he can!"

She glanced down at Peter. She said again, so softly that only he could hear, "Oh yes, he can."

About the Author

❖ ❖ ❖

JOANNA TROLLOPE, a descendant of nineteenth-century English novelist Anthony Trollope, is the author of historical novels and a study of women in the British Empire. *The Rector's Wife* is one of her six contemporary novels, and her second to be published by Random House.

PORTOFINO
by Frank Schaeffer

__ 0-425-14981-1/$6.99